FOREVER YOUR GIRL

MELANIE SHAWN

CONTENTS

Forever Your Girl
by
Melanie Shawn

Cover and Book Design by Wildcat Dezigns

Rev. 2.2

❀ Created with Vellum

1

"Can I tell you a secret?" the busty redhead whispered loudly over the sounds of the jukebox and people laughing, talking, and playing pool in JT's Roadhouse. The bar was exceptionally crowded, especially for a Wednesday night. "I'm not wearing any panties."

Jake wasn't sure if he should clue her in that half the bar knew that little "secret." Several times when she'd bent over the pool table to aim and shoot, she'd flashed a beaver shot. Telling her would probably be the right thing to do.

Nah.

If she were drunk, he would definitely clue her in and even make sure that she didn't embarrass herself—any more than she had!—or get into any trouble. But she was as sober as could be. She had to know that she was putting on a show. Besides, his brother Eric was the cop, not him. Firemen didn't *have* to arrest people for indecent exposure.

Not to mention, several guys from the station house were seated on the barstools that lined the wood-paneled walls surrounding the pool tables and they were enjoying the view. So instead of commenting, Jake just casually chalked his cue as a devilish smile spread across his face.

He knew that Carrie…or…Cassie…or…Candy or whatever her name was,

thought that she would be going home with Jake tonight. She'd been dropping hints about seeing his new house since she'd challenged him to a game of pool. Jake wasn't sure how he was going to break it to her that she would not be getting the grand tour of his abode anytime soon. Jake wasn't going to be bringing her home to his condo, which he still lived in—or to his new home, which he had not spent a single night in.

It's not that she wasn't attractive. Standing five foot six, she had gorgeous red hair that flowed all the way down to her lower back, big brown eyes—that she'd been batting at him all night!—and curves that reminded him of a pinup model. And it's not that he had an issue with her exhibitionist tendencies. If she wanted to give him a preview of the goods, hey, more power to her. She actually fit Jake's criteria for a hook-up hottie to a tee.

But Jake still wasn't interested. Since the day he'd gotten the keys to his new home three months ago—the home he'd wanted since he was ten years old and came across it his first day as a paper boy—he hadn't been "entertaining" as much as he normally did.

Or at all.

The truth was that he hadn't brought a woman to his *new* home since Lauren, his friend, a realtor who also happened to co-host *Home Sweet Vacation* Home, which showcased vacation homes of the rich and famous—had placed those two little keys into his hands.

"Your turn, Jakey," the redhead purred suggestively as she ran her fingers up and down her pool cue.

"Yeah, *Jakey*, it's your turn." Levi, who not only owned

JT's Roadhouse but was also one of Jake's good friends, smiled broadly as he set down another long neck on the tall round table in front of Jake.

Out of the corner of his eye, Jake noticed Little Miss Flash-A-Lot's eyes scan Levi from head to toe appreciatively. It didn't bother Jake at all that she seemed interested. In fact, it gave Jake an idea.

"Come here, sweetheart." Jake lifted his hand, motioning for the redhead to step closer. When she did, he asked, "Have you met Levi? He owns this place."

A flirtatious twinkle appeared in her big brown eyes as she said, "No, I haven't. Hi, I'm Courtney. I moved here about a month ago."

Courtney. Right! Jake knew it had been something with a *C*.

Levi grinned down at her. "Nice to meet you, Courtney," he said, his six-foot-four-inch frame towering over her. "Welcome to Hope Falls."

Courtney smiled seductively before coyly dipping her head. When she did, Levi glanced over at Jake with a questioning look in his eye. One that silently asked why Jake would be introducing this girl, who was obviously "a sure thing," to Levi after he'd already put in time with her.

Jake shrugged in response. He didn't have an answer for that. He just wasn't interested.

Levi shook his head a little, smiling as he walked back to the full bar—not one empty seat. Jake noticed several people already trying to get Levi's attention. When JT, Levi's uncle, had owned the bar, he'd always had at least two people, if not three, working—even on weeknights. Levi bought the bar almost two years ago and, except for a busboy, had run it on the solo tip. Jake didn't know how he did it.

"Jakey, it's your turn," Randy, the fire equipment

mechanic, sing-songed in a high-pitched voice.

Looking down at the table, Jake assessed his next move. He could easily end the game in four shots and head home. When the objective of the evening was *not* to find someone to share a couple hours with between the sheets, hanging out at the same bar five nights a week got a little old. But since the alternative was going back to his condo, turning on Sports Center, and being alone, he'd decided that playing pool at JT's was the way to go. The peepshow was an added bonus.

Leaning over, he lined up his shot. Then, gripping the pool stick a little too high, he pulled back and hit the cue ball just to the left, banking the six off the side, not sinking it into the corner—a shot he could have made one-handed!

Courtney giggled and jumped up and down, celebrating the fact that Jake had missed the shot. All four of Jake's fellow firefighters nodded their heads in thanks. Chris, the station's engine driver, even mouthed the words, "Thank you."

After Courtney bounced enthusiastically—causing her lady-lumps to almost spill out of her shirt—she began circling the table, running her fingers along the felted sides, "looking" for her next shot. Really, she was just putting on a show. Obviously, she loved the attention, and who was Jake to judge.

---~---

Tessa's nails dug into her palms as she gripped the steering wheel tightly. Her teeth were biting down on the inside of her cheek so hard she was scared she was going to draw blood. Breathing in shallow pants as she squeezed her thighs together, she tried desperately to concentrate on the small piece of the highway that was illuminated by her headlights. Her eyes were watering, causing her vision to blur, which made driving in these stormy conditions on mountain roads doubly dangerous.

Why? Why in the name of God and all that is holy did I decide to grab not one but two *twenty-four-ounce Mega Monster energy drinks in Sacramento?*

With a bladder the size of a peanut, she knew better. Sure, she'd almost fallen asleep several times on the long boring drive up the 5, but Tessa was quickly realizing that trying to hold in her bursting bladder while operating a moving vehicle—in the rain, at night!—was not proving that much safer than nodding off behind the wheel. Her wipers waved furiously back and forth in front of her as rain pounded down on her windshield. Tessa had never really given much credence to the idea that the sounds of water made you feel the need to pee more, but after driving for the last hour in the rain with a full bladder, she was definitely signing off on that theory.

"Okay, okay, okay, okay," Tessa repeated out loud to herself, trying to calm down. She talked to herself a lot. She wasn't sure why. Maybe it was left over from moving around so much as a kid. The life of an Army brat was nomadic. She'd been painfully shy as a kid, so making friends hadn't been easy. Especially given the knowledge that she would just have to do the same thing all over again in a year or so.

The trip down memory lane was not helping to keep her mind off the impending emergency she was facing. She really didn't think she could hold it in much longer without potentially damaging an organ or two. Just when she was either going to surrender to the panic and break down crying, or, you know, just pee her pants, she passed the wooden sign on the side of the highway that read "Welcome to Hope Falls Pop. 6,032."

Yes! She was almost there. *Thank God!*

All she could think about was making it to Sue Ann's Café, jumping out of her car, and running to the restroom. She hadn't been back to Hope Falls in close to thirteen years, but she did remember that the main strip Sue Ann's Café was located on was only about five miles past the city limits.

Just five miles. Which, with these nasty road conditions, meant about ten minutes. She just had to hold it for another ten minutes.

Easy peesy. Right? Right!

Just as Tessa was giving herself a much needed pep talk, the road curved sharply to the left, and as she turned, admittedly going about five miles too fast, her front right wheel dipped into a pothole, causing the car to jar suddenly.

Uh oh!

Tessa squeezed her thighs even tighter. Her bladder was so painfully full it felt like it was about to burst. She needed to face facts. There was a distinct possibility that she wouldn't actually be able to make it the ten remaining minutes to her destination without peeing in her pants.

Okay, she rationalized, *if peeing in my pants is the worst thing that happens today, it's not such a bad day*.

Tessa always tried to keep things in perspective. There were children starving, wars being fought, people dying and suffering beyond her wildest imagination; peeing her pants—although humiliating!—didn't exactly equal tragedy. Even on her personal bad-day scale it would only rank about a five.

She was still trying to convince herself that wetting

herself wouldn't be the worst thing to ever happen to her when a large sign appeared through the rain like a giant neon savior. JT's Roadhouse.

Yes! There would be no peeing of the pants today.

Loosening her death grip on the steering wheel, she turned into the gravel parking lot, which looked to be filled to the brim. She drove up and down the back two rows. No luck.

Come on. Where was the justice in the world?

She was about to resort to pulling into the handicap spot when she spied a space three cars down. Maneuvering into the blessed spot was sketchy at best. She was bouncing up and down, doing her seated version of the pee-pee dance, clenching her thighs together, and biting her lip as she tried to pull her PT Cruiser in straight. Straight didn't happen, but she was in between two cars and she hadn't hit them, so she was counting it as a win.

Quickly pulling her keys out of the ignition, she opened the door as far as she could without hitting the truck in the space beside her. Then, making herself as flat as possible, she slithered out of the car head-first like a snake. As soon as she cleared it, she slammed the door and shivered from the cold. For a split second, she contemplated grabbing her jacket from the back seat but just as quickly dismissed the idea. Bathroom. She was laser-focused on the pressing need to find a bathroom.

Stepping out, heavy raindrops fell over her as Tessa moved her feet as fast as she could across the tiny, wet rocks. This task was made significantly more difficult considering how badly she had to pee and the fact that she was wearing flip-flops—not the best shoes to navigate slippery gravel in the pouring rain while your bladder was about to explode.

When she'd left sunny, eighty-two-degree San Diego

this morning, she hadn't thought about how bad the weather would be up in the Sierras. Her mind had been totally consumed with other aspects of her return to Hope Falls. A brown-eyed, brown-haired, charming, sexy, painful aspect to be exact.

Just as she reached the entrance, the front door swung open as a young blond-haired, blue-eyed guy walked out with a tipsy brunette on his arm. Tessa quickly moved past them, almost bumping into the guy who didn't move to let her by.

"Hi," the guy said as Tessa scooted inside, his eyes giving her a thorough once-over.

Seriously?

Tessa's skin crawled at the unwanted attention. Not only did she not like being the object of perusal, but this guy had the nerve to check her out while another woman hung on his arm. What a *pig*. She quickly shook off the uncomfortable feeling. No time to worry about that. Right now, all that mattered was finding the bathroom.

As she stepped inside, Tessa realized that, although she'd passed by JT's more times than she could count the year that she'd lived in Hope Falls, she'd only been a seventeen-year-old senior in high school at the time and had never actually entered the twenty-one-and-over establishment, which meant that she had absolutely no idea where the bathrooms were.

A woman happened to be passing by and Tessa reached out and grabbed her arm. "Where are the bathrooms?"

Immediately picking up on the desperation in both Tessa's eyes and voice, the pretty redhead quickly directed, "Down the hall to the left."

"Thank you!" Tessa moved through the tables,

navigating as best she could on the wooden floors in wet rubber flip-flops.

Although she was aware that the bar was packed with people, she had tunnel vision. The patrons and sounds around her were completely muted. The only sound she heard was her brain screaming that she needed relief!

Tessa frantically pushed open the door marked 'Ladies' and saw that there was no line. "Thank God," she said aloud to herself.

She began unbuttoning her pants before she'd even closed the stall door. She sat down and all of the muscles in her body relaxed. *Sweet relief.*

Now that the emergency situation had been resolved, the reality that she was actually back in Hope Falls sank into her like the Titanic after it hit the iceberg. Dread filled her being and her palms moistened. Pushing her anxiety-ridden feelings down, Tessa decided this was not the time or place for a nervous breakdown.

Stepping out of the stall, she moved to the sink and washed her hands. Glancing up at the mirror, she almost screamed bloody murder at the image staring back at her. She looked like a drowned rat.

Raking her fingers through her shoulder-length hair, she tried to brush it out as best she could with her hand. It didn't really help. Luckily, she was rocking the no-makeup look. Otherwise it would be melting down her face right now and she would look like a drowned-rat with a scary clown face.

Okay, nothing she could do about her appearance now. She just needed to keep her head down, make it back to her car, and get to the safe haven that was Sue Ann's Café. That shouldn't be too hard. The bar was packed. No one would pay any attention to her.

2

"*WHY* CAN'T WE PLAY ONE MORE GAME?" COURTNEY whined as she stepped up to Jake and pressed her hands flat against his chest. The flirtatious redhead had just gotten back from the bar, where he'd seen her give Levi her number. "You said you'd play one more game. You can't leave."

He would tell her not to get her panties in a bunch, but since she wasn't wearing any, there was no point.

"Can't. I've got to be at the station house early," Jake explained as he grabbed his coat off the barstool.

"Please, Jakey." Courtney's whine had turned into a full pout, boo-boo lip and all. "I just want to play one more game. I almost won last time."

If she really believed that she'd almost beaten him in a game of pool, then either her IQ was several points lower than he'd originally given her credit for or she was delusional. Either way, his decision to introduce her to Levi was looking better and better.

"Yeah, come on, Jakey. One more game." Randy put

his bottom lip out. Chris and Peter folded their hands together in silent pleas.

Of course the guys wanted him to play one more game. It would give them more opportunities to look up Courtney's too-short skirt and down her low-cut shirt.

"Nope, I'm tired. I'm headin' home." Jake pulled on his North Face down jacket as they were all booing.

"You're no fun now that you're a white shirt," Chris yelled out.

Jake agreed that he had been different ever since his promotion to Fire Chief but only because it coincided with his purchase of the Shady Creek house, which he knew had been the true catalyst for his change in behavior.

"Old Jake just can't hang anymore," Peter goaded him loudly.

Jake smiled, shaking his head while lifting both his hands and flipping both Chris and Peter the double bird as he turned to leave. Before he'd even made it a step, he was stopped short by what he saw.

His brother Eric was headed his way, and he was in uniform, which meant he must have been covering someone's shift. Now that he was the Chief of Police, he normally dressed in a suit and tie. The stone-faced expression he wore made Jake's chest tighten.

"What's wrong? Are the girls okay? Mom and Dad?"

"Everyone's fine." Eric moved closer to him and lowered his voice, his tone in full "cop" mode. "Dispatch received several calls about a car swerving on the highway. One caller said that the vehicle turned into JT's parking lot. I arrived and found the vehicle that matched the caller's description parked in front, and I ran the plate…" Eric paused.

Jake waited, but Eric didn't say anything else. Maybe working all these doubles and planning his and Lily's wedding had fried Eric's brain. Slapping him on his shoulder, Jake cleared his throat. "That's a great story, bro. You feelin' all right? How much longer you got on your shift?"

Eric narrowed his eyes and sighed, "The vehicle is registered to—"

"Did you find the bathroom okay?" Jake heard Courtney's annoyingly high- pitched voice from behind him and felt her fingers wrap tightly around his bicep.

What the hell?

He turned to see why Courtney could possibly be touching him, and when he did, he came face to face with…

"Tessa Hayes," Eric said quietly.

Jake's heart slammed into his chest and his body went completely numb. He stood perfectly still, not moving a muscle. He didn't even blink out of fear that if he did she would disappear. Again.

She didn't, but in that moment, the entire bar disappeared. The entire world disappeared. All he could see, all that existed, was Tessa.

She hadn't changed much in the thirteen years, seven months, two weeks, three days, and about ten hours since he'd seen her last. Not that he was counting.

Her hair was a little shorter now, falling right at her shoulders, where it used to flow down to the middle of her back. Her cheekbones stood a little more pronounced on her rounded cheeks. She still had crystal blue eyes outlined with long, dark lashes, a button nose, and full lips that his body instantly responded to without getting permission from his brain.

"Hi, Jake," Tessa spoke softly, the way she had when they'd gone camping and she'd woken him up inside their tent to tell him that she wanted him to be her first. And then after, when she'd asked him never to let her go.

Her voice washed over him like the heated flames from a structural fire. Hot and consuming. Jake couldn't speak. He couldn't move. He couldn't breathe.

"Hey, Tessa." Eric moved beside Jake.

Tessa blinked, as if his brother's words had snapped her out of a trance. "Oh, Eric. Hi," she said, shaking her head as the corner of her mouth turned up in a half smile, the way it always did when she was embarrassed or feeling uncomfortable. Her eyes widened and she asked, "Wow, so you're a police officer?"

"He's the *Chief* of Police," Courtney chimed in. Even through his jacket, Jake could feel her nails dig into his bicep. She gripped his arm tighter as she extended her free hand and, in a not-so-friendly tone, introduced herself. "I'm Courtney, by the way."

"Oh, hi. I'm Tessa." She lifted her hand in a little wave then turned to Eric. Jake watched, captivated, as her face lit up the same way it had when he'd scored the winning touchdown at Homecoming or when his little sister Nikki had learned to French braid her own hair. Tessa genuinely *cared* no matter how small or big the accomplishment. "Police Chief. Wow, that's great. Congratulations."

"Thanks. How have you been, Tessa?" Eric asked warmly.

The light that had just sparkled in her eyes dimmed slightly. Maybe no one else would even notice. But Jake had.

"Oh, you know. Hangin' in there," she said with a tight smile, glancing between the three of them. Jake wasn't sure if she was just uncomfortable with the current situation or if it was more than that.

As she continued talking to his brother, Jake's eyes

traveled down her body. A *wet,* loose, long-sleeved white cotton shirt clung to her body, showcasing the curves that his body still ached for. She wore light blue jeans with a hole in the knee and pink sandals. Her delicate toes were painted a deep shade of purple.

Purple. That meant she was sad.

Jake's eyes flew to hers and he noticed things he hadn't at first glance. Dark circles under her eyes. A small wrinkle in between her perfectly arched brows. Her skin was paler than usual—or at least what he remembered as usual.

"I'm sorry for your loss. When did she pass?" His brother's question cut through the Tessa-induced fog that had taken up residence in Jake's brain.

"Almost nine months ago," Tessa's voice wavered and her eyes filled with moisture.

"Adeline passed?" The words came out of Jake's mouth before he could stop them.

Tessa sucked in a barely audible breath as her head jerked up to meet his gaze. Her vivid blue eyes wide and mouth open, she stared up at him silently.

Shit. He couldn't believe that, after all this time, those were the first words he'd spoken to her. Before he had a chance to say anything else, Tessa swallowed hard and confirmed, "Yes."

"I'm sorry," Jake's hands fisted at his sides. His first instinct was to pull her into his arms. To hold her and tell her that everything was going to be okay. That he would make sure of it. But the last time he'd done that, she'd left and hadn't come back until today. His need to touch her, to comfort her, was so strong he had to *actively* not reach out to hold her.

Her bright baby blues bounced between Eric, Courtney, and Jake. "Well, it was great seeing you guys and nice meeting you Courtney. Um, Sue Ann is waiting for me so… Bye." She started to step around them, but Eric stopped her.

"Listen, we got some calls down at the station reporting a white PT Cruiser swerving on the highway." Eric's tone wasn't quite in full on-the-job mode but it wasn't merely conversational anymore.

"Oh." Tessa's hands flew to her chest and she let out a forced laugh. "I probably was. But not because I'd been drinking," she quickly stated then laughed again nervously. "I mean…yes…I guess… Well…it was…*technically* because I was drinking. But not alcohol, just energy drinks."

Eric stared at her with a blank expression, and Jake knew that he had no idea what she was talking about.

Tessa had always had a tendency to ramble and not finish thoughts when she was nervous. The first time he'd kissed her, Tessa had spent five minutes talking about the gum she had been chewing—if he'd tasted it, how she would have spit it out if she'd known he was going to kiss her, even asking him if he wanted a piece. So he'd kissed her again until her Bubblicious bubble gum was the last thing on her mind.

Eric continued staring at her, probably trying to determine if her odd explanation was due to intoxication.

"She has a small bladder," Jake explained.

Tessa lifted her small shoulder in a shrug as a light blush crept up her cheeks. Her eyes darted to Jake's. "Yeah, that."

"Oh," Eric said as understanding dawned on his face.

"Ew gross," Courtney said with disdain as she somehow managed to plaster herself even closer to Jake. "She did ask me where the bathroom was when she came in. She looked panicked."

"Okay, soooo…" Tessa's plump lips made a perfect O

shape and Jake's body immediately took notice. His gut clenched and his pants were growing tighter by the second.

Damn, he'd missed her mouth.

Seemingly unaware of his body's response to her, she pursed her lips together and her brows lifted as she rocked back on her heels then onto the balls of her feet and clapped her hands together before she pointed towards the door.

"I'm gonna go."

He watched the sway of her hips as she navigated through the crowded bar. Her damp jeans had molded to her perfect ass. They didn't just showcase it, they advertised it. His palms tingled with desire to fill his hands with her firm backside. Thirteen years had not done anything to lessen his insatiable hunger for her.

The next thing Jake knew, his feet were moving quickly in her direction. He was vaguely aware of Courtney protesting his leaving but he ignored it.

"Tessa," Jake spoke just as she reached the door.

She froze, and he wasn't sure if she was going to turn around or just keep going. After several beats, she slowly turned her head and looked up at him.

When their eyes met, he realized he had no idea what he wanted to say to her. So many questions were clogging up his brain that he couldn't think straight. So he went with the first one he could clearly make out.

"Where's your jacket?"

"What?" she looked at him like he had just grown another head.

He nodded his head down towards her wet clothing.

"Oh," she said, gesturing outside, "it's in the car."

He continued staring at her, mainly because he just couldn't make himself look away.

Perhaps mistaking his silence for judgment, she explained in a defensive tone, "What? I really had to go."

Jake pulled one arm out of his jacket.

As soon as she saw what he was doing, her hands flew up in protest. "No, Jake, I'm fine. Really. My car is in the first row."

Ignoring her, he took it off and wrapped it around her small frame. He was careful not to touch her as he placed the coat around her shoulders.

"Seriously, I don't need this. I have a jacket in the car," she protested as she tried to shrug it off and move towards the door.

"Take the coat." His authoritative tone must have taken her by surprise because she stopped, looked back up at him, and then slowly slid her arms through the sleeves.

Jake's heart clenched as he looked down at her standing in front of him, drowning in his jacket, her purple toenails peeking out beneath her jeans. She looked so small and vulnerable. So many emotions flooded his system that he felt himself begin to shake from the power of it. Jake didn't shake. Not on the job and definitely not in his personal life.

Even under his large down jacket he could see her chest moving up and down with her shallow breaths, her clear blue eyes brimming with emotion. "Jake," she whispered hoarsely. His name sounded so good on her perfect lips. Too good. It made him begin to forget the last thirteen years.

That couldn't happen.

"Sue Ann's waiting for you," he snapped harshly as he reached above her and pushed open the door.

She flinched, either from the cold air that gushed in or the tone of his voice, but she quickly recovered. Her jaw tensed and she nodded her head once before turning and rushing to her car.

He stepped outside, drawn to her like a magnet, and watched as she glided across the gravel in her sandals. A small smile tugged at Jake's mouth. It looked more like she was ice skating than walking. Just as she slid into her car, Eric stepped outside.

"So Tessa's back," his brother said, stating the obvious.

"Yep." Jake almost felt like the last five minutes had been a dream, and he still wasn't sure if it was a nightmare.

"And she has your coat." Eric, again, pointing out a fact that Jake was well aware of.

Yep. Tessa was back. And she had his coat.

3

TESSA WAS SLIPPING AND SLIDING ACROSS THE PARKING LOT —Ice Capades style!—as fast as she could. She had a lump in her throat so big, she couldn't swallow. Her chest felt like a two-ton elephant was sitting on it and her stomach was so upset she thought that there was a very real possibility that she was going to throw up.

Of course she'd known that if Jake still lived here, she would inevitably run into him. In a town the size of Hope Falls, it was bound to happen. But why, *why*, did it have to be the second she'd crossed the city limits, after driving for twelve hours straight and looking like a hot mess?! And while he was with his girlfriend no less!

Over the last thirteen years, she'd imagined what it would be like if she ever got to see Jake again. She'd probably come up with close to a thousand different scenarios. She even had favorites.

The one that got the most repeat play in her mind was the one where she was in an airport, waiting for her flight. She would picture herself walking through crowds of people when, suddenly, she'd bump into a strong solid wall of a chest. Large protective hands would wrap around her shoulders to steady her. Her head would lift—in slow motion, of course! —to find that it was Jake she'd randomly run into. The electricity between them would be so palpable that neither of them could speak. So without saying "Hello," "Hi," or "How ya' doin?", he would just lean down and kiss her senseless. Then, after kissing her until she couldn't even remember her own name, Jake would tell her that he'd never stopped loving her and they would live happily ever after.

Not once, in all of the myriad of possible Jake encounters she'd conjured up, had she been soaking wet and looking like death warmed over while his brother questioned her about drunk driving and his girlfriend dry humped his leg. That had never even entered into her realm of possibilities.

Reaching her car, *finally*, she opened the door and had to scoot and shimmy her way in because there was barely any room due to her horrendous parking job. The large jacket she was wearing, thanks to Jake, certainly was not helping the tight fit either. And the cherry on top of this embarrassment sundae was that, although Tessa hadn't looked back, she knew that Jake was watching her awkwardly get into her vehicle. She could *feel* his eyes on her. Jake's energy was so strong that she'd always been able to sense his attention.

It didn't matter where they had been—in school, hanging out with friends, at his family's Sunday dinners—when Jake looked at her, her entire body came alive. It was like his powerful gaze was set to a frequency to which her body was subconsciously tuned. And it was becoming glaringly obvious that all the years they'd spent apart had done nothing to dull his visual superpowers.

Slipping into the driver's seat, Tessa quickly slammed

her car door like the boogie man was after her. She needed to get out of here and try to process her Jake sighting, but as she attempted to start the car, her hands were shaking so uncontrollably that she couldn't even manage to get the key in the ignition.

"Okay, okay, okay, okay," she said aloud to herself, trying to settle her frazzled nerves. Tessa had attempted—several times!—to break the habit of talking to herself, and, for the most part, had been successful. But it seemed that repeating "okay" to calm herself down was here to stay. It was the equivalent of a childhood security blanket.

As she sat in her car, a scent she hadn't smelled for years, but one that was as recognizable to her as chocolate chip cookies fresh from the oven or newly cut grass, surrounded her. It was Jake. Pulling the collar of the too-huge jacket she'd been forced to wear up to her nose, she inhaled deeply.

Oh God, that smelled good.

It smelled like safety. Like love. Like home. Like Jake.

Tessa realized, now, that she had not adequately prepared herself for what coming face to face with Jake Maguire—The Man—would be like. In her mind's eye, Jake was still seventeen. But—*news flash, brain!*—Jake was *not* seventeen anymore. He was an adult. A man. He must be at least an inch taller than the last time she'd seen him. His frame, while still lean, had some extra muscle added to it that made her lady parts quiver with awareness.

When Jake had taken off his jacket, his biceps had pulled taut against the cotton covering them and Tessa's mouth had filled with saliva. She'd had to swallow quickly so as to not drool over him.

His face still held its boyish charm but had matured into stronger lines and sharper features. He'd always been cute and handsome, but now he was so insanely sexy that, to use a phrase her Gran had always loved, "he could make a nun leave the habit."

There was one thing that hadn't changed, though. Jake's eyes. Those big brown eyes that Tessa used to completely lose herself in, were exactly the same. At seventeen, one look from Jake made every fear, every worry, every insecurity disappear. When she would look into his eyes, she'd know—*know*—that everything would be okay.

Well, until it hadn't been.

Shaking off unwanted memories, she tried to pull herself together. That was a lifetime ago. She wasn't here to drudge up the past. She just needed to get things in order with Grandma Adie's home and then she could get back to her life.

Sure, it was a Jake-free life, but those were the cards she'd been dealt and she had played a decent game with them. Tessa had made the best out of every shitty hand life had dealt her. She hadn't gone belly-up yet and she did not plan on leaving the table on this round.

With renewed strength, she put her key in the ignition and started the car. Glancing up—against her better judgment—she saw that not only was Jake watching her from under JT's awning, but that Eric had joined him. Both men stood stock-still, feet shoulder-width apart, Jake with his arms crossed and Eric with his hands clasped behind his back.

As she flipped on her windshield wipers Jake's face came into focus. Their eyes met, and not knowing what else to do, she held up her hand and gave a little wave goodbye. He nodded stiffly.

Wow. Could things be any more awkward?

She pulled out of the spot slowly and carefully—not only because the Chief of Police was watching her, but also because she couldn't afford for her insurance to go up due to her hitting a *parked* car.

Turning onto Main Street, Tessa headed to Sue Ann's. Her hands gripped the steering wheel tightly, once again. This time, it had nothing to do with her overconsumption of energy drinks. Part of her—a large part!—wanted to turn the car around, drive right back to sunny San Diego, and forget this day had ever happened. But she knew she couldn't. If she was going to have any kind of a future, she needed to be here.

Like Gran had always said, Tessa just needed to "deal with her life." Even if that meant getting her heart trampled by wild horses. Or more accurately, getting *pieces* of her heart stomped all over. Because Tessa's heart hadn't been whole for a long time.

Was it actually possible for a heart, that had been broken for thirteen years, to actually break more?

Well, it looks like I'm about to find out.

4

Jake rolled over in his king-sized bed and hit the button on his alarm, turning it off an hour before it was scheduled to wake him up. He had spent the entire night tossing and turning. Restless didn't even begin to describe it. Half of his sheets now lay on the floor beside his bed.

His sleepless night sucked for two reasons. One, Jake *loved* to sleep. He had never been one of those kids who complained about bedtimes. He'd always played hard during the day, and the second his head had hit the pillow, he'd been out. Now, as an adult, the 'playing' was a little different, but not any less exhausting, and the second his head hit the pillow, Jake was usually out for the count.

Two, he had a pile of paperwork waiting for him in his office that needed his complete focus. Technically, this was his day off. The department had moved to a modified Kelly schedule last year, which meant two days on, four days off. He was off for the next three days, but since taking on his new position as Fire Chief, the paperwork had seriously piled up.

Part of the problem was that his predecessor had left

everything in such a mess that it had taken Jake over a month to sort everything out. But also the weather this year had been particularly brutal. It had been an extremely dry summer, which had led to an exorbitant amount of wildfires. The winter had been uncharacteristically harsh, causing the department to be busier than Jake had ever experienced in his six years there. So after getting promoted, there had not been a lot of time for paperwork.

Jake knew that he needed to get up and get started on his day. But instead he lay flat on his back, staring up at the ceiling with only one thought in his head: Tessa.

Since seeing her last night, he hadn't been able to think of anything else. Their brief interaction just kept playing over and over in his head. Every word, every look, every movement was on repeat.

The bed jerked like an earthquake was rocking it and Jake lifted his head to see Lucky bounding towards him. Normally, his yellow lab didn't wake up until Jake's alarm went off, but he must have heard him turn it off.

"Morning, Luck." Lucky happily barked his greeting, and Jake smiled as he sat up and rubbed his dog behind the ears. Lucky rolled onto his back and flopped onto the bed. Jake gave him his morning belly rub then patted Lucky's chest, "Time to go out."

As he and Lucky made their way down the stairs of his condo, Jake couldn't stop thinking of all the different things he should have said last night. For starters, he would have found out what the hell Tessa was doing back in Hope Falls. That way he could avoid her, which was the last thing he wanted to do, but the only thing he could do.

Also, he should have asked more about Adeline. Tessa's grandma had always been good to Jake, even before Tessa had come to live with her. Adeline had been on his paper route and lived next door to his dream home on Shady Creek Lane.

When he was in middle school and would come to collect the money for the paper, Adeline would always have cookies and milk waiting for him. Sometimes the two of them would sit out on her porch and Jake would tell her about school and sports. He'd even told her about his desire to live in the house next door to her someday.

He hadn't seen her since he'd left for college the fall after senior year. In fact, the last conversation he'd had with her had not been a pleasant one. During his four years at UCLA, he hadn't come back to Hope Falls. He'd worked the entire time he had been in school, first as a waiter, then as a bartender. So when other kids had had breaks and had gone home to see their families, Jake had picked up more shifts to make extra money.

When he'd moved back after college, his mom had told him that Adeline had recently moved. She'd had to go somewhere with a better climate for her asthma and arthritis. He'd always wanted to apologize for his behavior the last time he'd seen her on her porch. Now, it was too late.

Jake shivered as he opened the sliding glass door and Lucky ran outside to do his business. Even after the door was shut, the chill continued as he moved across the kitchen, the Spanish tiles cold against his bare feet. He poured water into the coffee maker, threw in a filter and scoop of ground coffee beans, then pressed the 'on' button.

Jake had been trying to cut back on his coffee intake, but today he would mainline this stuff if he could. It was going to be a multiple-cup day for sure. As the familiar bubbling sounds of the coffee brewing began, Jake leaned against his granite countertop. Out the window, he watched as Lucky chased a squirrel up a pine tree and then ran around in a circle chasing his own tail.

Well, at least one of them was happy.

Why had she come back? The question just kept rolling around in his brain like a pinball being knocked around. He was pretty certain he wasn't going to get a moment's rest until he knew the answer.

Of course, the simplest solution would be to go over to Sue Ann's and see Tessa there. But Jake wasn't sure if seeing her again was the best idea. Sure, they had a lot of unfinished business to deal with, *but* he seriously doubted that was why she was in town. If it was, she wouldn't have looked like she'd seen a ghost when he'd turned around last night. No, Jake knew that *he* wasn't the reason Tessa was back in Hope Falls. He also knew that there was no way she was here to stay. So the best thing Jake could possibly do was keep his distance.

Lucky whined and scratched at the glass door so Jake opened it. As Lucky ran across the kitchen, he left huge muddy paw prints in his wake.

"Lucky, did you get into the flower bed again?"" Jake said in his sternest tone.

Lucky spun around and sat, displaying his best "good boy" face. His tongue was hanging out of the side of his mouth and his tail was wagging wildly, thumping against the wooden leg of the kitchen table.

"Stay out of the flower bed," Jake firmly instructed.

Lucky 'woofed' in what Jake could only assume was agreement. He, then, ran around the table several times, his nails clicking loudly on the tile, before heading to his bowl for breakfast.

Jake knew it was his fault that Lucky had not only been digging up the yard but also chewing up the furniture. He hadn't been exercising him properly. When he did, Lucky never got into things he shouldn't. Jake decided that instead of getting upset, he would be a responsible dog owner and take Lucky on a nice long run.

Plus, maybe the physical exertion would do Jake some good as well. Clear his head. Get rid of some of the anxiousness he was feeling. Hey, maybe between that and the boring paperwork he had to do all day, he would be so mentally and physically exhausted that he'd actually sleep tonight.

It was worth a shot.

---~---

Tessa made her way down the wooden staircase that led from the small apartment to the café below. The deliciously fragrant scent of freshly brewed coffee drifted through the air, and she let out an audible moan.

Yes, she was a caffeine addict. She could openly and freely admit that. Until she had a cup o' coffee, she was useless. Her brain cells only started functioning after she drank that first cup of the day.

And to face today, she would need it. She was meeting Henry, her Grandma Adie's lawyer, to go over Gran's will. Tessa was not looking forward to it. In fact, she'd been putting it off for almost nine months now. It felt like after she did that last final thing, her Gran would *really* be gone.

It might be delusional on her part, but the fact was that she just hadn't been able to face it. Now, she had no choice. Tessa knew that if she ever wanted to open her studio, she had to do this. So here she was. In Hope Falls.

But always one to look at the glass half full, she thought that at least the worst part of her visit was already behind her. She'd seen Jake and she was still standing.

Albeit a little unsteady due to the fact that she hadn't slept at all last night, but she was upright and mobile.

Last night, every time she'd closed her eyes, she'd seen Jake, heard Jake, and smelled Jake. Well, the smelling was not just in her mind since she'd gone to bed wearing Jake's jacket. Had that been the healthiest thing to do? Probably not. But she would be returning it today and she'd just missed him so much that she hadn't been able to help herself.

Stepping out of the hallway and into the dining room, Tessa couldn't believe how much this place still looked exactly how she remembered it. The tables all looked the same. Some square and some round, all covered by blue-and-white-checkered tablecloths, each one adorned with a vase of flowers in the middle. The walls were all painted muted shades of yellow with white accents.

Along the walls hung large framed pictures of the town. Her favorite was the one that had been taken in the 1920s. It was of Main Street, which, to this day, still had wooden sidewalks that, although she was sure they had been updated, looked exactly the same as the picture. Of course, there were more storefronts now. Sue Ann's Café was featured in the picture, although in the '20s, it had not been a café. It had been the Horseshoe Saloon.

Tessa found a seat next to the large picture windows in the front of the café and sat, looking out of the glass, soaking it all in. When she'd arrived last night, Sue Ann had already closed up, so Tessa had come in through the back entrance and gone straight upstairs—after spending about ten minutes convincing Sue Ann that it was just rain on her face and not tears.

Well, at least she had tried to convince her. Sue Ann had taken one look at the large, black North Face jacket she had been wearing and given her a questioning look that had made Tessa think she had known exactly who the owner of the coat was. But thankfully Sue Ann hadn't pushed her any further.

Not that Tessa was under some delusion that the entire town wouldn't find out about her mini-reunion with Jake last night—if they hadn't already. Even before social networking, gossip had spread around this town faster than the Road Runner ran away from Wile E. Coyote. She might not have been here for years, but she doubted that had changed.

Staring out the window, she did notice that the town looked to be a little livelier and more bustling than when she'd lived here before. She saw about a dozen people out and about on Main Street, none of whom she recognized, which was an odd feeling.

When she'd lived here her senior year of high school, within a week, she'd known everyone. It was *that* small of a town. But all the faces she saw now, as she looked out the window, were all new to her. A little spark of hope lit inside of her.

Maybe her return wouldn't be the talk of the town after all. Maybe she could slip in and out and not make even the tiniest ripple in the metaphorical water. Maybe she could meet with Henry, go over the paperwork, leave Jake's jacket with Sue Ann, and quietly get back in her PT Cruiser and be on her way.

"Tessa Hayes!" a loud female voice shouted.

Or maybe not.

Tessa turned her head and was pleasantly surprised at who the voice belonged to. Nikki Maguire had just walked into the café and was headed Tessa's way. Nikki was Jake's youngest sister. The last time Tessa had seen her, Nikki was a cutie who had just turned thirteen, had a full mouth of braces, and was a few inches shorter than she stood now.

Nikki must have been at least five foot six now, and she had grown into a beautiful woman. Tessa might not have even recognized her except that a few months ago, Nikki's picture had been splashed all over the news when she made headlines for dating a senator. There was some kind of brief scandal, but then the next thing Tessa read was that the two of them were engaged.

From the look on Nikki's face and the rock she was currently sporting on her left hand, things were going well.

"Oh my God! It's so good to see you!" Nikki exclaimed as she pulled Tessa into a tight bear hug. Stepping back, she asked with excitement, "What are you doing here?" Her eyes widened as she sucked in an audible breath. "Holy shit! Does Jake know you're here?"

Tessa smiled the first true smile she had had in a long time. It was so good to see that Nikki's lively spirit had not diminished in the last thirteen years—and neither had her colorful vocabulary. It made her chuckle a little. "Hi, it's good to see you, too. I'm here to meet Henry to go over my Grandma's will."

Sadness fell over Nikki's face as tears immediately sprung to her eyes. She shook her head slightly as her hands clutched at her chest. "Adie passed? Oh…I'm so sorry, Tessa." Again, Nikki's arms came around Tessa as her voice filled with emotion. "She was *such* an amazing woman."

Tessa had forgotten how much her Grandma had meant to the people in this small community. Over the last eight years of caring for her Grandma—*alone*—she'd lost sight of the fact that there were other people who had cared about her as much as Tessa had.

Nikki sniffed as tears fell down her face. She pulled a tissue out of her purse and blew her nose. "Sorry to get so emotional. It's just with having no grandparents that lived in this country, Adie kind of adopted me as her granddaughter."

Wiping her eyes, Nikki smiled as she said, "I remember that, whenever I would go to her house, she would just let me talk and talk. At my house, my family got tired of how much I had to say, which I can't blame them. I was *really* talkative. They would make little comments about it or just have this look on their faces that I could tell they were irritated. But not Adie." Nikki shook her head, smiling through her tears. "She always listened and would even ask questions. *No one* ever asked me questions. I think they were scared of how long it would take for me to answer."

Tessa felt her own eyes filling as her lips twitched up in a smile. "That was Gran. She had a way of making everyone feel *so* special."

Nikki nodded. "When did she…?"

"Oh, um, about nine months ago."

"I'm so sorry," Nikki repeated. And Tessa knew that she truly was. She could feel it radiating off of her.

But before Tessa completely lost it, she motioned to Nikki's left hand and asked, "So you're engaged?"

"Yes!" Nikki's entire face lit up like a bright, shining star. "Oh my God, you have to come to the wedding!" Her hands clapped together excitedly.

"When is it?" Tessa asked.

"Oh, we haven't set a date yet. Mike, my fiancé, is finishing out his term in the Senate and I am working on my Master's, full time. We are thinking early next year sometime."

"Congratulations on the wedding! Let me know when you set a date and I will definitely try to be there. What field are you getting your Master's in?" Tessa had always thought that Nikki could be anything she set her mind to. She could rule the world if she wanted. She was bright, beautiful and funny, and she just had an inner light that people naturally gravitated towards.

"Psychology," Nikki stated proudly.

"That's great, Nikki. You are going to help so many people," Tessa said, and she genuinely meant it.

"You know, you're just like her." Nikki's eyes once again got misty. "You make people feel special, too."

Tears fell down Tessa's cheeks at Nikki's words. She'd been back in Hope Falls for less than twelve hours and she felt as though she'd already been strapped in and gone on an emotional roller coaster ride.

Tessa really hoped this meeting with Henry was short and sweet. She wasn't sure if she could handle another twelve hours here.

5

Jake jerked his head up in confusion. Quickly taking in his surroundings, he realized, he was in his office. Sitting at his desk. With a massive crick in his neck.

A loud knock sounded at his door.

He must have fallen asleep while he was going over the paperwork. Looking down, he saw the file on the Crescent Road fire. One glance at his computer screen told him that he hadn't even inputted two pages before he passed out.

Again, there was a pounding at the door.

"Come in," he barked.

Jake rolled his neck from side to side, attempting to loosen it. He didn't know who his uninvited visitor was, but it had better be important. He wasn't even supposed to be here today. Normally when he was in his office with the door closed, the guys respected that and kept their distance.

The door swung open and his sister walked in with a very strange expression on her face. It was equal parts bubbling with excitement and etched with worry. His first thought was that she must have gotten pregnant and was scared to tell him.

He didn't *love* the idea of his sister having a baby before she was married, but hey, she was engaged. And Mike was a stand-up guy, and Jake knew that the man would take care of his responsibilities.

Jake made sure to keep his expression blank. He didn't want to ruin Nikki's grand "I'm pregnant" speech—knowing his sister's flare for the dramatics—by tipping her off that he'd figured it out. Plus, he thought it might be fun to give her a hard time about it. Act all shocked and shaken. That could be fun, and he could use some fun.

Stepping into his office without even greeting him, Nikki moved the pile of papers off of the green leather chair that was located in front of his desk and sat carefully at the edge of it. Her eyes lifted to meet his.

"I don't know how to say this," she began before taking in a deep breath and placing her hands flat on her thighs.

Here we go.

"Guess who I ran into at Sue Ann's this morning," she said slowly.

Sooo,—not pregnant.

How had Jake forgotten, even for the thirty seconds that it had taken Nikki to walk in and sit down, that Tessa was back?

"Tessa," Jake said flatly before turning his attention back to his screen. He hadn't wanted to talk to Eric about it last night and he sure as hell didn't want to talk to his sister, who had practically idolized his ex-girlfriend, about it now.

"You knew?!" Nikki exclaimed.

Jake nodded. He hoped that she would take the hint that this was not a subject he felt like exploring and leave.

"Who told you she was here?" His sister almost

sounded mad that someone had beaten her to the punch. And that's exactly what Tessa's return felt like. A hard punch to his solar plexus, gut, and balls.

"I saw her last night." Jake knew that Nikki would find out anyway. Half the town was probably talking about it.

"You did?!"

Jake nodded.

"Where? When? What happened?" Nikki shot the questions at him in rapid-fire succession.

Jake had always known when to pick his battles. And fighting Nikki on this by saying that he "didn't want to talk about it" or giving her half-assed answers was not going to fly. When his sister wanted information, she got it. She was relentless. Plain and simple.

The fastest way to get this conversation over and done with was to give her what she wanted.

"JT's Roadhouse. Last night. Nothing happened," Jake stated quickly.

"Nothing happened?" Nikki narrowed her eyes at him and tilted her head.

Jake shook his head no.

"Did you talk to her?"

"Briefly."

"What did you talk about?"

"Adeline. Tessa's small bladder. Her need to wear a jacket." Jake knew Nikki might think that he was just giving her the highlights but that *actually was* the sum of their entire conversation.

Nikki crossed her arms in front of her chest. "Are you trying to piss me off?"

"No, I'm trying to work."

"Jake, Tessa's here. In Hope Falls. What are you doing just sitting here like it's any other day?"

"Because it is."

"You don't want to go talk to her?"

"And say what, Nikki?" Jake looked at his sister. It might have sounded like a rhetorical question but it hadn't been. He had no idea what to say to her.

"I don't know!" Nikki's hands flew up in the air. "Find out how she's been. Ask her how long she's planning on staying. Tell her you never stopped loving her."

"What the hell are you talking about?" Jake never talked about Tessa. No one knew how he did or didn't feel about her.

"I know you still love her," Nikki said with a cocky expression on her face. It was the same expression she'd had when she was a kid and tried to blackmail him when she figured out that he'd been sneaking out.

How ironic that, at the time, he'd been sneaking out to meet Tessa.

"You don't know shit," Jake snapped as his jaw tightened. He wasn't trying to be a dick to his little sister, but he was not going to discuss this.

A wide smile slowly spread across her face. "Yes, I do. I wasn't sure until right now. I had a suspicion since that night at JT's when I was upset about Mike and you told me that if I walked away from him, I didn't deserve him. I thought it sounded a tad personal and I knew the only girl you ever really cared about was Tessa. And she left. I don't know what happened between you guys, but I do know that you would *not* be this upset if you didn't still love her."

"Why don't you go practice your psychology on someone else? I'm not upset. I'm just trying to work." Jake tried to keep his tone as even as possible. Frustration and anger were pulsing through him and he didn't want to take it out on Nikki. He knew she wasn't trying to be a pain in the ass. She just couldn't help herself.

"So if you're not upset, then you won't mind if I invite

her to Sunday dinner?" Nikki said with a challenging twinkle in her eye. "I'm sure Mom would love to catch up with her. You know how much she adored Tessa."

Okay, maybe she was trying to be a pain in the ass.

Jake shrugged nonchalantly. "Whatever floats your boat."

"Good," Nikki said with a smirk.

Jake could practically hear the gears turning in her head as she formulated some sort of plan. Well, she could plot and scheme until the cows came home. Nothing was going to change how he felt.

Nikki stood to leave, but just as she reached the door, she turned around and asked, "So what happened with Adie?"

Jake knew how much Nikki had loved Tessa's grandma. She used to spend hours upon hours at her house. They would knit, color, and bake. Everything a grandma does. He hated being the one to break the news to her. "She passed away."

"I know. Tessa told me. She said it was about nine months ago," Nikki spoke quietly, and Jake could tell she was getting choked up. "But do you know what happened?"

"No, I didn't ask." Jake knew he should have and guilt pressed on his chest.

"I didn't either." Nikki shook her head and wiped her eyes. "I was just so surprised to see her and then finding that out was just a lot to process."

Tell me about it, Jake thought. His sister was preaching to the choir. Jake didn't respond. He knew anything he said could send his sister off on a tangent, and he just wanted to be alone. Because, as she'd so accurately pointed out, Tessa's return was a lot to process.

He looked back at his computer and began to type.

Instead of taking the hint and leaving, his sister walked around the desk and threw her arms around his neck.

"I love you, Bubbas," she said, using the name she had called him when she was little. Apparently it was easier for a toddler to pronounce than "Jake."

He could feel the emotion radiating off of her. Nikki didn't show her emotional side that often. In fact, this behavior was very un-Nikki-like. But he knew that she'd always had a hard time with death. They'd been lucky enough not to lose too many people who were close to them, but when they were young and would lose a pet, Nikki took it harder than the rest of the family.

He wrapped one arm tightly around her. "I love you too, Nik."

As she straightened, she looked right in his eyes with steely determination. "I know. And I also know you still love Tessa. So man up, grow a pair and go talk to her."

And there she was. Nikki was back.

---~---

"Thirty *thousand* dollars," Tessa repeated slowly, trying to slow her heart that was about to beat out of her chest.

Henry moved his large cowboy hat and flipped through a few more papers. "That's what it looks like. The property tax has not been paid for quite a while. The interest and penalties accrued. Then, there is also the mortgage that is past due. Since you were given the home in the will, unfortunately you are now responsible for all of it."

Tessa felt like the walls of the quaint café were closing in on her. She couldn't believe what Henry was telling her.

After applying for a loan to open her studio and finding out that her credit score was so low, she'd gone to see a lawyer and found out about the house. He hadn't given her the details, just that Henry Walker was overseeing her Gran's estate. That was two days ago, and now here she sat.

"I'm so sorry about all this, darlin'. I had no idea Adeline had even passed until I got a call from that city slicker lawyer of yours. When the taxes started coming back unpaid, I tried to find your grandma, but I kept hittin' a brick wall. The last known address I had was the retirement home in Mission Beach. The letters were returned, and when I contacted them, they said they had no forwarding address for her."

Tessa heard the words that were coming out of Henry's mouth. But the only thing she could focus on was that number. She had built a pretty significant nest egg when she'd been on staff as a photojournalist for *Time* magazine. But it was gone now.

Over the six years that she had to stop traveling to take care of Grandma Adie full time, it had dwindled. Weddings, bar mitzvahs, and quinceañeras didn't pay quite as much as being a *Time* magazine photographer on assignment in war-torn countries. But she had still been doing okay until she had been forced to put her grandma in a nursing home the last four years of her life. That large monthly expense had steadily eaten up the rest of her savings.

"So what are my options as far as selling the house?"

"Well, it is your property. So you can do with it what you wish. I can call Lauren and have her meet you there this afternoon so you can take a look at the place. I'm sure she can give you the low-down as far as its value and such."

"Lauren Harrison?" For some reason, Tessa had thought that she was a TV host now. She was sure that she remembered seeing the pretty blonde on a commercial or a billboard or something. Or maybe she'd just imagined it. It was quite possible that, over the past few years, she'd begun having stress hallucinations.

"Yep. Well Harrison soon-to-be Stevens. She and Ben should be tying the knot any day now."

"Ben?" Tessa didn't remember a 'Ben' growing up, but Henry was referring to him as if she would know who he was.

"Her co-host on *Home Sweet Vacation Home*, Ben Stevens," Henry explained.

"Oh, okay," Tessa said, somewhat relieved that she wasn't going crazy after all. "Yeah. If you could have her meet me there at her earliest convenience, that would be great."

"Will do, sweet pea. Now you call if you need anything. I'm sorry again for your loss. That Adeline was one fine woman," Henry said as he stood and picked up his Stetson. Before he left, he paused and said, "It sure is good to see you home. This town looks good on you."

Tessa smiled and politely said, "Thanks."

She didn't have the heart to tell him that this wasn't her home. Sure, at one time, she'd thought that it would be. That she would make a life here. With Jake. But that all changed. Now, there was no way she could live here.

"More coffee, hon?" Sue Ann asked cheerily as she shuffled over to the table.

"No, I'm good. I think four cups in two hours is my limit."

"Everything okay?" Worry creased Sue Ann's brow.

No. Everything was not okay. But there was no way

Tessa was going to burden anyone with her issues. She would handle it alone. Just like everything else in her life.

"Yeah, everything's fine." Tessa tried to sound as upbeat as possible. Which was difficult since she was pretty sure she was going throw up.

"Well, you know me. I don't like to pry in people's business. And I tried to give you and Henry a little privacy." Sue Ann set the pot down as she slipped into the chair Henry had just vacated.

"I appreciate that. Thank you," Tessa smiled at her.

"But it's a small place and I did overhear a few things. Adeline was your blood, but she was also our family, and so are you." Sue Ann reached across the table and patted Tessa's hand supportively.

Tessa nodded, not trusting herself to speak. After being away for so many years, she wasn't used to this outpouring of emotion, and it was a little—a lot!—overwhelming.

Sue Ann gave Tessa's hand one more pat before she nodded decisively. Then she stood and grabbed her coffee pot. "Now, honey, if you need anything, anything at all, you just let me know."

Since Tessa didn't think it would be appropriate to ask if Sue Ann had thirty thousand dollars she could borrow, she asked instead, "Actually, do you know where I could find Jake?"

Tessa could pretend that she just needed to return his jacket, but the truth was, her world had just been turned upside down. And even though she knew it was a bad idea, she couldn't help herself. She just wanted to look into his eyes, even if it was only for a moment.

Sue Ann's eyes sparked with interest and her mouth twitched, but she quickly covered it with her response to Tessa's question. "Well now, if he's not at one of his houses—"

"*One* of his houses?" Tessa repeated. How many houses did he own?

"Well he has the condo and the house," Sue Ann explained, "but I would bet he's down at the fire station. Since he got promoted to chief, he's been there a lot."

Tessa shook her head. "So Eric is the Police Chief and Jake is the Fire Chief?"

A bright smile lifted on Sue Ann's face. "Yep. Those Maguire boys are good men. Rosalie and Sean did a good job."

"How are Rosalie and Sean?" Tessa asked as she stood and placed a twenty down on the table. She'd always loved Jake's parents.

Growing up, her house, no matter where it was, was always quiet. Her dad liked it that way and her mom did everything she could to keep her dad happy. When her parents moved to Germany her senior year of high school, she'd been so excited to be allowed to stay with her Gran. And her Grandma Adie's house had been much happier. There was always music playing and they had game nights where they would stay up late and play Trivial Pursuit and Scrabble. But as much as she loved it, it was still just the two of them.

When she'd go over to Jake's, there was always life, activity and noise. She remembered that Rosalie had always been in the kitchen. Usually, Amy had been somewhere reading. Nikki had always had two or three friends over. And Sean had always been fixing things, either in the garage, the yard, or the house—working on what he called his "honey-do" list.

"Oh they're doing pretty good. Sean's retired and they just celebrated their fortieth wedding anniversary not too long back. You should stop by and see them. I know they'd love that." Sue Ann winked at her before heading back into the kitchen.

Tessa thought about her suggestion as she headed upstairs to grab Jake's coat. Would his parents be happy to see her? Did they know what happened? Had Jake told them?

Well, there was one way to find out. She had to ask Jake.

6

Tessa stood in front of an unmarked door in the darkened hall at the back of the firehouse. Her entire body was trembling, and, for some reason, she instinctively knew that it was possible she was on the verge of hyperventilating. She wasn't sure how she knew that since she'd never experienced that before, but she did.

Why had she thought it would be a good idea to come see Jake? It *wasn't.* That much was clear to her now. What could she possibly gain by this little drop-by?

She wasn't even dressed for the occasion. She just had on jeans, Uggs, and a blue thermal. Not exactly va-va-voom. Not that she needed to be. It shouldn't matter what Jake thought about how she looked. He wasn't her boyfriend anymore. And he had a girlfriend.

Her fingers flexed at that thought, and she realized she was gripping his jacket so hard she was scared she was going to ruin it. She needed to simultaneously get a grip and relax her grip. Taking a deep, steadying breath, she took a step back from the door and tried to assess her options.

Biting down on her bottom lip, she shifted the weight of her feet and thought about the pros and cons of just setting the jacket down in front of his door and then hightailing it out of there. Yes, Jake would know she had stopped by, but he would just think it was to return his jacket. Sure, maybe the guys she'd spoken to when she had come in would think her behavior was a little odd. But she could just say that he hadn't answered the door. It was just a white lie. No harm, no foul.

Decision made. When she stepped forward to set the jacket down, something caught Tessa's eye from her peripheral vision.

"Sometimes he falls asleep in there. Just knock louder," the young blond-haired guy, who she thought had introduced himself as Chris when she'd arrived, appeared beside her. Then, like something out of a bad dream, before she could stop him, he hit his knuckles against the door three times. Hard.

"What?" she heard Jake's voice on the other side of the wooden barrier yell and her stomach dropped to the floor. He did *not* sound happy.

Yep. Definitely time to abort the mission.

She pivoted on her heels to turn and leave, because at this point she didn't care what anyone thought—she just wanted to get the heck out of there—when Mr. Blond-Super-Helper-Man aka Chris opened the door and announced, "You have a visitor." Then, he turned and walked down the hall, leaving her standing there. Alone.

The door swung open before she could escape. Her heart skipped so many beats it felt like it was playing hopscotch in her chest.

Jake sat behind his desk, typing at his computer. He was wearing a plain white short-sleeved t-shirt that was just snug enough that you could see the definition in his biceps and shoulders. Tingles spread from the top of her head to the tips of her toes. Tessa's mouth went dry. She didn't move.

After several moments of silence, Jake glanced up with a distracted-slash-irritated expression on his face. Until his eyes met hers. Then his stare hardened and his face went oddly…blank.

Oh boy, not good. She *really* shouldn't have come.

Words started pouring out of her mouth before she could stop them. "Um, here's your jacket. Thanks for letting me borrow it. I was going to get it dry cleaned since it got it wet"—Tess let out a forced laugh—"but…then I thought…that was silly. I mean, it's meant to be out in the rain. But if you want I can—"

"Tessa," Jake said, interrupting her inane ramblings. "Come in."

A shiver ran down her spine at his tone. His voice held so much authority and strength. He'd never sounded like that when they were teenagers. But they weren't teenagers anymore.

Her body responded before she had a chance to conference with her mind and her heart—both of which she was sure would have objected to "coming in." She took one small step just over the threshold of his office door. Jake's expressive eyes stared at her like she was being ridiculous—probably because she was!

Fine. You want me in. There. With this, she took two more steps until she was all the way in the office.

"Shut the door."

Jake's low voice might not have been intentionally sexy but holy-smokes-good-golly-Miss-Molly, it was. Those three words zipped and zinged a trail of tingly goodness all the way to her core. "Okay, okay, okay, okay" she whispered under her breath as she turned and closed the door behind her.

She could do this. It was just Jake.

Oh come on, a little voice piped up in her head with a sarcastic note. *Just Jake? That's like saying Jimmy Choos were "just shoes."*

Tessa made the executive decision to ignore that annoying little bugger, though, and stick to her original thought. Just. Jake. She could do this.

When she turned back around, she was surprised to find Jake's expression and demeanor looking much more relaxed. He had a small, knowing smile on his face and his eyes looked softer.

"What?" she asked, confused at his quick turnaround.

Her mind started spinning with reasons that he had looked so cold but now looked like Joe Cool. Maybe he hated being interrupted at work? No, that's stupid. Maybe he just didn't want anyone to overhear him being nice to her because of his girlfriend? No, that didn't sound like Jake.

"Nothing." He shook his head slightly and leaned back, motioning towards a green chair beside her. "Sit down."

She was having a really hard time concentrating on anything except his tingle-inducing shirt that fit tight in all the right places, but she did take note of the new level of bossiness he'd adopted. Last night it was "Take the coat." Today it was "Come in," "Shut the door," ""Sit down." Okay, she wasn't gonna lie, it was kind of hot, but would a "please" have killed him?

Tessa decided that, instead of pointing that out, she would take the high road. So she laid his coat on his desk and took her seat in the leather chair. This whole experience felt a little too surreal for her to process.

She was in Hope Falls. Sitting in Jake's office. And they were alone.

Having no flippin' idea what else to say, she simply said, "Hi."

"Hi."

A slowly building, wide smile broke out on Jake's face, revealing perfectly straight white teeth. And that's when it happened. Her heart, that was already broken in a million pieces, broke into a million more.

All because of that smile, the one that felt like it had been made just for her. That was the smile he'd had the first day they met, the first time he'd kissed her, the first time they'd made love, and the first time he'd asked her to marry him.

It was the smile she never thought she'd see again and the one she didn't know how she'd survived without the last thirteen years.

She *really* should not have come.

---~---

Jake could tell that Tessa was about two seconds from bolting. Something in the atmosphere of the room had shifted between them. He wasn't sure why she'd come by. But he did know it hadn't been to bring him his jacket.

He still couldn't quite get over how beautiful she was. She had a little more color to her cheeks today. And last night, when her hair had been wet, it had looked a little darker, but now it shimmered a light shade of golden blonde. His hands itched to reach out and touch it, like he had when she used to lay her head in his lap and he would run his fingers through its soft strands, his fingertips grazing her head.

Her eyes looked an even more brilliant and bright blue than they had the night before. They always popped whenever she wore the color blue. And her lips. Damn, they were the star of so many of his fantasies. Soft yet firm, plump and supple. He remembered the first time he'd kissed her. He'd thought he'd died and gone to heaven. He was by no means a virgin when they'd gotten together, but their first kiss had been the most erotic experience he'd had in his seventeen years.

When he'd looked up from his desk, she'd looked terrified. He'd even heard her whispering her "okays" when she'd closed the door, which she only did when she was trying to calm down. So he knew that, even though she'd come here, this visit wasn't easy for her.

When he'd first seen her standing perfectly framed in the doorway, he'd thought he was dreaming. That he'd fallen asleep again and dreamt of her coming to his office. It wasn't until she started rambling that he'd realized that she wasn't just a dream or some figment of his overactive imagination. She'd really been standing there, in the flesh.

Sitting here now, across from Tessa, he knew he had a lot to say, but Jake was at a loss of where to begin. He wasn't quite sure how to break the ice with her. What do you say to your soul mate after they've torn your heart out, chewed it up, spit on it, and disappeared for over a decade?

"How have you been?" he asked. He knew it was lame, but his natural charm was failing him at the moment.

"Fine." She shrugged her shoulders noncommittally but looked relieved that he'd spoken. Jake knew how much she hated awkward silences. "What about you? I heard you just got a promotion. I'm so happy for you.

Congratulations," she said with genuine happiness and pride shining through her eyes.

"Thanks." He cleared his throat, trying not to let her words affect him. He had to remind himself that whether she was proud of him or not made absolutely zero difference. Even if that was a lie, he had to tell himself that out of pure self-preservation. "What about you? Still taking pictures? Traveling around the world?"

Tessa was an amazing photographer. He had bought every *Time* magazine that her pictures had been featured in. But nothing from her had been printed in them for the last five years. He Googled her every once in a while—daily—to see if she'd moved to another publication, if she was freelance, any information at all really, but always came up empty-handed.

Tessa fidgeted in her seat. Her eyes were downcast, looking at her hands, which were folded in her lap. "No, not anymore. Just local stuff now."

"And where's local?" Jake asked. Maybe he shouldn't have. Maybe it would just make things worse if he knew where she lived. But there wasn't a day, an hour that went by, that she didn't cross his mind, and she was sitting here, in front of him, now.

He had to know.

"San Diego," she said as she tucked a piece of hair behind her ears.

"How long have you been there?" Jake felt his body tensing. He tried to temper his tone but he could hear a distinct hardness in it.

"Um, about eight years. Six of them full-time."

Six years. She'd lived in the same state as him for *six* years and she hadn't tried to contact him?! After she'd left to "see the world," he knew that her first stop had been New York. Then he'd heard that she'd spent some time in

Paris and Italy. He'd gotten her postcards. But she'd settled down—in California—and hadn't even bothered to pick up the phone?

Was she with someone? Is that why?

He looked down at her left hand. There was no ring, but maybe she just didn't wear one. "So are you married? Kids?"

A look of pain flashed in her baby blue eyes. Before he could ask if she was okay, it was gone. It happened so fast that he wondered if he'd actually seen it.

"Nope. On both counts." She smiled weakly. "What about you? Are you and Courtney serious? Do you have any kids?"

"Courtney?" Jake had no idea who she was talking about.

"Your girlfriend." When he didn't respond, she continued with a twinge of irritation in her voice. "The redhead. At the bar last night. You couldn't have missed her. She was the one attached at your hip."

"Oh, her." Jake tried to suppress his smile. If he wasn't mistaken, Tessa sounded jealous. It shouldn't make him feel like he'd just won a gold medal, but it did. As much as he enjoyed that feeling, this wasn't a game, so he set the record straight. "She's not my girlfriend. And no, I don't have any kids."

"Oh." Tessa brow's knitted in confusion as she sucked in a breath.

A small wrinkle appeared between her eyebrows. Jake's heart squeezed in his chest. He loved that little wrinkle. Whenever she'd been worried or concentrating way too hard, he used to softly brush his thumb over it and her whole body would relax at his touch. He'd always loved how responsive she was to him.

No. He couldn't think about that. Nothing good could come from thinking like that.

Pushing those thoughts from his head, he asked bluntly, "So why are you back?"

"Oh, um. I'm here to clear up some stuff with Gran's house," she explained.

"How long will you be here?"

"I don't know." She sighed, shaking her head slightly back and forth. Her hair brushed across her shoulders and the sweet scent of her shampoo made its way across the desk.

The room was silent except for the wind whipping against the window that sat behind Jake and looked out over the vast pines at the base of the mountain.

Conflicting emotions rioted through him. Anger. Happiness. Love. Hate. Fear. Joy. Pain. Pleasure.

He was so confused, he didn't know which way was up. So he decided to grab on to two absolute truths. She left. And she was leaving again.

That's what Jake needed to remember. Nothing would change those facts. No feelings. No words. No actions would change or stop those things. He knew that from experience.

Standing, he quickly moved towards the door and opened it. "Thanks for dropping off the jacket."

Her eyes widened as she looked up at him, seemingly taken aback by his sudden dismissal. She stood to her feet and smiled self-consciously. "Oh, no problem."

Looking down at the ground, she came around the chair and stepped towards the doorway. Just before she reached it, Jake closed the door, moving in front of her.

Her head snapped up and her eyes locked with his. Their bodies were mere inches apart. A flush rose up her cheeks, eyes dilating as she whispered, "Jake?"

"Why did you come here?" His tone held a dangerous edge to it.

"I told you, to go over my grandm—"

"Here," he snapped, "to see me."

Her lip quivered, either at his harsh tone or the question itself. Tears began filling her eyes. She stared up at him and she looked…lost. The sight of her vulnerability and pain melted some of the solid ice that encased his heart that she herself had caused.

"Never mind." He opened the door. It didn't matter anyway. Nothing she could say would change the last thirteen years.

She stayed where she was. Looking down to the ground, she took in a quivering breath and swallowed hard. A sad smile appeared on her face, and when she looked back at him, she shrugged as a single tear fell down her soft, smooth cheek. "I just… I just felt… I needed to… I thought…I wanted to…"

She was killing him. Watching her like this felt like someone was twisting a knife in his stomach. He wanted so badly to reach out and wrap his arms around her. Pull her close to him and hold her there. Forever. His jaw clenched and his hands fisted at his sides. "Just forget it."

Shaking her head, she wiped the tears from underneath her eyes and took in a deep breath. As she looked up at him with a renewed sense of determination, Jake felt like he could see all the way to her soul. "For a really long time, nothing in my life has made any sense. And then today…I just"—she sniffed and her breath caught in her throat—"wanted to come see you…to look in your eyes. You're what makes sense to me."

Jake saw more tears falling down her face before she turned and hurried out the door. He stood motionless, staring in front of him at the spot she'd just stood moments before.

He felt like the wind had been knocked out of him. Her words filled his mind, causing a fog of confusion and frustration to settle over him.

He was what made sense to her?! *What the fuck does that mean?*

Raking his hands through his hair, he stalked back over to his desk. He sat down and closed his eyes. Whatever was going on with Tessa—why she was here, why her life hadn't made sense, the pain in her eyes—none of it had anything to do with Jake.

They weren't together. They weren't even friends. She wasn't his. Even if it still felt like she was.

7

Tessa's day was not going well. But trying to be positive, she had to admit that the silver lining of the day was that she'd parked in the back of the fire station. So she'd been able to slip out the back door and get into the safety and privacy of her car without an audience of fire fighters witnessing her embarrassing outburst of emotions. She really didn't want it to start circulating around town that she'd left Jake's office bawling like a baby. Even if she wasn't going to be in town much longer, she would like to leave with at least a shred of dignity.

As she drove down Main Street and headed back to Sue Ann's, she got a text. It was from Henry and it said that Lauren would meet her at her grandma's house at three o'clock. It was only noon. She had a few hours to kill, and without even consciously thinking about it, she turned down Bluebird Road to the one place she'd missed almost as much as she'd missed Jake.

Jake.

Her entire adult life, Tessa had tried to convince herself that what she'd felt for him had just been teenage infatuation. Puppy love. That the reason her feelings and their connection had felt so intense was because they hadn't been dealing with real life yet. All of their energy and passion had solely been focused on each other.

Now, seeing Jake again, as an adult, while she was smack dab in the middle of "real life," disproved what she'd been trying to brainwash herself into believing. Which meant that, when she left here, she would go with the absolute knowledge that what she had felt with Jake was one hundred percent the real thing. She had not only loved him, but she was still hopelessly in love with him.

Also, the connection they'd shared was still so strong that she knew, just *knew*, he had to feel it, too. But when she looked in his eyes, she had seen how angry he was with her. Which, in all fairness, he had every right to be. Tessa knew he would never forgive her, and she would never dream of asking him to.

But being back here, seeing Jake again, still single, no *kids*… It made her question whether or not she'd done the right thing all those years ago. Had she made the right decision for both of their lives? At the time, it had seemed like the only option—if she'd truly loved him, which she had, she'd had to let him go. So he could be happy. But now? Now…she just wasn't sure.

As she pulled up under the large sign featuring a giant camera lens that read "Say Cheese" in the center, she saw a very familiar red VW Bug parked around the side. It hadn't even occurred to Tessa, until right this second, that Mary might not be here. Or even that Say Cheese might not even exist anymore.

It was strange, but when you left a place, especially one that felt so much like home, it just seemed like everything should be exactly the same as it had been when you returned. But, a lot of times, it wasn't. So seeing that Say

Cheese was still open and Mary's car was parked beside it, made Tessa want to do a happy dance. She was almost as relieved as she had been last night when she'd finally gotten to pee.

When she'd moved to Hope Falls her senior year of high school, Mary had been looking for a photography assistant and hired Tessa even though she'd had zero experience. From the first session she'd assisted on, Tessa was hooked. She'd loved it all. The equipment, lighting, angles, focus. It had become her passion overnight, and Mary had supported her every step of the way.

Climbing out of her car, she hopped over a large puddle that had formed in front of the sidewalk and practically skipped up to the front door. As she entered, the small bell that hung above the entrance rang. Tessa was flooded with warm fuzzies as she looked around the small lobby of the photography studio and saw that, aside from some of the pictures that hung around the walls, it looked exactly the same as she remembered it.

A tan couch with purple throw pillows sat against the side wall. There were two oversized chairs, one deep purple and one a walnut brown, that were positioned opposite the couch. And a round oak coffee table sat in the center, creating a warm and inviting sitting area for customers to look through their proofs or browse through the albums.

The walls were still painted a muted lilac with white trim. Dark chocolate brown curtains hung in the doorway, separating the lobby from the studio. And the best part was that the small coffee bar Tessa herself had built, still sat in the far left corner of the room. There was a fresh pot brewed, but oddly enough, the room didn't smell of coffee. It smelled as it always had, like cinnamon and cupcakes.

"Well, shut the front door and call me Sally. If it isn't

Miss Tessa Hayes?" Mary's voice sounded loudly from behind Tessa. "I heard you were back in town and hoped you would stop by, sweetie pie."

When Tessa turned around, she couldn't believe her eyes. Mary Higgins had not aged a day in the last thirteen years. Standing a good three inches shorter than Tessa, she still wore her hair piled wildly on top of her head in a loose bun. It was the same eye-popping shade it had been the last time she'd seen her. Of course the fact that she dyed it fire-engine red helped to hide grays, but her face looked exactly the same as well—a perfectly round circle with full cheeks, big brown eyes, a button nose, and penciled-in brows.

She was even dressed the same, wearing a loose-fitting pair of black slacks and one of her signature colorful animal sweaters. Today's featured a big peacock with its feathers spread boldly across her large chest. Tessa's favorite had been one that had showed bullfrogs on lily pads with a large heart in the middle of them.

"Hi, Mary," Tessa beamed as she threw her arms around her mentor and hugged her tightly.

Pulling away from her, Mary shook her head, making a tsk-tsk-tsking sound. "Have you been eating? You're thin as a rail."

"Yes, I have. I promise," Tessa assured her. Mary was always trying to "fatten her up" and "put some meat on her bones."

Reaching up, Mary cupped her hands, cradling Tessa's cheeks. She smiled up at Tessa like the sun was shining down on her. "Well, I didn't think it was possible but somehow you managed to get even prettier."

Tessa leaned into Mary's soft palm. She didn't want to start crying again, but she'd missed feeling nurtured and… special. Her Gran had passed nine months ago, but it had been well over five years since she'd had her faculties about her. Tessa had never imagined how painful it was to watch a person you love slip away slowly until they don't even know who they are, who you are, where they are. It was heartbreaking.

Mary's eyes grew worried when Tessa began tearing up, "You okay, pumpkin?"

"I will be," Tessa spoke in faith, because honestly she had no idea if she would be.

"Come on." Mary ushered Tessa to the couch. As soon as they were seated, she handed her a tissue. "So why do you look like you've got the weight of the world on your shoulders?"

"Oh, I'm fine. Just a lot of emotions are coming up being back here." Tessa tried to gloss over how she was feeling.

"Young lady, I may not have seen you in a month of Sundays but I do know that something is heavy on your heart. Is it Adeline's passing or your run-in with Jake?"

Tessa looked up at her in shock. "How did you—"

Mary interrupted, explaining, "Oh, well Stella over at the Pack 'N' Pay overheard Henry on the phone with Lauren talking about your grandma's place. Then she told Nadine, who gets her hair done by Rosemarie over at Curl Up and Dye, who came in to pick up an eight-by-ten of her granddaughter's christening and filled me in."

"Wow." The gossip train seemed to be moving full steam ahead in Hope Falls.

"And Marty over at Carson's Garage was at JT's last night. He went home and told Velma, who he's been shacking up with since his Margaret passed, God rest her soul, that watching the two of you reminded him of the people on her shows. You know how that woman loves her soaps. Anyhoo, he told Velma that he couldn't hear what ya'll were sayin' but that it was mighty entertaining. I ran into Velma, who went to go pick up Marty's blood pressure medication down at the pharmacy this morning. I was there getting my insulin."

"How are you feeling?" Tessa asked. Mary had been a Type 1 diabetic since Tessa had known her.

"Good days and bad days." She shrugged it off. "But I don't want to talk about my blood sugar. I want to hear about you. Tell me everything."

Tessa leaned back into the couch, curling her feet beneath her, and took a deep breath. If Mary wanted to know everything, they were going to be here for a while.

---~---

Jake was just shutting down his computer when there was yet another knock on the door. Seriously, this place was like Grand Central Station today. At least he'd already decided that there was no way he was going to get any work done. Not after Tessa had been there.

He still had several hours before basketball tonight so he thought he'd go home, grab Lucky and go on another run. In high school, when he'd been on the football team, Jake had always been exhausted when they'd had two-a-days—practice before and after school. He was hoping that a double-up on his running would have the same effect on him now.

But first, he had to deal with whoever was at the door. "Come in."

His brother walked in and shut the door behind him. He casually took a seat and leaned back in the chair, making himself comfortable.

"Can I help you with something?" Jake asked. He was really not in the mood to shoot the shit with anyone.

Luckily his brother really wasn't a talker, so he wasn't too worried.

"I just wanted to come by and make sure you were okay," Eric said.

"I'm fine."

"Really? Because I gotta tell you, I have never seen you look like you did last night when you saw Tessa." Eric's brow lifted.

Jake knew that his brother had developed a reputation for being a master interrogator on the force, but this was Jake's office, not an interrogation room, and whatever was or wasn't going on with Tessa was none of Eric's business.

"I was just surprised to see her," Jake answered honestly. He had been shocked as hell to see her in JT's last night.

Eric continued his line of questioning. "What happened between you guys?"

"You were there. Nothing."

"Not last night, smartass. In high school."

"Why do you care?" Jake wasn't sure what the sudden interest was. It's not like Eric could be interested in Tessa. He was engaged to Lily and happier than Jake had ever seen him in his life.

Eric leaned forward, resting his elbows on his knees. "Look, the few times I came home from school that year, you guys seemed inseparable, and honestly, the two of you kind of reminded me of Mom and Dad."

"What are you talking about?" Jake knew his brother had a point. He just wished he'd hurry and get to it.

"I'm talking about how you two were together. Anyone who was around you guys for five minutes could see it. You guys had this…connection. The only other time I'd ever seen it was between Mom and Dad. Then, you call me and tell me you're engaged and the next thing

I know she's gone and you turn into a man-whore asshole."

"Hey, I'm not an asshole." Jake wasn't even going to try and defend the 'man-whore' title.

"No, not anymore. But you were. For years," Eric stated flatly.

"So, what, do you want an apology? Did my brief stint as an asshole hurt your feelings?" Jake asked sarcastically.

"No, I want to know what happened."

"You know what happened. You just summed it up perfectly. We were together. We were happy. We were going to get married. She left." That was the story that everyone knew. The only people who knew the whole story were himself, Tessa and Adeline. And Adeline was gone now. So just he and Tessa knew. It was no one else's business.

"She just left? For no reason at all."

No *good* reason.

Jake knew his detective brother was not going to drop this so he figured he might as well tell him a version of the truth. "She realized that she didn't want to get stuck living in a small town. She knew that after school I planned on coming back here to live. She didn't want that. She wanted to see the world. So instead of going to school in Southern California, like we'd planned, she went to New York."

Eric sat there silently, his expression was unreadable. Jake couldn't tell if he was buying it or not. Jake was actually getting uncomfortable under his brother's stare and he hadn't even lied. He just hadn't told the *entire* truth. Jake actually felt a little sorry for the criminals his brother interrogated.

"Well, she's back now," his brother finally said.

"Not for long. After she gets Adeline's affairs in order, she's going home." Jake closed the files on his desk and unlocked the desk drawer he kept them in.

"Where's home?"

"San Diego."

"She's here now. Are you going to do anything about it?"

"Nope." Jake's patience was quickly running out. First his sister, now his brother. He was sure as soon as his parents found out she was in town, that they would be up his ass, too. Because they didn't know the whole story. How he'd gotten on his knees in the hospital room when she'd told him she was leaving and begged her to stay. He'd told her he would go with her. That he would do anything to be with her. That they could work it out.

She'd looked him right in the eye and told him to leave, to get out of her room. Screamed it, actually.

They didn't know how he'd gone back the next day but she had already been discharged. Or how he'd driven like a maniac to her grandma's house and then yelled at Adeline when she wouldn't tell him where Tessa had gone.

No one knew how he'd punched holes in his walls that night out of helpless frustration. Or how he'd gotten black-out drunk almost every night the first year of college just trying to forget her.

No, all his family knew was that they had been together. They had been engaged. Then she'd left. And that's all they ever needed to know.

8

Tessa pulled into her grandma's driveway next to a very nice Mercedes SUV she assumed belonged to Lauren. The expensive silver vehicle looked out of place parked in front of the rundown two-story house. Tessa's heart sank as she took in the peeling paint and the overall dilapidated appearance of the home.

It particularly stuck out like a sore thumb because the rest of the street had been well-maintained. A few of the houses looked as though they had even been renovated. As she stepped out of her car, she put her hand up, shading her eyes from the sun to try and get a better look at the house that sat next door to her grandma's. The blue house with white trim that Jake had wanted to buy since he was a kid. The house they had spent endless hours talking about raising a family in.

Jake's house.

Their house.

Tessa wondered who lived there. From what she could see through the large picture window that overlooked the mountainside it faced, there didn't appear to be any furniture in it. Hmm, maybe it was vacant?

A sound caught her attention then. She looked back just as the front door to her grandma's house opened and Lauren stepped outside. "They won't take less than one point five." She wore a suit that looked more like she should be on Wall Street as opposed to Shady Creek Lane. It was black and tailored perfectly to fit her willowy frame. Her hair was swept up without a strand out of place. Her appearance might have seemed severe and even out of place on someone else, but on Lauren it just worked. When their eyes met, Lauren waved warmly, then held up one finger indicating that she would only be a minute.

Tessa smiled and nodded, making her way up the wooden steps. As she reached the porch, she saw that her grandma's beloved swing was broken and one half was resting on the wooden planks below it. There were spider webs covering it. Only one of the cushions that Tessa had helped her grandma sew for the seat remained and it was tattered and sun damaged.

"Well, you can go ahead and write it up, but I'm telling you it's a waste of time. They won't take it." Lauren moved onto the far side of the lawn to finish her call, and Tessa took a fortifying breath before stepping over the threshold and into the house.

Tessa stared, in shock, at the only place that had ever been a home to her. Lauren had opened up some of the curtains, letting in the midday sun, but it still felt dark and gloomy. Dust covered every inch the eye could see. The few pieces of furniture that still stood looked to be in serious disrepair.

When Grandma Adie had first moved to San Diego, before the dementia had set in, she'd told Tessa that she had a property manager that would be looking after the house. Tessa had always meant to come up and check on everything or at least call and speak to someone at the real estate office that was handling the property, but her grandma's health had begun declining so rapidly that Tessa had been maxed out just trying to take care of her. Then, once she'd had to move Gran to a home, Tessa had spent all of her time picking up as many photography jobs as she could to continue to pay for her care.

"All right, sorry about that." Lauren walked back up on the porch, carefully stepping across the missing plank of wood in her six-inch heels, then entered the house with a friendly smile on her face. "Hi! It's been a long time, stranger. How does it feel to be back?"

"Hi." Tessa had no idea how to explain how it felt. "Yeah it's been a while. It feels…strange."

"I bet." Lauren nodded her head as her eyes widened. Her expression turned somber as she said, "Well I wish we were meeting under better circumstances. I'm so sorry for your loss. Adeline was an incredible woman."

"Thanks. Yes, she was," Tessa agreed. Since she'd cried enough for two lifetimes in the last day, she decided to direct the conversation to a less emotional topic. "Congratulations on your show. I haven't had a chance to watch it but I've seen the promos."

"Oh, thanks. It's fun. Not anything I would have ever expected to do, but like they say, life is what happens when you're busy making other plans. And what about you? Oh my gosh, that piece you did on Darfur. The image of the girl sitting beside her dying mother still haunts me today."

"Yeah, that was a tough shoot." It was also the last assignment that she'd been on as a photojournalist. The day she'd gotten home from that job had also been the first time the police called saying that they'd found her grandma wandering the streets, unresponsive.

"So," Lauren said, adopting a very professional tone, "I've looked over everything and it looks like, between the second mortgage and the back taxes, you owe one hundred and ten thousand."

The room started spinning at the sound of that number.

"Tessa." Lauren's voice sounded far away. "Are you okay?"

Tessa lips were tingling and she felt like she was floating. An arm wrapped around her and she was vaguely aware of her feet moving. Warmth from the sun hit her face and she squinted her eyes. She was outside.

"Tessa, are you with me?" Lauren asked from beside her.

Tessa's head felt heavy as she turned to look at her friend. She managed a weak, "Yeah." Slowly, her awareness returned. Lauren must have ushered her outside because she was seated on the grass in the front yard. She took in a few deep breaths. "I'm okay. Sorry. I don't know what came over me."

"I'm the one who should be apologizing. I shouldn't have just blurted out that number. I am so sorry, Tessa."

"No, it's fine. You were just doing your job. And I think that my lightheadedness had more to do with living on only energy drinks and coffee the last few days, driving for twelve hours straight, and getting no sleep last night," Tessa explained. She didn't want her friend feeling at all responsible for her passing-out close call.

Lauren did not look completely convinced but she dropped it. "Well, the good news is that there's not any structural damage to the house. I went ahead and had it inspected this morning after Henry called. A lot of the repairs are cosmetic. There is some plumbing and roof work that will need to be done. But mostly it just needs a deep cleaning and a few coats of paint to get it ready for sale.

"And the comps in this neighborhood are right at two hundred so you would not only be able to pay off the second mortgage and the taxes, you could have a little left over as well."

Tessa nodded, taking in the information Lauren was giving her.

"If you planned on selling," Lauren quickly added. "I just assumed that you wouldn't be holding on to it."

"Henry mentioned something about the bank taking it over. How long do I have before that happens?"

"You have forty-five days until they will be foreclosing on the property. But that is plenty of time. And I know that everyone will pitch in." Lauren pulled out her phone. "I'll get a hold of Amanda to put the word out. We can do a work day this Saturday."

There might be drawbacks like gossip and everyone knowing everything about everyone's business, but being a part of a small, tight-knit community definitely had its advantages as well. Not that Tessa was *really* a part of this community. But her grandma had been, so she kind of was, by default.

After Lauren finished typing on her phone, she looked up and announced with a small satisfied smile, "Done."

"Thank you, Lauren. I really appreciate it." Tessa had been handling things on her own for so long that having people rally around and support her was a nice change. But one she knew she absolutely could not get used to.

"Not a problem. I have to run to a production meeting, but we are having a book club meeting tonight at Amanda's at seven. You should come. Do you remember where Mountain Ridge is at?" Lauren asked as she pulled out a set of keys.

"Yeah. I learned to ride a horse at Mountain Ridge. Is Amanda running it now?" Tessa asked. As a teen, she'd loved going to the outdoor adventure park. There was horseback riding, kayaking, and nature walks. The summer she'd moved to Hope Falls, she'd been up there almost every day to take pictures, working on her craft.

"Yes, she is. Well, she and Justin Barnes."

"That cute guy that worked there?" Tessa remembered that she'd always seen him around fixing things.

"Yeah. After her dad passed, he left the resort to Amanda and Justin, and they reunited because of it. It's a very romantic story, but I'll let her fill you in. Can you make it tonight?" Lauren asked.

"I'll definitely try to." Tessa didn't want to commit to anything because she wasn't sure how she would be feeling this evening since the day was only half over and she had already had a mini breakdown and almost passed out. "Nikki mentioned it when I saw her at Sue Ann's this morning. It would be fun to catch up with everyone," Tessa said sincerely.

"Well, I hope you can make it. If I don't see you then, I will definitely be getting in touch with you tomorrow with plans for the work day Saturday."

"Okay, sounds good."

"Are you sure you are feeling okay? I can call and let them know that I'll be late." Concern laced Lauren's voice.

"No, I'm fine. Really. I have a protein bar and water in the car. I just need to eat," Tessa assured her.

Lauren's eyes narrowed for a moment before she said, "Okay. You have my cell, right?"

"Yep. I got it from Henry."

"All right. Call if you need *anything*."

"I will." Tessa waved goodbye to Lauren.

As Tessa watched Lauren climb into her SUV, she tried

to focus on the positives that had come from the conversation. There was no structural damage. She would most likely have help fixing the place up. She had a month and a half to get the house ready and then sell it. At least she had no doubt that, in Lauren's capable hands, the house would be sold.

Deciding to brave another look inside, she made her way back up the walkway. "Okay, okay, okay, okay," she mumbled under her breath. She could do this. Everything was going to be fine.

9

Jake's muscles were on fire as he ran up the incline on the steep hill and it just made him go harder. He was pushing his body further than he ever had. He didn't care about the pain that was shooting up his legs and back or the fact that he still had to go play a basketball game tonight. All he cared about was running.

He wanted to get lost in the rhythm of his feet pounding painfully on the pavement, the sensation of the wind harshly hitting his face, and the constricting ache of his chest, so tight, it seemed like he could not get oxygen. All of those things felt better than thinking about Tessa.

Running had always worked as a very effective form of cheap therapy for Jake. It cleared his head until there were no thoughts at all. Just him and the road. He'd spent the last thirteen years trying to outrun a ghost, and most of the time he'd been fairly successful. Especially since he'd stopped using alcohol to do it. But now that ghost was alive and well, right here in Hope Falls, and it was proving to be much more challenging.

Lucky, however, could not have been happier about his

efforts. Two runs in one day was his version of doggie heaven. Jake saw Lucky's tail disappear around the bend of Shady Creek Lane. When Jake had first rescued Lucky, they had always taken this route so Jake could run by and see the house that he one day wanted to own. To this day, every time they went on a run, his golden lab headed this way.

Jake came up around the bend just moments after his four-legged boy, but Lucky was nowhere to be seen. He passed the huge oak tree that stood tall in his front yard, which Lucky always peed on—marking his territory—and there was still no sign of him.

Then he saw him. Lucky was standing over someone who was lying on the grass. As he moved closer, his heart slammed in his chest. It was Tessa. She was unconscious.

His feet moved faster than they had ever carried him before. He had just reached her when she started blinking her eyes and moving her head to get away from Lucky's kisses.

"Sit," Jake instructed his dog, who immediately stopped licking Tessa all over her face and sat down with a huff. His tail wagged wildly and he was whining, but he was sitting.

Jake fell to his knees and leaned over her, staring down as he asked, "Tessa. Tessa, can you hear me?"

Her lids fluttered open and her blue eyes looked up at him. Her pupils were slightly dilated and her skin was really pale. But she was awake.

"Jake?" she whispered. Her face scrunched in confusion as she lifted her hand and ran her fingers along her cheek. "Were you licking me?"

"No. If I were licking you, it wouldn't be on your face." Memories of his tongue tasting every inch of her body began flashing in his head.

Fuck. He needed to knock that shit off. He'd just found Tessa lying unconscious, so the last thing he needed to be doing was picturing her naked while he licked her from head to toe. Damn, he was doing it again.

She made a small grunting sound, confusion still clouding her beautiful face as she tried to push up on her elbows.

Placing his hands on her shoulders, he gently held her in place. "Just lie still, Tessa. Do you know where you are?" He needed to see how aware she was of her surroundings. It was good that she knew who he was and had been somewhat aware of Lucky licking her, but that didn't necessarily mean she was lucid.

Her eyes darted from side to side and her fingers spread out on the ground beneath her before her beautiful baby blues looked back up at him and she said, "Um, I'm outside on the grass?"

"Good." The corners of Jake's mouth pulled up in a grin. He reached down and held her wrist to check her pulse. "Do you happen to know where that grass is located?"

"I would if you'd let me sit up," she said, her tone indicating that she was stating the obvious.

Her pulse was strong. He checked her pupils—they looked good. She was getting a little color in her face and she was being a little smart-assy, which was a good sign. But he didn't want to let her up just yet. "Do you know what happened? How you ended up on the grass?"

"Um," she sighed and closed her heavy-lidded eyes. He was about to say her name and make sure that she hadn't gone to sleep—he didn't know if she had a concussion or not—when her eyes popped back open. "Oh yeah, I was going to the car to get food. After I looked through the house, I started getting dizzy."

"When's the last time you ate?" he asked, his tone coming out a little harsher than he'd meant it to. It was just that he knew that when Tessa got busy or stressed, she forgot to eat.

Her eyes rolled up as if she were trying to remember.

"If you have to think about it, it's been too long," he pointed out.

She looked at him with renewed fire in her eyes. "When's the last time you ate?"

"Two hours ago," he stated immediately, "and I'm not the one sprawled out on my ass in the front yard."

"Good point," Tessa begrudgingly conceded.

That was one of the things he'd loved the most about Tessa. She was reasonable. Even if she had been mad at him or had hurt feelings about something, they'd always fought fair. No matter what the circumstance had been, she would listen to his point of view with an open mind. And even if she hadn't agreed with it, she would at least try to see his side of things.

That was a rare quality to find in someone. Whether you were male or female. He could just add it to the list of things that were uniquely Tessa.

"So can I get up now?" she asked, pulling him out of his nostalgic thoughts.

"Oh, yeah." Jake wrapped his arm around her shoulder, supporting her neck as he helped her sit up.

When she was fully upright, the new seated position brought her face to face with him. He didn't remove his arm just in case she needed it for balance—or maybe because she felt so good that he couldn't bring himself to let her go. It was probably the latter.

"Thanks," she said as a flush rose up her cheeks and she licked her lips.

He knew she wasn't doing it to be purposefully

seductive. Tessa didn't play games the way other girls did. But that didn't mean that seeing her pink tongue swipe along her full lips didn't make him harder than a steel rod. It did.

Jake closed his eyes for a moment, trying to get his body under control. Unfortunately, it didn't have the desired effect, because as soon as his vision wasn't in play, it seemed to trigger all of his other senses to come bursting to life.

The warmth of her breath fanned across his face, smelling sweet like peppermint. Her silken hair brushed against the back of his hand as his thumb, of its own accord, rubbed in slow circles around the soft skin at the base of her neck, where he'd reached out to support her. Her delicate shoulder was nestled perfectly in the bend of his arm.

It felt so right to hold her like this. Too right. If anything happened between them, it wasn't regret that he was scared of. His fear was that it would destroy him. He had to do something before he *did* something.

Opening his eyes, he avoided eye contact as he placed his arm beneath her knees and stood, picking her up off the ground.

"Jake!" she cried as her arms flew around his neck. "I can walk."

"Good," Jake responded but did not put her down.

Lucky barked happily while trucking along beside them as Jake stalked towards his house.

"Oh, you have a dog?" Tessa asked excitedly. "Hi, handsome boy!"

"Hi," Jake answered.

"Shut up." Tessa playfully but weakly swatted Jake's shoulder. "What's his name?"

"Lucky."

"Hi, Lucky. You're such a handsome boy."

Lucky barked and jumped up to try and get closer to Tessa.

"Down," Jake said firmly, shifting his weight so he could grab his keys.

Tessa looked around, and when she saw where they were standing, her eyes flew to his. "What are you doing?"

"Taking you home." Jake hadn't meant to phrase it like that, and he wanted to kick his own ass for letting those words escape from his lips. Apparently, he was not immune to Freudian slips.

Tessa didn't seem to notice his verbiage. She was focused on something else entirely. "You live here?" Her eyes grew wide with shock.

"Kind of," Jake answered honestly.

"What?" Tessa asked as they stepped inside his unlived-in house.

Jake carried her through the front room that was completely bare of furniture to the back of the house, where a lone couch sat. As gently as possible, he set her down in it and moved across the hardwood floors, his sneakers squeaking loudly on them, to the kitchen.

"Wow." She looked around the large space. "So you really bought this place, huh?"

"Yep," he said as he opened the cabinets to take inventory of what little food he kept there. Looks like peanut butter and jelly was on the menu this afternoon.

"Did you just move in?" Tessa asked.

"I haven't moved in yet." Jake spread the peanut butter on a slice of wheat bread and tried to disconnect himself from all of the uncontrollable feelings that he was having from Tessa being here, in his house. The one they'd talked about raising a family and growing old together in.

"Oh. When are you moving in?" Tessa asked.

"I don't know." He brought her the sandwich and a water and sat beside her.

"I have a protein bar in my car," she said as she took the paper plate and water bottle.

"Eat," he responded.

She looked at him for a beat, and he thought for a moment that she was going to refuse to eat it, but then she took a bite.

They sat silently while she ate. Well semi-silently. She was ooing and awwing over Lucky, who was sitting beside her in seventh heaven as she fed him bites of her crust.

"Thank you. For everything," she said sincerely after she chewed the last bite and took a long drink of water. "Well, I should let you get back to"—her eyes scanned him—"your running."

"Tessa, wait."

She froze for a moment, half off the couch. Then, slowly she sat back down.

"What?" she asked uncertainly.

Good question. Jake realized he didn't know why he'd stopped her. He just wasn't ready for her to go. But since he had, he might as well get some information.

"Why were you at Adeline's?" Yes, it might be a stupid question. Obviously if Tessa was in Hope Falls, she would want to come by and see her grandma's house.

Tessa sighed. "She left the house to me in her will."

"And that's bad?" Jake would have assumed that Tessa would have expected the house to be left to her. Or maybe any reminder of Hope Falls was just bad to Tessa.

She looked at him and he could tell that she was battling with whether or not to talk to him about what was going on with her. He waited. He wasn't going to beg. He'd done that before and he wasn't about to do it again.

"Do you really want to hear about this?" she asked.

"Yes." Of course he did.

Seemed like they were both full of stupid questions today.

---~---

Tessa ran her fingers through Lucky's soft fur as he snuggled his large head against her thigh. She was torn about opening up to Jake. None of this was his problem, but she was scared that he would take it on as his—and she was equally scared that he wouldn't.

But this was Jake. If he wanted to know what was going on, then the least she could do was tell him. She owed him that much.

"I owe over a hundred thousand dollars on a second mortgage and back taxes. The bank is going to foreclose in forty-five days if I don't come up with the money. But the good news is Lauren feels like, with some TLC and minor repairs, I should be able to sell it for, at least, that much." She tried to sum up the situation as succinctly as possible.

"You said Adeline passed nine months ago. Why did you wait so long to take care of this?"

Tessa knew that it was a fair question. She would have asked the same thing if she were in Jake's shoes. Still, that didn't change the fact that it really pissed her off. He had no clue what she had been through the last nine months. Or nine years for that matter.

But she'd decided to tell Jake what he wanted to know. "I just found out about the house three days ago. I was trying to get a loan to open up a studio in Mission Beach and was denied for bad credit. When I looked into it, I found out about the will and the house. Then I found out how much money I owed a little earlier today, when I met with Lauren to discuss the house."

His facial expression didn't change as he asked, "So what's your plan?"

"Well, I was still formulating one when I passed out cold, but so far it looks like I will fix up the house and sell it. I don't really see any other options."

"So you can buy your studio?"

"So I can get out of the mountain of debt I've just found myself in and try to salvage my credit score," Tessa clarified.

"And buy your studio," Jake repeated coldly.

Okay, obviously Tessa wasn't one of Jake's favorite people, and it wasn't like she'd known him as an adult. But it still surprised her that he was being so…unfeeling. She had just lost her grandma. Jake knew, more than anyone, how much she had meant to Tessa. She would have thought that he would find it in his heart to be just a little sympathetic towards her.

Oh well. She'd gotten by without his caring for the first sixteen years of her life and for the last thirteen. She didn't need it now. "First I need to take care of the house. Once that's done, I'll figure out my next move."

As soon as the words move came out of Tessa's mouth, Jake's face flinched, but he quickly recovered and was wearing his newly favored mask of neutrality before she could blink. His big brown eyes, the ones she used to lose herself in, stared at her blankly.

"So you're staying in town while you fix it up?"

His expression might be unreadable but he sure didn't sound too happy about that scenario. But it's not like she had a lot of options. It wasn't like she could commute from San Diego every day to work on the house. Even though she was pretty sure he wouldn't like her answer and would not be throwing her a welcome home party anytime soon, she confirmed, "Yep."

"Where?"

Seriously. "Sue Ann's. Until I get the house to the point where it's habitable."

Jake shook his head. "You can stay here."

"What?!" Tessa's raised voice caused Lucky to lift his sleepy head and bark. She began petting him behind his ears and he lay right back down and closed his eyes. Slicing her gaze back to Jake, Tessa searched his eyes to try and find some clue as to what could possibly have motivated him to say something so outrageous.

"It makes the most sense. I'm not moved in yet and it's right next door to Adeline's. That way you can get done what you need to do and get back to your life."

Jake's explanation did nothing in the way of clearing up Tessa's confusion. First of all, Sue Ann's was only about a three-minute drive away. So she didn't really think that the six-minute—round trip!—commute had anything to do with his offer. Then the way he'd said "get back to your life" with more than a hint of disdain told her that he still resented the fact that she'd left and was going to be leaving again, so why would he want her staying in his vacant house? Which begged another question.

"Why haven't you moved in?"

Jake didn't reply. Instead, his body tensed and he leaned forward on the couch, resting his elbows on his knees. Dropping his head in his hands, he raked his fingers through his thick brown hair and sighed loudly.

It always broke Tessa's heart to see Jake upset. He was always so happy, the life of the party, always wearing a smile on his face. So any time he looked angry, hurt, upset, or confused, it seemed magnified to her since it was in such complete opposition to his normal state. She would do anything to put the smile back on his face.

She did recognize the irony in the fact that the time she'd seen him the most upset, she had been the one who had caused it. But it had been *for* him…even if he didn't know it.

Without even thinking about it, Tessa reached out and rubbed her hand up and down his back in comfort. His shirt was damp with sweat, and she could feel the muscles in his strong back rippling beneath her featherlight touch. Her mind began wandering to what his bare skin would feel like. Look like. Taste like. Her fingers began tingling with arousal just as Jake suddenly jerked to a standing position and walked to the kitchen.

Tessa pulled her hand back quickly, as if she'd touched a hot stove. Which, metaphorically, she guessed she had. Jake was *hot,* and touching him could only lead to her getting burned. Looking down, she began petting Lucky again and tried to shake off her intense physical reaction to Jake.

It had always been like that with them. Just being in his presence had never failed to cause her body to come alive with passion and desire. Then, the second they'd touch, electric bliss would spread through her. Like his body was a living, breathing live wire.

When he'd carried her into the house earlier, she'd still felt like she had been coming out of a deep sleep. She hadn't been fully present. It had felt more like she had been sleepwalking—or being sleep-carried.

But just now when she'd touched him, she realized that, if anything, his effect on her had increased—not decreased—in the thirteen years they'd been apart.

Great. That was just what she needed. One more thing

to add to her list of things that sucked. No, she shouldn't look at it that way.

Tessa had made the decision over a decade ago when it became glaringly obvious that she would *never* get over Jake and that no man would ever come close to taking his place in her heart, that she would just be grateful for the fact that she'd had that once-in-a-lifetime love. Some people lived their whole lives and never experienced even a tenth of what she'd had with Jake.

"So you'll stay here," Jake pronounced as he leaned casually against the black slate countertop of his kitchen island. His hands rested on the sleek black counter on either side of him and he crossed one ankle over the other, appearing to be the poster boy of cool, calm, and collected.

But Tessa knew Jake. He was far from relaxed and calm. The vein in the left side of his neck, that only popped out when he was extremely aroused or really pissed off, was popping out something fierce. She'd loved that vein. When they would make love, she would lick from the bottom of it to the top where it disappeared beneath his earlobe. He would always growl with male appreciation and grow bigger inside of her.

It would also make an appearance when he was mad over a bad ref call when he'd played football or when his friends would talk about how hot his little sisters were. One quick glance down to his sweats told her that Jake was not suffering from the same reaction to her as she was to him, so that meant that he was really pissed off.

"I can't stay here, Jake," she replied firmly. Talk about a daily reminder of what she could have had. Staying here would be a cruel form of emotional and mental torture.

"Why not?" Jake crossed his arms, causing the thin

cotton material that covered them to pull taut, and the sight made Tessa's pulse race.

Holy hot tamale!

Standing in front of her, all six foot two of him, Jake wasn't just sexy. Sexy she could handle. No. He was toe-curling, spine-tingling, panty-melting, mouth-watering, forget-your-name-and-birthday *sexy*. It made it very difficult to carry on conversations with him. Always had.

"What?" Tessa asked since she had completely lost her train of thought.

The corner of his mouth twitched. Damn it. She'd been caught.

"Why won't you stay here?" he asked again.

Since he hadn't answered her honestly the first time, she decided two could play the question game. "Why do you want me to stay here, Jake?"

They stared at each other for what felt like an eternity. She *hated* awkward silences, but she was not about to answer first. Nope. If he wanted to know why she couldn't stay here—which she would have thought was obvious!—then he needed to tell her why he even wanted her there in the first place.

Again, his large hands raked through his hair in frustration. "I don't know," he said, and he looked back at her, holding his hands out then dropping them back down. "I just do."

The lost look in his gorgeous brown eyes crushed the remaining pieces of her heart. In that moment, she knew. It didn't matter what staying in this house would cost her. If that's what Jake wanted—*needed*—then she had no choice.

"Okay," she agreed. "I'll stay here."

A look of equal parts relief and sadness crossed his face before he nodded, pushed off the counter, and walked past her, casually saying, "All right, good. Let me show you where everything is."

Right. Because a grand tour of her ex-boyfriend-slash-love-of-her-*freaking*-life's house—the one they had planned on living in and raising a family in but was now vacant (even though he *owned* it)—that he was insisting she stayed in while she fixed her grandma's house next door after he'd just found her passed out on the lawn and made her a peanut butter and jelly sandwich, was perfectly normal.

She was sure this was how lots of people were spending their Thursday afternoons.

10

"Wait a minute." Eric's breathing was labored as he passed the ball to Jake. "She's staying in your house?"

Jake easily grabbed the basketball, juking around Justin before lifting his arms over his head, aiming, and shooting. He watched as the ball flew in the air, making a perfect arch before swooshing into the net. No rim, all net. It seemed that his double run and zero sleep were not affecting his basketball game in the least. He'd just managed to put in the winning shot, making that three W's in a row.

"Yes, she is," Jake answered his brother, trying to hide the smile that kept wanting to spread across his face every time he thought about her there.

"Why?" Eric sneered, not even trying to disguise the disapproval in his tone as the guys all walked off the court.

They played every week now. Sometimes it was two-on-two or, like tonight, it was three-on-three. Tonight Jake's team consisted of himself, Eric and Matt, their sister Amy's boyfriend. They were playing against Ryan and Luke, who were newbies, having only lived in Hope Falls a couple of years, and Justin, who'd they'd known since they were kids. All six guys walked off the court to where their gym bags were lined up against the wall.

"She needs to fix up Adeline's place so she can sell it," Jake explained.

"I thought she was staying at Sue Ann's," Eric stated with an accusatory tone.

"She was." Jake sliced his eyes to his brother, clearly communicating this was not a subject that was up for debate.

"And?" Eric asked, not letting it drop.

"And now she's not." Jake pulled out his white towel and wiped his face.

Jake didn't expect Eric to understand why he'd asked Tessa to stay at the house. Hell, he didn't even understand. Why would he think anyone else would? It had just felt like the right thing at the time.

All these years, he'd had no idea where she had been. Sure, he'd see her pictures in the magazines from all over the world, so he'd had a vague knowledge of where she'd been. He'd gotten a few postcards from her, too. But for the last thirteen years, he had no idea if she had been okay. If she had been happy. If she had been sad. If she had been stressed. If she had been eating enough.

That entire time, it had felt like a part of him, a physical part of his body as vital as his arm or leg, had been missing and there hadn't been anything he could do about it. Out of sheer self-preservation, he'd had to shove those feelings down into the dark recesses of his soul and lock them up there. He'd had to try and trick himself into feeling like a whole person.

Then today, when he'd run up and seen her lifeless form lying on the ground, it had hit him. What if he hadn't been there? What if she'd still been in San Diego or

New York or some third-world country? What would have happened to her? It made him crazy thinking about it.

And then when he'd touched her, the fear that had been coursing through him changed to something else completely. His entire body had come alive again. It was like he'd been sleepwalking through life and the moment his thumb had brushed across the soft skin at the base of her neck, he'd woken up. Lifting her into his arms and carrying her to his house had been a combination of surreal and heartbreakingly sad.

As he'd carried Tessa over the threshold into his home, it struck him that carrying her over the threshold, as husband and wife, was a scene he had imagined countless times. And here, he had actually done it. Only Tessa wasn't his wife. He wasn't her husband and they weren't starting a life together. She'd been half conscious and more interested in Lucky than she had been in the fact that he had been carrying her at all, much less carrying her over "the threshold."

Taking care of her, getting her water, fixing her a peanut butter and jelly sandwich had felt right. Like for the first time in his adult life, he was exactly where he was supposed to be, doing exactly what he was supposed to be doing.

It had pissed him off. Because that wasn't his life. She'd left once and she was going to leave again.

Then, when she'd reached out and rubbed his back the same way she had when they'd been a couple, he'd allowed himself a few moments to absorb it. To *feel.* But he knew from experience that her soft, comforting touch was like crack to him. If he allowed himself to take a hit, he'd suffer painful withdrawals without it.

He needed to keep his distance and be close to her at the same time. He just wasn't sure how to accomplish that.

Somehow, her staying at *his* house, the house that should have been theirs, even if he wasn't there, was the only solution he could come up with.

Was he thinking straight? Probably not. Was it the smartest move to have her sleeping in his bed, in his house? No. Jake couldn't make sense of everything right now. All he knew was that he'd wanted her there, and since she'd agreed, he'd felt about a thousand pounds lighter.

"What's her name again?" Justin asked. Jake did not feel like continuing this conversation, but he couldn't blame Justin for asking since Eric wouldn't drop it.

"Tessa Hayes," Jake and Eric replied in unison.

"That name sounds familiar," Justin said, narrowing his eyes as if he were trying to place her.

"She only lived in town senior year," Jake explained. Justin was his brother's age so he had already graduated when Jake and Tessa were seniors.

"So this is your ex-girlfriend?" Matt asked as he sat on the corner of the bleachers.

"Yes," Jake answered, trying to keep his tone light. He liked Matt. He was a good guy. He had no idea how sensitive this subject was to Jake.

"So are you guys getting back together?" Matt asked optimistically.

"No," Jake shot back harshly as he reached into his bag and pulled out his sweats. That wasn't going to happen, and he didn't want people getting the wrong idea or rumors spreading because she was staying in his house.

When he looked back up, all three men were staring at him with odd expressions on their faces.

"What?" Jake snapped.

"Nothing," Justin and Matt answered, shaking their heads, but Jake saw the what-the-hell-is-his-problem looks they were exchanging.

Jake grabbed his bag and turned, his sneakers squeaking on the hardwood flooring.

As they were all making their way out of the gym, Justin stopped abruptly. "Hold on. She's the photographer, right? I remember her coming up to Mountain Ridge, all the time, to take pictures." Then, a second phase of recognition dawned on Justin's face as he continued, "Wait, wasn't she the girl Parker caught you with in the tent?"

Yes.

"She's a photographer." Jake didn't respond to part two of his question.

"Parker caught you with Tessa in a tent?" Eric, always the "detective," just had to ask.

"I don't remember." Jake kept walking.

"Bullshit," Eric laughed, catching up to him, "What happened? Do Mom and Dad know?"

Jake could not believe his brother was playing the "do Mom and Dad know" card. As kids, that was how they all held power over each other. It was basically their version of blackmail. Well his, Eric's, and Nikki's anyways. Amy never did anything wrong, and even when she caught her siblings doing something, she never threatened to tell.

"There's nothing to know." No way was Jake going to talk about that night. It was private.

Well, sort of. After Parker found them, he did call Adeline. But for some reason, she didn't get Tessa in trouble or tell Jake's mom and dad. She'd just sat them both down and talked to them about being responsible.

A lot of good that did.

"So you guys comin' to JT's?" Justin asked, obviously attempting to change the subject. Which he should, since he was the one who'd brought up the night in the tent to begin with.

"Hell yeah. Losers buy. I'm there," Jake said, hoping they had navigated off the topic.

"You sure you don't need to check in with the missus first?" Eric asked.

Jake knew that he was just busting his balls. But the thing that pissed Jake off was that his brother was only an asshole when he didn't agree with what someone was doing. What in the hell was Jake doing that was so wrong?

He was helping an old friend.

End of story.

11

Tessa pulled into the small parking lot of Mountain Ridge Outdoor Adventures and saw that not only was Lauren's car already there, but six others were there as well. She was running late, as per usual. Jake hadn't wasted any time taking off after he'd shown her around his home. Before leaving though, he'd given her strict instructions to lie down and get some rest—after taking her vitals once more and checking to see if her eyes were dilated so he could "rule out a concussion."

She'd promised she would, and oddly enough…she had. As soon as Jake and Lucky had left, she'd taken a quick shower. After lying on the grass and walking through her grandma's dusty, spider-webby house, she'd felt really grimy. And since she'd planned on leaving after she'd met with Henry, her suitcase had been packed in her trunk, so she'd had fresh clothes to change into.

Either the former owners, or Jake, had renovated the house, so there were upgraded appliances and fixtures throughout, but they had outdone themselves in the master bath. Jake's shower was like heaven in water form. Not only was it large enough to hold eight easily, it also boasted dual massaging showerheads, a skylight window, dark brushed-stone tiled walls, and a bench seat in the corner that had been perfect for shaving her legs. The room also had barrel ceilings, natural stone heated flooring, an electric towel warmer, and two wood-framed mirrors sitting atop rock crystal his-and-hers basin sinks with warming lights in the ceiling.

Tessa could have lived in just that room and been perfectly happy. It was larger than her first apartment in New York had been. The only thing it was missing was a claw-footed bathtub. Tessa had always dreamed of a claw-footed bathtub. She thought her desire might have stemmed from reading all those historical romance novels as a teen. They had just always seemed so decadent to her.

Although if there would have been one there today, she might have fallen asleep in it, which would probably not have been safe. Because as it was, she'd barely made it to the large king-sized bed in Jake's room before it had been lights out.

The only reason she'd woken up when she had was because Sue Ann had called to see if she would be staying another night. When Tessa told her that she wouldn't be needing the room, Sue Ann had asked if she was leaving town. Tessa had said that she wasn't. To which, of course, Sue Ann had asked, "Then where are you staying?" When she'd told her that she would be staying next door to her grandma's at Jake's, she'd tried to downplay the "Jake's" portion of things and play up the "next door to my grandma's" part. Still, Tessa distinctly heard a smile in Sue Ann's voice when she'd cheerily told her that was "just lovely" and to "let me know if you kids need anything."

Tessa sighed as she climbed out of her car and made her way up the familiar dirt path leading to the front door of the main house. Nerves began flittering in her stomach. Other than Nikki and Lauren, whom she'd only briefly seen today, she hadn't seen any of these girls in over a decade. Two of the women in the room would be Jake's sisters and the rest were his friends.

She wasn't sure what they knew about her past or present. Nikki had seemed friendly enough today. But maybe that was because she'd been so young at the time that Jake hadn't told her about what had happened. Or maybe he had.

Also, what would they think about the fact that she was staying in his house? Because now that Sue Ann knew, Tessa would happily put money on the fact that half of Hope Falls was probably aware of her current living situation.

Oh well. She wouldn't be in town long and she was only staying at the house for Jake.

Well, that wasn't completely true. Sure, it had started out that way. But now, it definitely didn't hurt that after forty-five minutes in Jake's bathroom she was as relaxed as if she'd had a two-hour massage in a luxury day spa. Not that she'd ever been to a luxury day spa, but she'd imagined it.

As she stepped up onto the porch, the door swung open. Nikki rushed outside and pulled her into a hug. "You made it!" Nikki exclaimed happily.

"Yep," Tessa nodded as she followed Nikki inside.

As she walked into the large living area, Tessa was greeted with hugs galore from the girls she hadn't seen yet upon her return—Karina, Amanda, Sam and Amy. Every one of them was saying how happy they were to see her and how sorry they were about Adeline. Tessa was having a hard time taking it all in as well as getting over how grown up everyone looked.

Of course she'd seen Karina in magazines and on television. Karina Black was a huge pop star now. But when Tessa had known her, she had been just Karina Blackstone, a quiet, dark-haired sophomore girl who always carried around her guitar. Tessa did remember, though, that they'd had photo lab together and Karina was always making her laugh. She had a very dry sense of humor and quick wit.

Tessa had watched, with the rest of the world, as Karina skyrocketed to fame. Her debut album had gone platinum—and so had every album she'd released since. But after a decade of touring and "Hollywood life," Karina had returned to Hope Falls, where she'd met Sue Ann's grandson, Ryan. Apparently, from what Sue Ann had said when she was filling her in on all-things-Hope-Falls this morning, Ryan and Karina had had a bumpy start but they were now happily engaged, living together, and even touring together.

Then there was Sam, the Olympic medalist snowboarder. The fiery redhead had been extremely competitive when Tessa had been a T.A. in Sam's P.E. class. Tessa still remembered the teacher, Miss Langley, having to give her a pep talk whenever Sam hadn't performed up to her self-imposed high standards. Tessa was sure it was that drive that had helped her achieve all the success she'd had.

Sue Ann had told her that Sam was now engaged to Luke Reynolds, who was also an Olympian. They had both bowed out of the competitive circuit and were running the ski program at Mountain Ridge. If it weren't for the red hair, Tessa wasn't sure she would have recognized Sam on the street. Her freckles had faded and her cuteness had transformed into stunning beauty.

Amanda didn't look like she'd aged a day since the last

time Tessa had seen her. Her blonde hair and fresh face looked exactly how Tessa remembered her. Tessa had always thought that she resembled one of the porcelain dolls her grandmother had collected.

She saw Amanda and Justin's wedding picture hanging on the wall. It made Tessa's heart fill and ache at the same time. It was great to see that she had gotten her happily ever after, but at the same time it made Tessa wish that she had gotten hers as well.

"What'll you have? White or red?" Lauren asked, holding up two bottles.

"Oh, none for me. I'm driving," Tessa said.

"I can take you. I'm just having water," Amy offered as she lifted her bottle in the air.

Amy looked different as well. Jake's little sister had worn glasses and always had her hair pulled up in a ponytail with her nose in a book when Tessa had known her. Now, her light brown hair flowed beautifully around her face. She no longer wore her wire-framed glasses, and Tessa noticed for the first time how large and blue her eyes were.

From what Sue Ann had told her, Amy had just recently started dating and now lived with Henry's nephew, Matt, who, like Amy, was a teacher at the high school. Sue Ann had said—in a whispered voice—that Matt had lost his wife, tragically, years earlier and had moved to town to start over. From the glow Amy had, it looked like things were going well.

A glass of wine did sound like the best thing since the invention of Twinkies, but she had to decline. "No, it's okay. I've got my car."

"Oh, it'll be fine in the parking lot." Amanda assured her. "You can come pick it up tomorrow."

"Are you sure?" Tessa asked both Amanda and Amy.

Both girls nodded in unison.

Well, who was she to turn down a ride and a glass of wine? Especially after the day—no scratch that, *years*—she'd had. "Red."

Lauren's lips turned up into a small smile. "Girl after my own heart. All of these lightweights always go white."

From the looks of the three empty bottles of Pinot Grigio on the table, Lauren was not kidding.

Tessa heard the front door opening behind her just as a girl, who looked exactly like a young Sofia Vergara, walked through the door. Her long dark hair hung loose, she didn't have a stitch of makeup on, she wore black leggings and a loose sweatshirt, and somehow she managed to look more put together than Tessa did when she spent hours getting ready.

"Hey! Sorry I'm late. The senior ladies wanted me to show them how to give a lap dance after Burlesque class."

Tessa almost spit out her wine. Luckily, she only choked a little bit. It's not that there was anything wrong with lap dances. It was just not something she usually heard in the same sentence as "senior ladies."

"Please tell me Renata was not one of them," Karina said flatly.

Tessa remembered Renata Blackstone as a stern disciplinarian. She was tall and thin and always wore her long hair pulled back tight and braided down her back. She was Karina's grandmother, and she had raised her. Tessa didn't know where Karina's parents were, but she did remember going out to the reservation where Karina had lived, nestled in the hills beside Hope Falls, to do a photography project with her.

Somehow Tessa could not imagine the Renata that had given Tessa a stern talking to for wearing too much eyeliner, getting tips on lap dances.

The gorgeous dark-haired girl pursed her lips and her eyes widened before repeating verbatim with a flat tone, "Renata was not one of them."

Karina moaned and shook her head. Tessa laughed. She'd only been around this new girl for a minute and she already liked her.

Nikki popped up from her seat. "Tessa, have you met Lily, Eric's fiancé?"

Tessa smiled as she stood and held out her hand. "Oh, no, it's nice to meet you."

Lily's face lit up. "You, too. I've heard so much about you."

"You have?" What could she have possibly heard? Tessa had only gotten to town yesterday.

Tessa's reaction must have seemed like more than just surprise because Lily began explaining. "Oh no, nothing bad. Sorry." Lily waved her hands like she hadn't meant to say that. "Eric just told me that you were Jake's 'one that got away.'"

The room went quiet and Tessa could feel everyone's eyes on her. Her cheeks started burning and she was sure that they were bright red.

Lily looked around the room that was so quiet, they could have heard a pin drop. "I'm sorry. Should I not have said that?"

"No, it's fine," Tessa said. She knew that Lily hadn't meant anything by it. Changing the subject, she asked, "So you teach dance lessons?"

Lily nodded as Karina jumped in, explaining, "She got roped into it by Henry. Lily is an ah-may-zing dancer and I hired her to do my winter tour. She moved here from Sacramento on what was supposed to be a temporary basis, but within a week of being here, Henry had her teaching classes and Lauren rented her the house next door to Eric. Poor Lily didn't stand a chance. Once Hope Falls claims you as its own, it's like the Bermuda Triangle. You can't escape."

I did, but not because I wanted to.

Then Karina added, "Case in point: Sam, Lauren, Justin, me, and now you. We all came back."

"Oh I'm just here for a little bit. Until I can fix up the house and sell it," Tessa provided, quickly setting the record straight. She knew that conversations like these were what turned into rumors, and she didn't want anyone—Jake!—to hear false information.

A knowing twinkle lit in Karina's eyes as one brow arched. "We'll see."

As Tessa looked around the room, she could see that all the ladies had similar looks of keep-telling-yourself-that on their faces. But that was only because they didn't know what she knew.

She couldn't live in Hope Falls and not be with Jake. Since she couldn't be with Jake, she couldn't live in Hope Falls. It was that simple.

12

"So what happened in the tent?" Eric leaned his head in and asked quietly with an I'm-your-big-brother-so-you-have-to-tell-me look in his eye. Eric might not be a detective anymore, but the reason he had been so successful was that, when he wanted information, his pursuit to gain it was relentless.

Looking around the lively bar, Jake knew that no one was paying attention to his and Eric's conversation. The rest of the guys were in a heated sports debate.

"Tessa and I went camping up at Mountain Ridge after Prom. Parker found us. That's it," Jake answered.

Eric stared at him, trying to read Jake's expression.

Getting a little irritated, Jake continued, "That's ancient history. Why the hell do you even care?"

Eric lifted his mug of cold beer to his mouth and took an unhurried swig. "No reason."

No reason, my ass.

"Girls are on their way," Luke declared as he typed on his iPhone.

Every Thursday, the girls all had a "book club

meeting" while the guys played hoops. Then afterward they would all meet up at JT's. Usually, this was the portion of the evening when Jake would find someone to go home with since everyone coupled up with their significant others. Eric used to be his wingman, but now even he was engaged. However, being on the solo tip had not slowed Jake down.

Yet, tonight, he had zero interest in starting up a conversation with one of the half dozen girls who had been undressing him with their eyes since he had been there. The only girl on his mind was Tessa. He didn't want anyone else, but he couldn't have her.

He also didn't trust himself to leave right now. It was too early and he was sure that if he got behind the wheel, he would drive right over to his house, the one that was currently being occupied by the one girl he wanted and couldn't have. If he waited a couple hours until he knew she'd be asleep, it would be less of a temptation to go see her.

Well, that was his plan anyway.

So he figured that he'd hang out with Nikki. Her fiancé, Mike, was a senator and was back in Washington. He figured they could play some pool, maybe throw darts. Anything to kill some time.

"Sorry, guys. I'm slammed," Levi said as he dropped off a pitcher they'd ordered about fifteen minutes ago.

"No worries," Jake assured his friend. "You should really think about getting some help in here."

"Yeah, I think it might be time," Levi agreed before he turned and went back behind the packed bar.

"Do you want to dance?"

Jake felt a tap on his shoulder as he looked up to see Darla, who Jake lovingly referred to as the leader of the B.B.B. (Bleached-Blonde Bimbo) clique.

"Not tonight, sweetheart." Jake winked at her and smiled. He wasn't trying to be a dick. It was just that one, the double run, no sleep, and physical basketball game was catching up with him, and two, he knew the only dance she was really interested in was the horizontal mambo and she needed to find a different dance partner for that one.

"Please," she purred, "it's my birthday."

Shit.

"Come on, Jake." Eric elbowed him with a challenging gleam in his eye. "It's her birthday."

Damn. When had his brother become such an asshole?

"All right, birthday girl. One dance." Jake stood and wrapped one arm around Darla's waist, leading her to the dance floor as he flipped his brother off behind his back.

Jake could hear Eric chuckling. All the years Jake had been a smartass to his brother, he'd thought it was really funny, but now that Eric was stepping up his smartass game and Jake was on the receiving end of it, it wasn't quite as amusing.

Just as he, Darla, and her fake double D's reached the center of the dance floor, the music slowed and the opening chords of Peter Cetera's "Glory of Love" began playing through the speakers.

What the…? Is this some kind of a joke?

Jake looked around, but everyone was minding their own business. Of course they were. Why wouldn't they be? No one else knew that this had been Jake and Tessa's song.

It had started out as a joke because the first time they'd hung out, they'd watched *The Karate Kid*. It was one of the few VHS tapes Adeline had owned. Then, since Jake had done morning announcements at school senior year, he had taken the opportunity of dedicating and playing 'Glory of Love' to Tessa the next morning.

Since that day, it had been "their" song.

Darla wrapped her arms around his neck and began seductively swaying against him. Jake moved his hands to her lower back and held them there loosely. He tried to step away and put some distance between them, but the birthday girl was having none of it as she molded her body to his.

Jake couldn't remember the last time he'd heard this song. It had to have been years. When it would come on the radio, he'd turn it off. If it started playing in a store he was at, he'd leave.

What were the chances he would hear it and be forced to listen to it the day after Tessa showed back up in town? A hundred to one? A thousand to one? A million to one?

Whatever it was, the chances were slim. Now, as he listened to the lyrics, he realized how much he'd wholeheartedly believed in them as a naïve seventeen-year-old. How much he had needed her and would have done anything for her.

But it really didn't matter how he'd felt then or still felt now because she'd walked away. Left him. So now, here he was dancing with Darla. On her birthday. In a bar.

Life hadn't quite turned out how he'd planned.

---~---

"No, it's fine Amy. I don't mind. Really," Tessa assured Amy.

This was why Tessa always drove her own car and never drank. Because of situations like this. Now she was stuck going to JT's when all she really wanted to do was go home and go to bed. Well, maybe she'd take one more shower first because, seriously, that shower was incredible.

"Okay, good. I can't wait for you to meet Matt," Amy grinned and a blush rose up her cheeks.

Tessa was so happy that Amy had found someone who could make her blush at the mere mention of his name. She'd always been so sweet and quiet. Eric had been in college the year that she'd spent a lot of time at the Maguire's house, so it had just been Jake, Amy, and Nikki there. And Tessa remembered thinking at the time that Amy seemed to be overlooked a lot or just not *seen* because her siblings were so loud and outgoing.

If the glow Amy had was any indication, Amy had definitely found someone who saw her. Tessa was looking forward to meeting him and the rest of her friends' significant others. But there was a voice in the back of her head screaming that Jake would probably be there.

No one had said as much and she hadn't asked. But if he wasn't at work, then chances were he'd be with his friends and brother.

What would she say to him? How should she be around him? What would he say to her? How would he be around her?

This whole situation was so bizarre. She didn't know how to just *be* around him. Part of her just wanted to have it out with him once and for all. Lay all her cards on the table and let him do the same. But another, *bigger*, part of her just wanted to leave with the memory of who Jake had been to her intact and unvarnished. That memory had gotten her through so many bad times in her life that she honestly didn't know if she could face the rest of life without having it to hold on to.

If they had it out, who knew what can of worms she would be opening. What if he hated her for what she'd done all those years ago? Or worse, what if he really didn't care at all? Tessa knew that it was strange to think that his not caring would be worse than hating her, but that is how she truly felt.

Her biggest fear was to find out that their one year together didn't mean anything to him. That would devastate her.

"So where are you living now?" Amy asked.

"San Diego," Tessa replied.

"Do you like it there?"

"It's beautiful, and you can't beat the weather," Tessa spouted. It was her go-to answer whenever anyone asked her about San Diego. But the truth was the constant seventy-degree weather was kind of boring. She liked seasons and she missed snow.

She remembered the first time it had snowed the year she lived in Hope Falls. Jake had known that she had been waiting, like a kid, for Christmas. So the first snow that year, he'd come over to Adeline's and woken her up at five a.m.

If she closed her eyes, she could still feel his hand brushing against the side of her face as he'd whispered softly, "*Wake up, beautiful. I have something to show you.*" She'd thought it was a dream when he'd picked her up in his arms—not unlike he had earlier today—and carried her down the stairs. She'd only really woken up when he'd set her down and helped her into her coat, boots, and gloves.

Then they'd gone outside and played in the snow. Afterward, they snuggled under a huge throw blanket on the porch swing, sipping hot chocolate Gran had made them, and watched the sunrise while it snowed. It was one of the best memories of her life.

Jake had talked about their future. Getting married.

Having kids. The same things he always had said when he'd held her in his arms and promised her forever.

Honestly, a small, totally selfish part of her had been happy when he'd told her that he wasn't married and didn't have kids. Which she could fully admit was not only ironic but also insanely hypocritical since the reason she'd done what she had was so that he could be happy and have a family.

Gravel rumbled under the tires as they pulled into JT's parking lot. Tessa's head was spinning and she didn't think it had anything to do with the two glasses of wine she'd had back at Amanda's. Nope. Most likely it had to do with a certain brown-eyed, sinfully sexy, heartbreakingly hot man-of-her-dreams-slash-soul-mate.

She needed to stop thinking about him. Distraction. That was the name of the game from here on out. Looking around, she saw that the parking lot was just as crowded, if not more, than it had been last night.

Holy cow!

She'd only been in town for twenty-four hours. How was that even possible? It felt like it had been a full week, at least.

As she shut the car door, Tessa immediately put her hands in her jacket pockets as her body shivered from the cold.

"Looks like we beat the other girls here," Amy observed as the two girls hurried across the parking lot as quickly as they could to get to the heated comfort inside.

As they stepped inside the dim bar, the level of noise was much higher than Tessa had remembered it being last night. But in all fairness, she had been mainly concentrating on not peeing her pants and then in just a little bit (a lot!) of shock at seeing Jake, so it could have been this loud.

Even over all the white noise of people laughing, talking, and playing pool and darts, Tessa clearly heard *their* song playing. She thought maybe she was having stress-induced delusions, but it did seem like the song was actually playing as she followed Amy over to a table that was brimming with testosterone and ridiculously good-looking men, only two of whom Tessa knew. She was both relieved and disappointed that Jake wasn't one of them.

She said 'hi' to the guys she knew—Eric and Justin, both of whom had odd expressions on their faces. She thought maybe she'd spilled wine on herself or something, but when she looked down, she didn't seem to have any stains that she could see. Then, Amy introduced her to Karina's fiancé, Ryan, Lauren's fiancé, Ben, Sam's fiancé, Luke, and finally her fiancé, Matt. Matt was the only one Tessa didn't recognize at all since she'd seen Ryan on YouTube videos with Karina and Ben on the TV show ad with Lauren. She'd actually owned a Gatorade poster of Luke as a teenager when he'd won his first gold medal.

After all the introductions, Tessa excused herself to use the restroom because, let's face it, she really did have a small bladder. As she weaved through the tables, she glanced up and her world stopped spinning on its axis.

Jake was slow dancing. With a blonde. To *their* song.

Tessa would have thought it couldn't get any worse but then…it did. The blonde giggled at something he said, tilted her head up, and kissed him. On the dance floor. In front of everyone. With *their* song as the soundtrack.

Images of the night that she'd come back to Hope Falls before she'd left for New York, started flashing in her head. Jake in his truck with some blonde. Two weeks after she'd broken up with him and left. *Two weeks.* Two weeks that she'd spent crying herself to sleep, and she'd come back to find him screwing a blonde in his truck that was parked at *their* spot.

Tessa reminded herself that that was thirteen years ago. She might have had a right to be upset about him moving on so quickly then, but she had no reason to feel anything about his behavior now. Yet she did.

Turning on her heels, she quickly made her way back to let Amy know that she was tired and was going to call it a night. Amy tried to insist on driving Tessa home, but she lied and told her she'd already called a cab. Then she waved a quick goodbye, told everyone it had been nice meeting them, got the hell out of there, and didn't look back.

13

Jake jerked his head away from Darla the second her over-glossed lips touched his. He'd had enough. As much as he didn't want to hurt her feelings, he was done being groped. After several attempts to shoot down her advances using subtlety and humor, Jake knew he was going to have to be blunt.

"This dance is over." Jake pulled away from her and started to move off the dance floor.

Her hands wrapped around his wrist and she tugged on his arm pleading, "Please, stay. I'll behave. I promise."

Yanking out of her grasp, he said firmly, "Nope. Sorry. Three strikes and you're out, birthday girl."

"Jake," she loudly whined his name.

He ignored her.

She'd already grabbed his ass, tried to grab his junk, and planted an unwanted kiss on him. Sure, maybe most guys wouldn't be complaining about a hot blonde getting frisky, and maybe it made him the pussy that he was, but so be it.

He'd just sat down when he noticed Amy sitting beside

Matt. His sister was smiling at him weakly. He nodded his head. "Hey, sis."

She waved and began talking just as Eric leaned forward, casually saying, "You just missed your new tenant."

"What?" Jake looked at his brother, not sure what his comment meant but already not liking the cocky tone in his voice.

"Tessa was just here," Amy clarified.

"Was?" Jake hadn't been gone more than a few minutes. How could he have missed her?

"She left right after she saw you making out with Birthday Barbie over there." Eric nodded to the dance floor.

Jake stood so fast the back of his knees almost knocked his chair over. He was halfway across the bar when he heard Amy saying something to him about Tessa catching a cab. He kept going.

He pulled the door open and heard a familiar voice. It was Chris, his engine driver, saying, "…love to give you a ride."

Oh hell no.

Coming around the corner, he saw the back of Tessa's blonde head. It was shaking no. Her voice sounded friendly enough, but her tone was clearly broadcasting an I'm-not-interested signal. "No thanks. I'm fine waiting. Really."

Atta girl.

Chris looked up, and the moment he saw Jake, his expression turned from *Hey, baby. How you doin?* to *Oh shit.* "Hey, Chief." Chris nodded and moved around Tessa. Then, because he could obviously read the room, Chris quickly went inside the bar.

Tessa didn't turn around. Her back was facing him as she looked out over the parking lot.

"Tessa?" Jake wasn't sure what he was doing out here or exactly what he wanted to say to her. He had absolutely nothing to feel guilty about. It's not like he'd done anything wrong. So why did he feel like he needed to apologize?

She didn't speak, so Jake reached out and grasped her shoulder, gently turning her to face him. When she looked up, his feeling the irrational need to apologize increased by about a thousand percent.

Her large blue eyes had small pools of water in them as she put on a brave face and smiled up at him. "Hey," she said quietly as she wrapped her arms around herself. The gesture could very well have been out of necessity because it was cold outside, but it seemed protective to Jake.

Either way, he wanted to get her out of here. "Come on."

"What?" Her brows knitted as she looked up at him.

"I'm taking you home," Jake said, taking a step towards his SUV.

Tessa tilted her head and tucked her hands in the crooks of her elbows, crossing her arms. Her posture and demeanor changed on a dime. Staring at him like he'd just offended her somehow, she said, "No. You're not."

He repeated her earlier question. "What?"

"You don't have to worry about me. I called a cab. You should go back to your date," Tessa said flatly, her tone clearly conveying her unhappiness at the thought of him with someone.

A few moments ago, it had been killing him to see Tessa upset. But right now he was having a hard time not smiling over the appearance, once again, of the green-eyed monster. He knew it was wrong to feel any joy or satisfaction about Tessa being upset at *all*. Yet, as much as he couldn't help it if it made him a pussy to not want Darla groping and fondling him, he couldn't help it if it made him a dick to enjoy the fact that it had made Tessa jealous to see it.

Still, he didn't want her to get the wrong idea. "I'm not with her."

"Really," Tessa said with sarcasm dripping from her voice. "Wow. You coulda fooled me. Do you think blondie knows that you're not *with* her?"

"Tessa." Jake felt like he was getting whiplash from his constantly changing emotional state over the last sixty seconds.

First, it had broken his heart to see her in pain. Then, he'd been a little *too* happy to see her jealous. Now, he was starting to get pissed off because he didn't have to answer to *Tessa* or anyone about his actions.

He was just about to say so when the Fabulous Four appeared out of nowhere. Lauren, Karina, Amanda, and Sam all stepped up on the curb and happily greeted Tessa and Jake.

"What are you guys doing out here in the cold?" Amanda asked, being her usual bubbly self.

"Waiting for a cab," Tessa answered

"We were just leaving," Jake said at the same time.

All four of the women stared silently at both of them. Then, a slow smile spread on Karina's face. "Alrighty, then. Well, you kids have fun."

The four went into the bar, and Jake could hear their whispers and giggles. Seriously, it felt like they were all back in high school. In more ways than one.

He and Tessa stood staring at each other for a few moments before he finally said, "There's only one cab driver in town, and believe me, you do not want to get into his car. Let me take you home."

Tessa bit the inside of her lip, and he saw her weighing the pros and cons of his offer. She closed her eyes, and when she opened them, she was wearing an expression that he would have expected to see on someone walking a plank. She sighed as if resigning herself to her fate and said, "Fine. If you really don't mind."

"Not at all." Jake placed his hand on her lower back as they made their way to his Yukon. His ever-fluctuating emotions were still in action because, once again, happiness flooded his system. He *loved* that he could always reason with her. Well, that and the feeling of her lower back under his palm.

He loved that, too.

---~---

Tessa sat silently in the passenger seat, looking out the window as they passed through downtown Hope Falls. The city had placed twinkle lights in the trees, adding to the quaint small-town charm that was uniquely its own. The shop windows were all darkened, but there was a strip of lighting on the wooden sidewalks that gave everything an ethereal glow.

She could pretend that she was just enjoying the scenery, but that would be a flat-out lie. In her heart she knew she was just being a total *brat*, plain and simple. Which was frustrating because it was very out of character for her, and if she saw someone else behaving like she was, she'd think they needed to get over themselves. But for some inexplicable reason, she just couldn't stop the "I'm a brat" train now that it had left the station.

Logically, she knew Jake had interrupted his night to play chauffer and take her home. Whether or not he was really "with" the blonde was not the point. He didn't owe her a ride home or a place to stay and he certainly didn't owe her an explanation about his personal life. She'd forfeited that right a long time ago.

She just couldn't help being upset. Seeing Jake with someone else made her want to scream. Or cry. Or hit something. Or someone. Preferably blonde.

Which was ridiculous. Her behavior was ridiculous. She could practically hear Grandma Adie's voice in her head saying, *Now that boy has done nothing but been good to you, Tessa Avery Hayes. You better knock that nonsense off and act right.*

It's not that she was just imagining that that's what her grandma might say. Grandma Adie *had* said that. Multiple times. In fact, every time Tessa and Jake would get into a disagreement and Tessa would go and tell her grandma, those had been her exact wise words of wisdom. She'd always taken Jake's side. But in fairness, his had been the right side to take.

Deciding to heed her grandma's advice, Tessa cleared her throat and turned in the heated leather seat, pulling her leg up underneath her in an effort to appear casually relaxed and grateful. "Thanks for the ride."

Jake didn't look over at her, his attention directed at the road illuminated by his headlights in front of them, but she did see a twitch in the corner of his mouth. "So you're talking to me now?"

"I wasn't *not* talking to you," Tessa defended. Sure, that was total BS, but whatever. He didn't know that. Actually, he probably did. Jake had always been able to read her like a book.

Instead of calling her on her blatant lie, he did something that took Tessa by complete and utter surprise. Jake—gasp!—apologized. "I'm sorry if what you saw upset you. Honestly, I'm not with that girl. I was only dancing with her because it's her birthday. And she kissed me, not the other way around. And I didn't put that song on the jukebox."

Tessa was speechless. For several reasons. The Jake she knew did not apologize for things. Mainly because he never did anything wrong, but still. He hadn't done anything wrong this time either. And he'd remembered *their* song.

Now she *really* felt silly for the way she'd reacted. "You don't have to apologize. Who you kiss or kisses you, who you dance with, is none of my business."

"I know I don't have to apologize," Jake said as he turned onto Shady Creek Lane. "I know it's none of your business. But it still feels like it is."

Jake's words caused goose bumps to pop up on her skin, and Tessa's palms grew damp as her heart started beating so fast, it felt like it was trying to set a world record. She knew exactly what he meant. It *did* still feel like it was her business, but she'd never expected him to say that.

Tessa turned back around, facing forward as the large SUV pulled up the driveway in front of the house. She felt like she should say something. But what?

Before she had a chance to come up with anything brilliant, Jake continued, "It feels like a lifetime has passed and also like no time has passed at all."

"Yeah, it does." That was *exactly* what it felt like.

They both sat staring at the house they had planned to have their happily-ever-after in. The heavy atmosphere could be cut with a knife. Tessa had so many things she wanted to tell Jake. To ask Jake. About him. About them.

But when she opened her mouth, the only thing that came out was, "Why haven't you moved in here yet?"

Jake let out a small forced laugh. "I don't know," he said as he raked his hands though his hair. Then, leaning his head back against the headrest, he placed his hands on the steering wheel.

Tessa watched as his large fingers wrapped around the wheel and she felt a pull deep inside of her. She hadn't forgotten how those fingers felt on her body.

Trying to distract herself, she glanced up at Jake. Bad move. With his head tilted back, it gave her a perfect view of the sexy lines of his neck. Her lips tingled with a desire to press her mouth against his exposed skin. She saw the shadowed line of his vein protruding out and running down into the hood of his sweatshirt.

Her pulse quickened as her eyes—acting on their own accord!—darted down to his lap to determine if his sexy neck vein was making an appearance because he was mad or if maybe it was because, like her, he was turned on.

Ding, ding, ding! We have a winner. Tessa saw the large, bulging evidence that Jake was, in fact, still physically affected by her. A thrill swept over her and tiny firework-like tingles exploded throughout her body. She couldn't tear her eyes off of his lap, which was growing bigger by the second.

"Tessa." Her name rumbled from deep his chest.

Her eyes shot up to his and the look she saw there caused her center to spasm with arousal. His eyes were filled with hungry, predatory need. He'd never looked at her like that when they were teens. This was the look of a man, a man who knew what he wanted and exactly how to get it.

Tessa wasn't sure who moved first, but they moved towards each other, meeting over the console. Jake cradled her face in his hands, his fingertips wrapping around the back of her neck and kneading in an erotic massage.

Closing her eyes, Tessa gave in to the all-consuming passion that was rioting through her. With Jake, it had always been like this. One touch, one look, one word and her body lit up with fire, burning only for him.

She could feel his heavy breath fan across her face, and her lips tingled with anticipation. He rested his forehead against hers, and she opened her eyes. His large brown eyes staring back at her sent a delicious tremor racing through her.

"Jake," she whimpered in need.

His strong jaw tensed as his name left her lips and his fingers clenched, holding her tightly in place.

"Fuck," he grunted loudly as he pulled away from her and was out of the car, slamming the door behind him.

Tessa blinked several times in shock. The next thing she knew, he was at her side of the car swinging her door open. When she looked up at him, his gaze was unreadable. She wasn't sure if he was pissed off or if they would be continuing their "moment" inside the house.

Realizing that there was only one way to find out, Tessa placed her feet on the side bar and then prayed that her shaky legs would support her as she stepped down onto the driveway. Her prayers were answered and she was able to stand. Jake shut the door and started up towards the house. She followed, taking in his broad back as his long legs carried him in measured strides.

He'd always had a lean, athletic build as a teen, but now his body looked as though it had filled out in all the right places. She could only imagine what he looked like beneath the layers of clothes he wore. She'd seen glimpses of his arms, his neck, and all it had done was make her eager to see more.

Hopefully, when they got inside, she would.

Jake silently opened the door and motioned for her to go inside. She did. As she passed him, her shoulder brushed against his chest, and just that innocent, fully clothed contact had her on the brink of exploding.

Moving inside, she only made it a couple of steps before she heard Jake say from behind her, "Goodnight."

Spinning around, she saw the front door closing, leaving her alone. She watched as the deadbolt turned, locking into place. Reaching out, she held on to the staircase railing as she listened to Jake's key pull out of the lock and his heavy-booted footsteps as he walked back down the path.

She slumped against the wall and slid down until her butt hit the tiled entryway. The loud engine of Jake's SUV roared to life. Then, the sound slowly faded.

As she looked around the dimly lit, mostly empty house, tears began to slip down her cheeks. Not because Jake hadn't come in and they hadn't made love tonight. As much as she wanted him, she knew that was probably for the best. No, she was crying out of grief. For the life they lost. For the life they could have had.

14

Jake's head was pounding so hard, he thought there might actually be a demolition crew smashing in the walls of his brain. He tried to swallow but his mouth was dry like he'd eaten an entire bag of cotton balls. His stomach was knotted in pain and nausea. His whole body ached.

A groan escaped him as he rolled to his side and struggled to open his heavy-lidded eyes. A sliver of sunlight shone in brightly through the small, parted space in the dark drapes covering his bedroom window. Even that tiny amount of light caused him to squint and immediately regret his decision to open his eyes at all.

Harsh sounds of a bell ringing and raucous knocking thundered down his ear canal. Lifting his arm, which felt like dead weight, he pulled a pillow over his head to try and mute the offending noises.

Lying perfectly still on his back, Jake took in steady breaths in hopes that the nausea rolling through him would pass. He couldn't remember the last time he'd felt like this. It had to be when he'd been in college.

"Wake up, Sleeping Beauty," his brother's voice boomed.

"Go away," Jake said into the pillow that was still covering his face.

He heard two steps, some fabric rustling, then another two steps before the only thing that was protecting him from the harsh realities of the world was yanked off of his face.

Jake hissed as he rolled his head to the side to try and avoid the intense rays of sunlight shining brightly through his now wide-open window.

"Get up," Eric commanded. "Meet me in the kitchen. We need to talk."

The blurry outline of his brother turned and Jake watched the dark figure leave his room. Eric was usually not such an asshole, but the past couple of days, his brother had definitely been displaying a-hole-like tendencies. Jake wanted nothing more than to tell his brother to kick rocks and go back to bed, but he knew that Eric wouldn't leave and it would just draw out this little meet and greet. So even though his entire body was screaming in protest, Jake sat up and carefully lowered his legs off the side of the bed.

When his feet hit the cold hardwood floor, he rested his hands on his down comforter and pushed up. Jake stood gingerly, giving himself time to adjust to the entire world tilting on its axis.

Breathing in through his nose and out through his mouth, he walked slowly down the stairs and into his kitchen, where he found Eric leisurely sitting at the breakfast table, eating a Danish, with Lucky sitting beside him, begging for a bite.

"Sit." Eric motioned to the seat pulled out across the table from him. "Drink."

Jake noticed a piping-hot cup of coffee sitting in his black Batman mug on his white oak kitchen table, and the tempting smell of roasted coffee beans overrode his instinct to tell Eric to go to hell and not bark commands at him like he was a dog.

Sliding into the chair, Jake sank down and leaned his elbows on the cold wooden surface of the table. Closing his eyes, he lifted his warm java-filled mug with both hands, bringing it to his mouth. The second the hot liquid touched his lips, he began feeling more alert. After several drinks of the strong coffee, the hangover-induced fog he'd been navigating through began clearing up.

When he opened his eyes, he found his brother staring at him with a smug look on his face.

"What?" Jake asked defensively.

"You look like shit," Eric stated bluntly.

"Thanks." Jake set down his mug. "Is that what you came over to tell me?"

"No, I thought you might need to talk," his brother said calmly as he finished off the last bite of his breakfast.

Jake's eyebrows rose as he shook his head. "Nope. I'm good."

"Really?"

"Yep," Jake confirmed with a nod of his head.

Truth was, he was confused as shit and furious at himself for still wanting Tessa as much as he did. Last night in his truck, he'd been seconds away from stripping her out of her clothes and burying himself inside of her in the driveway of the home that he owned and did not live in.

Then when he'd gotten home, he'd been so tempted to drive back over to her that he kept having to stop himself from grabbing his keys. So in an attempt to go numb, he'd started drinking. It had started with a glass of whiskey, but if memory served, he'd finished off the entire bottle and then some.

"Rough night?" Eric asked, his gaze falling on the empty bottle of Jack Daniel's tipped over on its side and about a dozen empty beer cans sitting on Jake's granite countertops.

Jake didn't feel like justifying his bender to his big brother, and it pissed him off to be questioned about it. Eric had no idea what the hell was going on in his life.

"Eric, if you have something to say to me, say it."

"Actually it was *you,* little brother, who had a lot to say last night—or this morning. Why don't I let you do the talking?" Eric picked his phone up off the table and pressed on the screen then turned it around.

Jake was stunned to hear his own drunken voice coming from the small device. At the beginning of the message, he sounded mad and wasn't making much sense. He was rambling, speaking in broken sentences, talking about love and how unfair life was. And then, when he thought it couldn't get any worse, he heard himself slurring, "*…she lost the baby and just left. Who does that?! How could she leave me after that?*"

Jake reached across the table, pulled the phone out of his brother's grasp, and pressed delete.

"She was pregnant?" Eric asked, but it was more of a statement than a question.

Jake didn't look up at his brother. His gaze was focused on his fingers that were wrapped tightly around Eric's phone. Jake nodded.

"And she lost the baby?"

Jake nodded again.

"And then she left," Eric concluded.

Sighing, Jake figured that since his brother knew this

much—thanks to his own dumbass drunk-dialing!—he might as well tell him the whole story.

Taking a deep breath, he just started talking. "About a month after high school graduation, we went to The Train Museum in Sacramento. We'd been there about an hour when Tessa started complaining of stomach cramps. I was barely able to get her to the car in the parking lot before she started crying and I saw blood between her legs. I remember how bright red it looked against the pale blue shorts she was wearing. I got her in the car and then I raced towards the hospital I'd seen from the freeway on the way to the museum. I ran red lights and was doing about seventy. When I finally got her there, everything happened so fast. They took her out of my arms and rushed her back into the ER. They wouldn't let me go back with her because I wasn't family."

Jake set the phone down on the table and took a deep breath. A knot formed in his throat and his hands fisted, remembering the fear that had rushed through him and how completely powerless he'd felt when there had been nothing he could do to help her. Clearing his throat, he continued. "She was so scared when they wheeled her away. She was reaching out her hand, begging me to go with her. Not to leave her.

"I didn't know what to do. I called Adeline. I don't even remember how long it took her to get there, but the next thing I knew, she was sitting beside me in the waiting room, telling me everything was going to be okay. She kept going up to the front and asking to see Tessa, but they told her she was in surgery. It was dark outside before they came out and told us that Adeline could go back and see her. She tried to convince them to let me go, too, but they wouldn't.

"From the moment Adeline walked through the sliding

glass door until she appeared again, I just paced. Back and forth. I felt like I was coming out of my skin. I didn't know what to do with myself. She just *had* to be okay. I remember the look on Adeline's face as she came out of the doors. Everything stopped. I tried to ask if she was okay, but I couldn't speak. She assured me that Tessa was resting comfortably and was going to be all right as she ushered us into a small waiting area off the hall. After we sat down, she told me that Tessa would be okay but that she'd lost a lot of blood and that she'd lost the baby."

Jake looked up at his brother, who was staring back at him with a blank expression. "I had no idea what she was talking about. Adeline must have seen it on my face because she said, 'You didn't know, did you?' I told her I didn't. She said that she didn't think Tessa had known either because if she'd had any idea she was pregnant, she would have told one of us."

"Do Mom and Dad know?" Eric asked.

"No." Jake shook his head. "Just me, Adeline, and Tessa knew about it. Her parents were still in Germany, and I told Mom and Dad that I was on a camping trip.

"She was placed in ICU and I wasn't allowed access to her until that Monday. I didn't leave the hospital all weekend. I just stayed there, waiting to see her. Adeline kept coming out and giving me updates. When she was moved to a regular room, they finally let me go back.

"I remember how small and pale she looked lying in the bed. I was so relieved to finally see her, but when I saw the look in her eye, I knew something was wrong. I moved beside her and leaned over to kiss her forehead but she moved away from me. When I sat down, I tried to hold her hand but she pulled it away from me.

"I told her I loved her and how sorry I was for what she went through. I told her she was going to be okay now, that we would be okay. She wouldn't even look at me at first. She just stared out the window and told me that this whole thing made her realize what she really wanted and that it wasn't to be married and have kids. She said that she didn't want to be tied down. She said that when she left the hospital she wasn't going back to Hope Falls. She wouldn't tell me where she was going. She just said that she didn't want to be with me anymore and that we should both move on with our lives."

Jake stared down at his coffee cup sitting on his kitchen table and wrapped his fingers around the warm ceramic. "I tried to reason with her and tell her that she'd been through a lot and she might feel like that right now but that we could work it out. She wouldn't listen. Finally, she did look at me. She screamed at me to get out of her room and leave her alone. Nurses came and escorted me out of the room. Adeline was in the hall and she said it would be best to give her some time. She told me to go home, get some sleep, take a shower and come back and see her the next day. She promised she'd talk to her and call me with any updates.

"I hadn't slept or showered or eaten in days, and I felt so lost. So I listened to her. I went home, took a shower, ate, and slept for twelve hours. As soon as I woke up, I got in my car and drove back to the hospital in Sacramento. I got there at noon but she wasn't there. She'd been released earlier that morning. So I headed back to Hope Falls thinking that I must have missed the call from Adeline, but when I got to her house, Adeline told me that Tessa wasn't there and she wouldn't tell me where she was. I freaked out. I couldn't believe what was happening. I searched the whole house. She was gone."

Jake was surprised that he actually felt better after telling his brother what had happened. He'd never talked about it before, but now he was thinking that maybe he should have.

"And that's the last time you saw her?" Eric asked in a tone that Jake was sure many a criminal had been interrogated with.

Jake nodded as he confirmed, "Yeah. That's the last time I saw her. Until the other night at JT's. She sent me postcards from Italy and Paris. They just said that she was thinking of me and hoped I was happy and doing well."

"Have you talked to her?" Eric's tone softened to sound more like a brother and less like a police investigator.

Jake shrugged. "There's nothing to say."

Eric's arm reached to the counter, and before Jake even saw it coming, an empty beer can tagged him right in the head.

Jake's hand flew up too late to block it. "Hey! What the fu—"

"I knew you could be an idiot, Jake, but I didn't think you were really that stupid."

Jake threw up his arms. "She left. Now she's back because she *has* to be and then she's going to leave again. End. Of. Story."

His brother slowly shook his head at him. "Jake, I know that I have been giving you some shit. Making you dance with Darla. Getting in your business. But I was only doing that because I wanted to see what *this* really was. If it was something real or just a memory that you couldn't let go of."

Eric leaned forward on the table with an earnest expression on his face. "This is real, Jake. You love her. I've never seen you move as fast as you did when you thought Tessa had left last night. Or be less interested in a blonde with a huge rack as you were when Darla came to ask you to dance. And I know you didn't listen to the rest of the message but it went into great detail about everything that you miss and *love* about Tessa. Great. Detail."

Jake covered his face with his hands and rubbed them up and down. How could Eric know the whole story and still be giving him shit about her? He should be on his side.

"Look," Eric said as he stood, "you guys have some serious unfinished business here. If you ever plan on moving on with your life and finding happiness, you need to deal with it. Yes, she might leave again. But she's here now. Talk to her—before it really is too late." Eric slapped him on the shoulder as he headed out of the kitchen towards the front door. When he got there, he turned back before opening it. "I am sorry that you went through all that. Losing the baby. Losing Tessa. I wish you would have told me sooner. You shouldn't have had to deal with that alone. You were just a kid. But when you talk to her, try to remember that she was a kid, too, when she lost a baby she didn't even know she was carrying."

With those words, his brother was gone. Jake winced at the loud cracking sound of the door shutting, still feeling the effects of his hangover.

He laid his head on the cool surface of the table until Lucky started crying and scratching at the sliding glass door.

"Sorry, boy." Jake felt bad that it was so late in the day and he hadn't been out yet. He decided he would take him on a run to make it up to him. Maybe he could sweat out some of the alcohol he'd ingested the night before and clear his head a little bit, because Eric's words were playing over and over in it.

"…she was a kid, too, when she lost a baby she didn't even know she was carrying."

15

"Thank you so much for going shopping with me," Tessa told Nikki as they grabbed the last bags out of the trunk.

Nikki shut the trunk of Tessa's car and they headed into Jake's house. "Oh please, you never have to thank me for going shopping, even if it's for cleaning supplies. Also, as much as I enjoy being able to go to school full time, I get a little stir-crazy shut up in my house taking online classes."

Tessa could understand that. Nikki had always been adventurous, even as a pre-teen. It made sense that she'd been a flight attendant. Seeing the world. She was always on the go. But now that she was working on her Master's in Psychology, she didn't have much time for adventures anymore.

"Do you think it's weird that Jake doesn't live here?" Nikki asked as they unloaded the bags in the front room.

Tessa normally hated talking behind people's backs, but in this case she just couldn't help herself. She was just so happy that someone else felt the same way she did. "Yes!" she exclaimed.

Nikki eyes lit up, apparently happy to find someone else to discuss the subject with as well. "Every time I ask him about it, he gives me a different reason-slash-excuse. Amy and I even surprised him by getting him the couch and a new bed. We figured that, since the old ones had been so well used, he could have a new "slut-free" start. We told him he could burn his old stuff. But even cootie-free furniture didn't get him excited about living here."

Tessa must not have covered her reaction to Nikki talking about Jake's colorful, slut-filled past.

Nikki's eyes widened in horror. "Shit, I'm sorry. I don't have a filter."

Tessa waved her hand dismissively. "It's fine."

"None of those girls meant anything to him." Nikki bit the inside of her lip.

She appreciated Jake's sister trying to make her feel better, but the facts were the facts, and the little bit she'd heard in the few days she'd been back in town had told her that Jake had been a busy boy. Very busy.

Still, she didn't want Nikki to feel bad or think she'd upset her. Trying to assure her, she said, "Seriously, it's fine. Jake and I are… Or, um, we were…just kids. It was a long time ago."

Nikki slowly nodded her head, not seeming entirely convinced. Then she said, "I really thought you guys were going to get married. I used to imagine what the dress I would wear at your wedding would look like."

Tessa smiled. She remembered that Nikki always used to ask what her wedding colors were going to be. She didn't realize then that it was because she had been picturing herself in the wedding.

"You guys were really perfect together," Nikki said with a hint of sadness in her voice. "He hasn't been the same since you left."

Tessa's head shook slightly back and forth. There was no way that was true. Jake was so strong and he lived his life to the fullest. Fun should seriously be his middle name.

Grandma Adie had told her he'd left for college a month after she'd left and that he hadn't really come back to visit that much before he graduated. College changed people. They matured. "He just grew up, that's all."

Nikki's face grew serious. "I know my brother, and I'm telling you, it's not "he grew up." It's he's never gotten over *you*."

Tessa didn't know what to say. She hadn't gotten over him either. But none of that mattered, and there was no way she could explain that to Nikki. Part of her wished that what Nikki was saying was true, that Jake really did still feel the same way he had. But another part saw how tragic that would be if it was, in fact, the truth.

Before she had time to process her feelings on the matter, she heard "Freak Me Baby" by Silk playing loudly. Nikki started busting out laughing as she pulled her phone from her pocket as the explicit lyrics rang out in the cavernous house.

Nikki answered the phone, grinning from ear to ear, her face lit up like the Rockefeller Center Christmas tree in New York. "How could you possibly have changed my ringtone?"

Tessa picked up a few of the bags and went into the kitchen to give Nikki some privacy. While she was unpacking them, she thought about what Jake's sister had said.

Could it be true that he hadn't got over her?

Last night, she really thought that something was going to happen between them. But he'd left. If he still had feelings for her, wouldn't he have stayed?

"Sorry about that." Nikki was glowing as she came

around the corner. "Mike is on his way. He just got into Oakland."

"Nice song," Tessa teased her, motioning to her phone.

"I know, right?" Nikki laughed. "He's so funny. He keeps changing my ringtone."

"What if your parents heard it?" Tessa asked, feeling like she was back in high school again, worrying about Rosalie and Sean's reactions to something.

Nikki's hands flew up in the air. "My mom is the one who changed the ringtone for him when I was at her house this morning. You don't understand, my parents drank the Mike Gowan Kool-Aid. They adore him. They are proud card-carrying Team Mike members." Nikki laughed as her eyes danced with happiness. "He really is pretty amazing. I can't wait for you to meet him at the work party tomorrow."

"Isn't he only in town for the weekend?" Tessa asked.

"Yep. He has to fly out again on Monday morning."

"I don't want you two wasting your Saturday helping me fix up the house. You should be spending quality time together." Tessa truly appreciated her friend's willingness to help her, but she didn't want her sacrificing precious time with her fiancé for it.

"Are you kidding me? Mike's a politician. Well, for another six months anyway. He lives for this kind of stuff."

Tessa knew that Nikki was joking about Mike 'living' to fix up houses, but she did ask, "What do you mean, only six more months? He is not running for re-election?"

Nikki shook her head. "Nope. I don't think that politics was ever what he dreamed about going into. It was almost more of a family obligation. And things with his family have been a little tense since the campaign manager scandal. So when his term is up, he's going to move up here to Hope Falls and start his own practice, put his law degree to good use."

"Wow. So you guys are going to live here then? In Hope Falls?" Tessa asked. As a kid, all Nikki had talked about was getting out of the small town. She would dramatically say that she'd rather die than end up living here for the rest of her life.

"Yep," Nikki replied happily as she began helping Tessa unpack the bags. "I know I used to think that staying here would be like *Groundhog Day*, that I would be bored to death. But now, as an adult, I honestly couldn't imagine living somewhere else. I mean, of course, if Mike had wanted to remain in politics, then I absolutely would have adjusted. But since he fell in love with Hope Falls too, then I guess I'm just a lucky girl. I get to be with the love of my life, live in the only place I've ever called home, and be surrounded by family."

"You deserve it, sweetie." Tessa was happy for Nikki. She deserved every happiness this world had to offer.

Nikki chuckled. "I think you are the only person on this earth that calls me 'sweetie.'"

Tessa laughed and shrugged. "You are a sweetie—to me. I think I might always see you as that thirteen-year-old girl who was my shadow."

"I can deal with that," Nikki smiled.

When they'd laid out all of the supplies, Tessa pulled up the list that Lauren had emailed to her this morning. "Okay, well I think that everything is here. We should be all set for tomorrow."

"All right. Mike and I will be here bright and early." Nikki hugged her before she turned to leave.

"Thanks. See you tomorrow." Tessa looked at everything she'd purchased and started collecting the receipts to put in an envelope.

She couldn't believe how quickly everything had added up. Between the cleaning supplies, paint, and flooring, her bank account was running on fumes. Luckily, her roommate Molly's boyfriend had just moved in the week before Tessa had left. When Tessa had called Molly to let her know that she'd be longer than expected, Molly had told her that Rick would just pay her portion of the rent and utilities for as long as she was gone.

But even with those bills not hanging over her head, Tessa needed to bring in some extra income. Maybe she would call Mary and see if she had any work she could throw Tessa's way. And she'd also ask Sue Ann if she needed any help at the café.

Between her finances, the house, and Jake, Tessa's stress level was running into the red. But she would try and pick up some part-time work, and hopefully, after tomorrow, the house would be in much better shape. So with plans in place to work on two of the three blood-pressure-increasing situations in her life, she decided that instead of dwelling on the third, she would go to her new favorite place in the *whole* world. The master bathroom.

It was her tiny piece of heaven on earth. For now.

16

JAKE PULLED INTO THE DRIVEWAY AND HIS CHEST tightened in pain when he saw that Tessa's PT Cruiser was not parked in it. It was only six a.m.

Where could she be? Had she decided to stay at Sue Ann's? Had she not come home last night? Or worst of all, had she left town?

Jake was trying to calm his racing pulse as he looked up and saw Tessa's car pulling in beside him. Relief washed over him at the sight as he let out a breath he hadn't even known he had been holding. Maybe Eric had been right. Maybe he and Tessa did need to talk.

He stepped out into the crisp morning air.

"Hey." Tessa stood beside the driver's side of her car and waved, her big blue eyes peeking out from beneath her worn blue LA Dodger's baseball cap. Jake grinned. That had been their only source of contention. He was a San Francisco Giants fan and she was a Dodgers fan.

"I see your taste in baseball hasn't improved." Jake walked around the car.

"No, it hasn't. Because you can't improve on perfection. And my boys are perfection," Tessa smiled cockily.

"Really? How many World Series championships have *your boys* won in the last five years? Oh, that's right—zero. And the Giants have won…oh, that's right—three. That does not sound perfect to me."

He moved in front of her and rested one arm on her open door and the other beside her on the roof of her car. She stood between his arms and crossed her arms over her light grey sweatshirt.

"Perfection is not always measured in wins."

"That sounds like something a loser would say," Jake teased.

Tessa gasped. "I am *not* a loser."

"No"—Jake tilted his head and tugged the bill of her baseball cap down—"but your team is."

"Psshh." Tessa adjusted her hat then reached up and pushed his chest hard with both hands. "Whatever."

Instead of backing up from the force of her shove, instinctively Jake moved forward, wrapped his arms around her small frame, and pulled her towards him, closing the small space between them. It wasn't until she sucked in a startled breath and looked up at him, her body pressed tightly against his, that he realized what he'd done.

Her slender fingers fanned out across his chest, and even through the several layers of clothes he wore, he could feel the touch. The connection. His body was filled with a deep ache as his heart beat erratically.

Her eyes widened as his hands flattened against her lower back and his thumbs traced the line along the hem of her jeans. It felt like every ounce of blood in his body rushed below his belt. He could almost hear it like a raging river in his ears. The only other sound he heard were the pants of his labored breathing.

Her sky blue eyes looked up at him the same way they had when she was seventeen. Filled with passion, lust, and —unless Jake was reading it wrong—love.

At that thought, his fingers gripped over her rounded backside and his thumbs slipped beneath the hem of her sweatshirt, grazing along the soft skin of her lower back. The moment they touched skin to skin, Tessa's eyes closed and her full red lips parted as a whimper of need escaped her mouth. His grip tightened and he pulled her harder against him, his rock-hard erection pressing against her pelvis through the layers of their denim jeans.

Jake almost felt lightheaded with his fevered, hot desire. All he'd ever wanted, all he'd ever needed, was here in his arms.

His love. His passion. His heart. His soul. His Tessa.

"Tessa," Jake rasped.

Her eyes opened and locked with his. He felt a tremor run through her body and it caused his rock-hard shaft to twitch in his pants. He wanted to feel her trembling body, naked, beneath him, while he was buried inside of her.

In the back of his mind, Jake knew that he might regret this. A small voice—that sounded a lot like his brother's— was in his head saying that he needed to *talk* to her before anything happened. Warning signals were going off in his brain, cautioning Jake that this wasn't a good idea.

But Jake didn't give a shit about any of that. Looking into Tessa's baby blue eyes, caressing the smooth skin on her lower back, his hands filled with the rounded globes of her perfect ass, Jake could only think about kissing her, making love to her.

His head lowered slowly and he felt her rising up on her tiptoes. Just as their lips brushed, a loud honk sounded in the air, startling Tessa and causing her to jump back from his arms.

Turning, they saw not one, not two, not three, but about a dozen cars pulling onto the street. It was led by Eric's truck, which held not only Lily, but also Shadow, their golden retriever, between them. They were followed by what looked like the entire town of Hope Falls.

As the cars all found parking spots on the small street and people began getting out, Tessa looked up at him with a questioning look. He could see that she was worried about what he might be thinking. In that moment, Jake knew his brother was right. They needed to talk.

But this wasn't the day. Not wanting her to think that he was upset about what had just happened—or almost happened—between them, Jake said dryly, "Thanks."

Tessa's eyes widened at his insincere tone.

"This bad boy is gonna be real fun to walk around with all day." He motioned down to the large bulge his straining erection was causing in his jeans.

Tessa's hand flew over her mouth as she giggled, "Sorry."

"Don't be." Jake shrugged. "It's a permanent condition when you're around."

She stilled and searched his eyes. Even though he hadn't meant it to be a serious statement, he could see that his words affected her and she was trying to see if he was serious.

Did she really not know how he felt about her? How could she not know?

"Hey, kiddos." Sue Ann bustled around the car and, just like that, Jake's boner deflated.

Well, at least that problem's solved.

"I brought sandwiches for lunch. Where do you want me to have Ryan put them?"

"Oh, thank you so much!" Tessa exclaimed. Then she looked up at Jake, her hand gesturing inside the car. "I got donuts for everyone. Do you mind if we put the food in your kitchen and let people eat there? It's a lot cleaner than Gran's."

Jake wanted to say, "It's your kitchen, too. Do whatever you want." But it wasn't. He needed to remember that. So instead he nodded as he reached past her and pulled out several pink boxes of donuts. "Sure. I even have some fold-up tables and chairs in the garage we can put out."

"Perfect," Sue Ann said cheerily before she yelled over her shoulder, "Ryan, go ahead and bring the food into Jake's."

As Jake was turning to bring the donuts inside, he felt Tessa's slim fingers wrap around his bicep. He turned and she said, "Thank you. You didn't have to do any of this."

"Yes, I did," Jake answered honestly. Turning and walking up to the house, Jake realized that she really didn't get it.

Time. Heartache. Distance. None of that had changed the fact that he would do anything for that girl. His girl.

---~---

"Thanks, again." Tessa lifted her arms to hug Lauren, who, at five foot six inches, stood a good four inches taller than her. "I don't know how you do what you do. I am in serious awe of your organizational skills. Because of you, we got more accomplished today than I would have in six months."

"Well, we had a lot of people helping." Lauren waved her hand dismissively.

There was no way Tessa was going to let her downplay her role in today's massive renovation success. "Even if I had this many people helping me every weekend, it still would have taken me, at least, a month."

This morning, Lauren had separated everyone into work groups and designated leaders. Tessa watched in amazement as every hour she would check in with each of the group leaders and get status updates. Then she would prioritize the next hour accordingly.

She had designated runners who would go out to get supplies when needed. Also, she'd assigned four-person lunch and breakfast cleanup and serving crews that had made the mealtime transitions seamless. Lauren Harrison was a force to be reckoned with.

Lauren was scrolling through her iPad when she announced, "I think that we accomplished all of the heavy-lifting jobs that don't have to be done by professionals. I will get estimates on the roofing and plumbing to you by Monday."

Tessa wanted to cry. It felt so good to have someone other than herself taking care of details for once. "Lauren, I seriously don't know whether to kiss your feet or elect you for sainthood."

A small smile pulled at Lauren's still perfectly applied lipsticked lips. "Well, I haven't had a pedicure in a month, and believe me, I am no saint," she said with a wicked gleam in her eye as Ben and Jake made their way up the driveway.

The guys were coming back from taking a load of flooring they had pulled up from the bathrooms to the dump.

Ben stepped up and pulled Lauren into his arms, planting a kiss on her that would make a porn star blush. Lauren looked a little dazed when he pulled away. Ben leaned close to her, resting his forehead against hers, and said in a low voice, "I've been waiting to do that all day."

"Damn, Ben." Jake smiled at their friends as he stepped beside Tessa, his hand resting on her lower back, sending all kinds of mixed messages to her brain and lady parts. "You couldn't have waited 'til you guys got home?"

"No." Ben shook his head, looking not at all embarrassed about his PDA.

A small blush rose on Lauren's cheeks. "He likes it when I get organizational."

"Well, that's one I haven't heard before," Jake laughed. "But you definitely found the right girl if that's what gets your engine running."

"Hell yeah I did," Ben said, and with that, he lifted Lauren over his shoulder in a fireman's carry and slapped her rear end.

Lauren shrieked but she wore a huge smile on her face as her fiancé carried her down the driveway. Lauren lifted her head and waved. "Bye! Call if you need anything!"

"Thanks, again," Tessa called out, "for everything!"

As Jake and Tessa stood at the top of her grandma's driveway and watched as their friends drove down the street, the energy between them shifted. Like it did every time they were alone.

She was scared to look up at Jake and she was equally as scared not to. Everything between them was so… unsettled. And she had no idea what to do to settle it.

"Have you done a grand inspection?" Jake's deep voice rumbled beside her as his thumb rubbed in circles around her tailbone.

She shook her head as she braved a look up into the milky chocolate pools of his eyes. "No. I was knee-deep in kitchen cabinets all day. I just came up for air. Lauren was giving me progress updates."

He tilted his head towards the front door. "Let's check it out."

Tessa wasn't sure why he was being so nice to her. He had to be angry with her. Sure, she got the physical stuff. When things got *heated* between them, it didn't confuse her at all. But the rest of it? She just had no idea what was going on in his mind.

Which was odd, considering that historically he'd been the open book out of the two of them. Sure, Jake had always been able to read *Tessa* like a book. But part of what made that special was that other people couldn't. They would take her at face value or, like her parents, not really consider her at all. Growing up, she'd been expected to do what she was told and not only *not* have an opinion about it, but also be happy about it. So, she'd learned to smile through anything and hide what she was truly feeling. Sometimes she did such a good job even she didn't know what she really felt.

Until Jake. She could say or not say whatever she wanted, but somehow he always *knew* what was really going on inside of her. He'd seen her like no one else, not even Grandma Adie, had.

She'd only ever been able to hide what she was really feeling from him once. Thirteen years ago. When she'd lain in the hospital room and told him that she didn't love him anymore and to get out.

As Jake opened the door to her grandma's house, Tessa was once again struck by just how much had gotten accomplished that day and how different everything looked. The old green carpeting had been pulled up and the hardwood flooring, that had been original to the house, had been polished. All of the walls were empty, cleared of pictures and paintings. There were white spots throughout from where the holes had been patched.

As they walked up the stairs, she saw that the loose boards on the third and fourth steps had been fixed. Both upstairs bathrooms had new flooring, and to Tessa's surprise, the master even had new fixtures.

"Wow. I still can't believe all of this got done in just one day." Tessa looked around in disbelief.

Jake nodded. "It's amazing what Lauren can do with a few spreadsheets and an iPad."

"Right?!" Tessa agreed with a little laugh.

"How does it feel?" Jake asked. "Being back here. In this house."

Tessa paused, wanting to figure out how to explain her feelings in exactly the right words. But she could only come up with two. So she looked at him and shrugged. "Surreal and different. It's just not the same place without Gran."

Understanding flashed on his handsome features. His eyebrows lifted as his gaze dropped to the floor. He placed his hands in his pockets and rocked back slightly on his heels.

He looked unsure of himself, which was very un-Jake-like. It was starting to make Tessa a little nervous —well, more nervous than she already was being alone with Jake! —when he looked up and asked, "Do you want to get a pizza?"

Those were probably the last words that she'd expected to come out of Jake's mouth. Okay, well maybe not the *last* words, but they did surprise her nonetheless. "Sure," she agreed automatically.

"Do you mind if we go to my condo? I need to let Lucky out."

"Yes, that's great!" she said, perhaps a little too eagerly. But she couldn't help it. She wanted to see where Jake lived. And there was the added bonus of getting to see Lucky. She'd formed an instantaneous bond with that handsome guy when he'd curled up beside her after she'd passed out.

At her lightning fast response Jake's lips parted and his perfectly white teeth shone in a smile that she hadn't seen on his face since she'd been back in Hope Falls. It was one of her favorite smiles. It was his you-are-the-cutest-thing-to-ever-walk-this-planet smile. Every time he'd flashed it, she'd felt like the luckiest, most special girl in the world. Right now was no exception.

After closing up both houses, Jake insisted on driving them both, which she'd thought was ridiculous because then he'd just have to drive her back home tonight.

Unless he planned on her staying with him tonight.

Oh boy. Just when she felt the butterflies in her stomach beginning to wage a full-on wing-war of flutters, he said from beside her, "So how have you been? Really?" His tone was even and serious.

In an instant, her excited nervousness turned to dread. She knew he'd added the "really" because he didn't want her to answer with a generic "good" or "fine." He honestly wanted to know how she'd been. *Really*.

Tears began filling her eyes, but she instantly tried to blink them away. There was no reason for her to get emotional. Her life hadn't been *that* bad. It hadn't been easy but it could have been a lot worse.

Instead of trying to spin it through her deeply embedded glass-half-full filter or give in to the woe-is-me emotional wave she was riding at the moment, she decided to go the "just the facts, ma'am" Joe Friday *Dragnet* route. "Well, the last six years have been a challenge. Gran's dementia progressed rapidly. She was initially misdiagnosed with Alzheimer's, but within a few months, they changed her diagnosis to vascular dementia." Tessa let out a forced laugh, "Which is basically all the fun of Alzheimer's with the added bonus of strokes.

"I took her out of the retirement home she'd moved into after leaving Hope Falls and tried to care for her at home. I stopped traveling, gave up my position at *Time*, and didn't take on any freelance work that took me out of Southern California. I hired two nurses to care for her in shifts when I was on a shoot. That lasted for a while. Up until the night I woke up to find that she'd walked right out the front door and it took us four hours to find her. I knew, then, I was not equipped to care for her."

Tessa sniffed and felt Jake's large hand cover hers where it rested on the center console. As much as she appreciated the comforting gesture, she didn't want him to feel sorry for her. She'd managed.

"I'm so sorry," he said, sadness filling his voice as he brushed his hand over hers.

She shook her head and pulled her lips up into a smile. "It's fine. It took three different assisted living homes before I found one that I was happy with the care she received. So for the last few years, I just worked locally. Weddings, mostly. I sold my condo and moved in with a roommate, and if I wasn't working, I spent my time at Ocean Gardens with Gran."

"Where are your parents? Didn't they help?" Jake asked.

Tessa looked out the window. She didn't want him to see the tears that were forming in her eyes. "After Germany, Dad retired and they decided to move to Belgium. They call on my birthday and Christmas, but other than that, I don't hear from them."

"Damn, Tessa, I'm so sorry." Jake's voice, his touch, all should have been a comfort, but somehow were just making her feel more alone. Because she knew that she couldn't get used to it.

This time in Hope Falls was just a small reprieve from her life. A hiatus. A vacation from reality. She needed to remember that.

17

Jake could see Tessa yawning out of the corner of his eye. He knew that the right thing to do, the gentlemanly thing to do, would be to take her home. But he didn't want to. And if that made him a selfish prick, he decided he could live with that.

Tonight had been one of the best nights he could ever remember having. After Tessa had opened up to him on the way over, he'd made it his personal mission to make sure that she had a night where she could just be. So they'd ordered a pizza and played with Lucky, and were now lounging on the couch, watching movies.

And as hard—literally and figuratively!—as it was to be near her and not touch her, kiss her or make love to her, tonight had reminded Jake of the other reason that he'd been so devastated when Tessa had disappeared from his life. He'd not only lost the girl he loved more than life itself, he'd lost his best friend, too.

Tessa was hilarious and smart. She always called him on his shit. The optimistic way she looked at life was contagious.

"Oh my gosh," Tessa said as another—loud—yawn escaped her. She lifted her hands over her head and moaned as she stretched like a cat. Her back arched, and with her hands raised, the hem of her shirt pulled up, revealing the fair skin on her stomach. Lowering her arms, she snuggled into the corner of the couch and tucked socked feet underneath her. "I can't stop yawning."

"Because you're exhausted," Jake said, pointing out the obvious.

A smile appeared on her face as her big blue eyes peeked up under dark lashes, looking over her shoulder at him. "Ya think?"

Damn, she was so cute. Jake wasn't sure what he was going to do when she left again, but right now he was really enjoying the fact that she was here. In his condo. Beside him. And he knew that it would be all kinds of bad if he touched her the way he *really* wanted to, but that didn't mean he couldn't touch her at all.

"Come here," he said as he grabbed a throw pillow that was beside him and placed it on his lap.

Her eyes widened, and for the first time tonight, she didn't seem completely calm and relaxed. She probably had no idea what his intentions were. And to be honest, he wasn't totally clear on them himself. Jake just knew he needed to touch her.

"Come here," he repeated, patting the striped pillow that lay on his thigh.

Slowly, she pushed off the armrest where her head had been resting on the other side of the couch. Sitting up, she looked at him as her chest rose and fell rapidly. She nervously licked her lips.

Jake was sure as hell glad that he'd grabbed the pillow because his body's reaction to the way that she was looking at him, her labored breathing, and the sensuous sight of her licking her lips would have been clearly visible if he hadn't. He wasn't sure what she was going to do. Of course, he knew if he wanted to, all it would take was reaching out and pulling her to him and she would be putty in his hands.

The day he'd found her passed out, the night he'd given her a ride home, earlier that morning in the driveway—all it would have taken, any one of those times from Jake, was one kiss and it would have been game, set, match.

But this was different. They weren't face to face, mere inches away from each other. They weren't even touching. Of course there was sexual tension between them—as always—but he wanted to see if she trusted him and herself enough to just be close to him.

His body was strung tight with need, but that's not what this was about. This was just about needing to be close to her. His arousal was going to have to take a back seat for once. It wasn't happy about it, but Jake needed…connection.

Taking a deep breath, Tessa lowered onto the pillow and laid her hand gently on his thigh. Jake let out a breath of relief as he began running his fingers through her soft hair.

She moaned at his touch and his hard-on grew harder than he'd even thought was humanly possible. Looking down at her as the light from the television flickered off her face, he was mesmerized by her beauty. His eyes roamed over her delicate jawline, the sexy slope of her neck, her gorgeous profile. He felt overwhelmed. Not just with how badly he wanted the girl lying on his lap, but also with how much he loved her.

"That feels so good," Tessa said, her voice sounding sleepy as her eyes grew heavier.

"Does it?" Jake heard the need in his voice.

"Hmm mmm," she murmured her confirmation.

Knowing he might not like the answer but having to ask anyway, he said, "So what's the plan? Did Lauren give you any idea how long the sale might take?"

"Nope, she didn't. There are still a couple of big repairs to be done. And caring for Gran the last few years ate up my savings, so I'm gonna stay here and work part-time until I make enough money to finish the house and put it up for sale." Tessa's voice was growing quieter and her languid blinks were becoming longer and longer.

"Where are you working?" Jake asked. She'd only been in town a few days, and he hadn't heard about her getting any job.

"Um, I asked Mary if she had any jobs that she could throw my way," Tessa said as she shut her eyes and didn't open them again.

Oh, that made sense. She'd worked for Say Cheese in high school and Jake knew how much she'd loved it then.

"And I was going to see if I could pick up shifts at Sue Ann's, but today Levi said that he could use some help at the bar, so I'm gonna work a few nights a week at JT's…" Her voice trailed off and her breathing slowed.

Jake continued raking his fingers through her hair, mainly because he couldn't help himself. As much as he didn't like the idea of Tessa working in a bar, he did like the fact that she'd said she was going to work a few nights a week. It indicated that she planned on being here for weeks—plural!

Eric's words kept echoing in Jake's head. "*You need to talk to her… She was a kid, too, when she lost a baby she didn't even know she was carrying.*"

Maybe his brother was right. Now that Jake knew that she was going to be sticking around for a little while, at least, he should just talk to her. See where her head was at now.

Jake knew that his brother was definitely right on one count—he needed to deal with this. The only thing he was worried about was making sure that things didn't get physical between them. Because if that happened, he didn't think he could handle it when she left. Again.

18

"Jake, are you sure about this?" Tessa fidgeted in the seat beside him.

"For the twentieth time, yes," Jake assured her. He hated seeing her stressed again. Today had been perfect. After she'd woken up on his couch that morning, he'd made her breakfast and then taken her back to the Shady Lane house so she could shower. They'd spent the day taping off rooms at her grandma's house to get it ready to paint.

Lucky had come with them and had not left Tessa's side. They'd played music and Tessa had even danced with Lucky, who had barked happily while standing on his back legs, his paws resting on Tessa's shoulders.

Days like today were how Jake had pictured his life. He'd never cared about being rich or famous. All he'd wanted were days exactly like this.

"I can stop by and see your parents another time. It doesn't have to be for Sunday dinner."

"Listen, my mom has laid down the law. She's pissed that no one told her about the work day yesterday and wants to see you," Jake had mixed feelings about Tessa being at Sunday dinner. As happy as he was that Tessa was here now, sitting beside him, he knew that once she sat down at their family table, Sunday dinners would never be the same again.

"Nikki said that your dad's health has been poor off and on, and he would have overdone it if he'd come yesterday."

"Right, but try and explain that to my mom." Jake pulled up in front of his childhood home and saw that his siblings' cars were all there. He looked over and saw Tessa's expression at all of the cars parked in front of the house. "Plus, you don't want me to be the odd man out, do you?"

"It's your family. You're not the odd man out." Tessa was wringing her hands in her lap.

"Are you kidding me? Eric has Lily, Amy has Matt, now Nikki has Mike, my parents have each other and even Laverne has Shirley." Jake opened the door and got out. He knew that prolonging their entrance would only give Tessa more time to let her nerves go crazy.

"Laverne has Shirley?" she asked as he opened the door and she stepped onto the running bar.

"My parents' corgis, Laverne and Shirley," Jake explained as he placed his hand on her lower back and guided her towards the house.

Tessa's face lit up as Jake shut the car door. "Oh, I love it. That's too cute."

Before they'd even made it onto the brick path that led to his parents' colonial-style home, the front door flew open.

"*Tesero*!" his mother Rosalie cried out as she ran down the steps and threw her arms around Tessa. In Italian, *tesero* meant darling or treasure, and after about a month of Jake and Tessa being together, his mom had started calling her that.

Seeing his mom's face as she practically smothered Tessa in her embrace caused a knot to form in Jake's throat. As a teen, he'd liked the fact that his parents had loved Tessa as much as they had. But as an adult, he appreciated how rare it was to find someone who so seamlessly fit into the dynamics of his family.

His siblings had been able to pull it off. But Jake hadn't had one relationship that had even made it to Sunday-dinner status. Of course, in all fairness, he hadn't actually had a real relationship. Unless you counted hooking up with the same girl multiple times a relationship, which he didn't.

Jake watched as his mom linked arms with Tessa, talking nonstop as she practically dragged her up the steps to the house. Sean, his father, was waiting in the doorway.

"Oh, me darlin'. Aren't you a sight for sore eyes. It's been donkey's years since I seen ya last." His father's Irish brogue was sounding even heavier than it normally did, which tended to happen when he got emotional. His father hugged Tessa tightly. When he released her, he pointed to Jake, "Boyo here has been banjaxed since ya left."

Tessa looked at Jake with a questioning glimmer in her eye, probably having no idea what his dad had just said. Jake stepped beside her and wrapped his hand around her waist. Leaning down, he whispered in Tessa's ear, "He said he hasn't seen you in a long time and that I was wrecked when you left."

He was concentrating on keeping his voice low because lately, whenever the kids translated their father's Irish-isms in front of their dad, he got a little offended. He was getting sensitive in his old age.

When Jake straightened, he saw the look of surprise in

Tessa's eyes. It took him a moment to realize what had put it there. Did she really not know what her leaving had done to him?

"Now that everyone's here, let's eat!" his mom yelled out happily.

As Jake and Tessa took their seats at the table, Jake was struck by how, with her beside him, it felt like the final piece in his family's puzzle was in place. He knew it wasn't a thought he should dwell on, so instead he focused on saying hello to his brother, sisters, and their significant others. Tessa was doing the same.

"Before we eat, I have an announcement," Amy spoke loudly, which was very out of character for his quiet bookworm sister. She cast a nervous glance towards Matt, and Jake noticed he winked at her supportively. As Amy stood and took a deep breath, she glanced down at the table while her hands covered her stomach.

"Mama mia, you're pregnant!" his mother screeched.

"What?!" Nikki cried out. "Is that true?"

Amy looked down at Matt, who promptly stood up and placed his arm protectively around her. "Yes, and we're getting married."

There were screams of joy, mostly from his mother, and Jake sat speechless looking at his little sister. She was going to be a mom. The first one of his siblings to have kids. He was going to be an uncle. Uncle Jake.

Everyone was up and out of their seats, congratulating and hugging Amy and Matt. Nikki and his mom were crying. Jake stood, hugged his little sister, and shook Matt's hand.

It was a relief that both his sisters had found good guys. Jake knew that Matt would take care of both Amy and the baby. And when the time came, he knew Mike would do the same for Nikki. He didn't see himself having to kick either of their asses in the future.

"And we are getting married in two weeks." Amy dropped yet another bombshell. "The day after the Policeman/Fireman Ball."

"Two weeks, Amalia? How is that possible?" Jake's mom shrieked in horror.

"We just want a small wedding, but we want to do it as soon as possible"—Matt reached down and rubbed Amy's belly lovingly—"for obvious reasons. And that will give my family enough time to drive up from Arizona."

As everyone started settling down, once again taking their seats around the table, the food began to get passed around.

Nikki asked, "How long have you known?"

Amy smiled up at her soon-to-be husband. "Just a week."

"A week?!" both his mom and Nikki repeated. Loudly.

Amy nodded happily, not affected at all by their reactions. "Matt wanted to tell everyone the second we found out, but I needed time to process the news before I told anyone."

Jake's dad sniffed, and everyone's faces turned towards the head of the table, where tears were pooling in his old man's eyes. "Well, this is just something fierce. I'm going to be a daideo."

"And I'm going to be a nona." His parents looked lovingly across the large table at each other.

"Okay, not to make this about me, but..." Nikki began, and everyone laughed because Nikki did have a tendency to make things about herself, "by a show of hands, who thought that it would be me who would end up knocked up out of wedlock?"

The chuckles continued as most of the hands at the

table rose, including his parents'. His mom patted Nikki's arm as she lovingly added, "I have to be honest. I am just so relieved you didn't end up on that show Teen Mom."

"Thanks, Mom." Nikki's voice was laced with sarcasm.

Out of the corner of Jake's eye he saw, Tessa dip her head down.

Shit.

Jake squeezed Tessa's knee beneath the table and she looked up at him with a small, sad smile on her face. They stared at each other for a moment before Tessa got pulled into the "is it a boy or girl" debate that his sisters, Lily, and his mom were having.

Jake reached out to grab the bread basket his brother was handing him and the knowing look in Eric's eye told him that he hadn't missed the moment that Jake and Tessa had just shared. His brother's words once again played on repeat in his head. "*…she was a kid, too, when she lost a baby she didn't even know she was carrying.*"

In his heart, Jake knew they needed to talk about what had happened. He'd almost brought it up while they had been working on the house earlier today but he'd enjoyed his time with her so much that he hadn't wanted to ruin it by bringing up such a sensitive topic.

He had to be at the station at nine tonight and he would be there for the next few days. So if this was going to happen, they'd have to talk about it as soon as they left here. Jake couldn't avoid it any longer. It was time they both faced what they'd lost.

---~---

"Okay, Mom. She already promised. We have to go." Jake pulled on Tessa's arm, rushing them out the door.

Tessa looked up at him, her brow furrowed in question before hugging Rosalie once more and assuring her, "I will come to Sunday dinner for as long as I'm in town, Mrs. Maguire. Cross my heart."

Jake's mom squeezed her arms around Tessa, hugging her so tightly it almost cut off her air supply. Then she pulled back and pinched Tessa's cheeks affectionately as she said, "Oh, my *Tesero*, it's so good to have you home."

Tessa tried to hold back the tears as she smiled down at Rosalie's large brown eyes—that reminded her so much of Jake's!—her rounded cheeks, and full pink lips. This woman was everything Tessa had always imagined a "mom" should be. She'd accepted Tessa as one of her own from practically the first time Jake had brought her home.

"Okay, bye, Mom. Love you," Jake said, practically dragging Tessa out of the house. He seemed to be on a mission to get them out the door.

His mom and dad stood on the porch and waved goodbye. After spending the entire afternoon and into the evening with Jake's family, Tessa's heart was full. She'd forgotten just how "at home" she'd always felt at his house. And even all these years later, she still felt the same.

As Jake opened the door to his Yukon and she stepped up into the SUV, she tried to push down all of those pesky, wistful thoughts that were trying to pop up like a jack-in-the-box in her mind. Most of them were centering around the theme that days like this could have been a normal Sunday. That this could have been her life. Her family.

Shaking off those thoughts, Tessa waved at Mr. and Mrs. Maguire as they pulled away from the curb.

"I have to be at the station in an hour," Jake said, his tone sounding so serious that it sent off an alarm in her head.

"Oh." Tessa turned towards him to see if she could get a clue as to what he was feeling. He stared straight ahead at the darkened road illuminated by his high beams, his jaw held tight and his expression unreadable. She softly said, "I can get a ride from your condo if you don't want to take me back to the house."

He turned to her, his face scrunched in confusion. "No, I can take you. It's fine."

Her left shoulder shrugged as she brushed her hair back behind her ear. "Okay. You just seemed stressed, so I was trying to help."

Jake shook his head slightly back and forth, exhaling loudly out of his nose like she'd missed the point. She was sure that she had, and she still had no clue what he was upset about.

"We need to talk." Jake's tone sent a chill down her spine. Her stomach felt like it was on the spin cycle and her palms dampened.

He looked upset. And he'd just said the four dreaded words that anyone in a relationship of any kind hated to hear. We. Need. To. Talk.

Those two things coupled together did not bode well for this being a happy convo. Her mind started racing as she tried to figure out what he could possibly be mad about. Was it the fact that they'd stayed at his parents' house for so long? Jake had tried to make an escape each time one of his siblings and their significant others had left. But his mom kept holding them up until it was just the four of them and Laverne and Shirley.

Rosalie had had so many stories, photos, and even a

video of her and Sean's fortieth wedding anniversary party that she'd wanted to show Tessa. Tessa had happily listened, looked, and watched. Even when the camera had turned on Jake, who had a brunette up against the wall at the rec center after Nikki had given a very heartfelt toast to their parents. Sure, it had made her sick to her stomach to see Jake's tongue shoved down some hoochie's throat, but she'd smiled and laughed as if it hadn't affected her in the slightest.

Or maybe it wasn't that at all. Maybe Jake was upset that she'd agreed to go to Sunday dinners for as long as she was in Hope Falls. If that were the case, then she would just make up an excuse to tell Jake's mom. Tessa totally understood if Jake didn't want her there. It was *his* family. Not hers. And as much as she wished things were different, she was not a part of it.

Or maybe it was…

"Tessa." Jake's voice sliced through the white noise of worry and questions that were throwing a loud party in her head.

Turning to look at Jake, she realized that they were seated in the driveway at his house on Shady Creek Lane. Wow. That was fast.

He hadn't killed the engine, but she reached out to grab the door handle anyways.

"Do you mind if we talk here?" he asked.

Oh boy.

Taking a deep breath, she settled back against the leather seat. She watched as Jake's long fingers adjusted the heat that was blowing into the truck.

"Is that good? Are you comfortable?"

She nodded, unable to speak. Not only had a large knot formed in her throat, but she was scared that if she opened her mouth at all, her stomach would interpret the move as a "fire away" order and she'd throw up all over the console.

Yep. Mouth shut was definitely the safest route.

"We haven't ever talked about what happened," Jake stated. His voice sounded strong, but as he looked at her, she could see the look of uncertainty in the chocolate pools of his gorgeous eyes.

Jake didn't specify what he was referring to. He didn't have to. Tessa knew. Shaking her head, she agreed, "No, we haven't."

"How far along were you?"

Jake's question caught in her chest, causing it to ache with pain. Forcing herself to speak, she quietly said, "Eight weeks."

"You were two months along?" Jake breathed.

Tessa nodded.

He cleared his throat. "And you didn't know?"

"No. Not until I woke up and they told me what had happened." Tessa remembered how terrified she'd been when they rolled her away. When she closed her eyes, she could still see Jake standing in the hall of the hospital, arguing with the nurses that he needed to be with her.

Then everything had happened so fast. Several different nurses and doctors had asked her questions. She had tried to answer them all, but she'd been in so much pain. The last thing she remembered was them calling her name before everything had gone black.

"Did they say why it happened?" he asked.

Tessa had known that this question might possibly come up and had already decided just how much to share with him. It had been his baby, too, so she felt it was only right to tell him about that portion of her diagnosis.

Okay, okay, okay, okay. It was just information. She just

needed to open her mouth and give him the information. "It was an ectopic pregnancy."

"A what?" Jake asked, his brow furrowed above his nose.

"It means that the embryo attached to my fallopian tubes. It never made it to my uterus," Tessa tried to explain without letting herself get emotional.

"Why did that happen?"

Damn. This was the part that was going to get tricky. The doctors had told her that she'd been born with a congenital abnormality in her fallopian tubes. Which would have been bad enough to hear, but then they also said that she'd had a ruptured ectopic pregnancy. Her fallopian tube had burst. They'd rushed her to surgery, then, to stop the bleeding. The surgery had been successful as far as they had stopped the hemorrhage, but the outcome had ultimately sealed both Jake's and Tessa's fates. She would never be able to have children.

When she didn't answer, Jake asked, "Was it something I did?"

Tessa stared at him, not having any idea what he could possibly mean. "What?"

His eyes searched hers as if looking for the truth. Then, as if a verbal dam broke, words started spilling out of him. "I've played it back over and over again. I took you horseback riding after graduation and then we went white water rafting the weekend before. Plus, we were having a lot of sex. You should have been resting—"

"Jake, no." Tessa reached out and placed her hand over his. "It wasn't any of that. Nothing we did or didn't do caused it. There was *nothing* we could have done. It was just one of those things."

She would never forgive herself if Jake felt any guilt over what had happened. It wasn't his fault. None of it was his fault. Thinking about him carrying that around for all these years broke her already broken heart even more.

Jake sat in front of her, silent, except for his audible breathing. She would do absolutely anything to take away that tortured look in his eye.

"Do you ever think about what things would have been like? If you hadn't…" Jake's voice trailed off.

"Lost the baby," Tessa finished.

Jake looked at her, nodding once.

As she let out a forced laugh, the tears that had been threatening to rise up and fall began spilling down her cheeks. She sucked in a choppy breath as she said, "Yeah. I think about it. Every. Day."

Jake's jaw tensed. He stared at her and it felt like he saw down to her soul. His nostrils flared as he breathed heavily in and out of his nose. Before she knew what was happening, he wrapped his strong arms around her and pulled her against him.

Tessa melted into his solid form. Her head rested on his shoulder as tears poured from her eyes. Her fingers dug into the safety and solidness of the arms that were embracing her.

"It's okay. I'm here," Jake soothed her as she sobbed against him. He ran his fingers through her hair, and with his other hand, he rubbed up and down her back. She let go of everything she'd been holding on to for thirteen years.

Pain. Sadness. Fear. Loss. Heartbreak.

She'd pushed it down. Buried it deep inside of her. Now that it had made its way to the surface, she was scared she wouldn't be able to find her way out of it. That it would take her under like quicksand.

Tessa clung to Jake like he was her lifeline. Because he was. He always had been.

Even in the years they'd spent apart, when life got hard, which sadly was more often than not, Tessa would close her eyes and imagine Jake holding her. Just like this. Whispering that he would always be there for her. That everything would be okay.

After what seemed like forever, just as her sobs were beginning to subside, Jake's phone went off.

"Shit," he said under his breath.

Tessa opened her eyes and the digital clock told her that they had been parked there for over an hour. Pushing away from him, she wiped her eyes as she apologized. "I'm sorry. You're going to be late. I don't know where that came from."

"Don't be sorry. That was thirteen years overdue," Jake said. Reaching up, he cupped her face and brushed his thumb across her still damp cheek.

She leaned into his hand, loving the feel of his skin against hers.

"I really wish I didn't have to leave," his strained voice rasped.

"Me, too," Tessa breathed.

Cursing under his breath, he pulled away from her and came around to open her door. Tessa shivered from the cold as they walked up the short path to the front door. She wished more than anything that Jake didn't have to leave, but the heated floors and spa-quality shower were not bad consolation prizes. She could almost feel the water pouring down on her as if she were already standing under the pulsing stream of the showerhead.

"Are you going to be okay?" Jake asked as he opened the front door to let her in.

The last thing she wanted was Jake to be distracted and worrying about her. Fighting fires was a dangerous occupation. He needed to have his head in the game. So, attempting to put his mind at ease, she curled her lips up into her brightest smile as she said, "Oh yeah. That showerhead is calling my name."

Need and hunger filled his eyes as his lips turned up into the exact same smile she'd seen spread slowly across his face the first time he'd seen her in her cheerleading uniform senior year. Now it held the added bonus of being surrounded by the panty-melting stubble sprinkled across Jake's handsome face.

"Showerhead, huh?" His husky tone held just a dab of playfulness.

Tessa felt her eyes widen like saucers and her cheeks heat as she realized what she had said sounded like. "No, not like that! I just meant that I was going to take a shower."

He winked at her as he shut the door. "Sure ya did."

"Jake," she laughed as she planted her hands on her hips and stood in her most indignant stance, but the door clicked shut as his name left her mouth.

She walked up the stairs as she heard him pulling out of the driveway. Her phone beeped in her pocket and she pulled it out. It was a text alert, and it was from Jake. It read: *Have a nice shower…I never thought I would be so jealous of a showerhead.*

Tessa laughed. She was tempted to text something flirty back but instead just went with a smiley face emoticon and the same sign off she used to use when she wrote Jake notes in high school: *XOXO*.

19

It had only been twenty-eight hours since Jake had dropped Tessa off, but he felt like it had been a week since he'd seen her. Normally, he loved being at the firehouse. Jake loved his job and he loved the people he worked with.

They'd only had two calls, both of which were medical, and he'd been able to finally catch up on some of the paperwork that had been piling up on his desk. Which was a miracle in and of itself because the only thing that was occupying his mind was Tessa. He kept replaying every moment he'd spent with her since she'd walked into JT's that rainy night almost a week ago.

Jake knew that if they spent any more time together things would get physical between them. What Jake didn't know was if that was a good idea or not. His body had voted and it had come back with a resounding *yes*. His heart and mind were on the fence about the situation.

Logically, Jake knew that even if his heart and mind voted yea and it was two to one in favor of keeping things platonic between himself and Tessa, the second he saw her again, that would all be out the window. Their connection was just too strong, too real, too deep.

What Jake felt for Tessa was so much more than just a crazy-strong attraction, or being drawn to her like a magnet, or even craving her like an addict craves his next hit. No, with Tessa, it felt like she was a part of his soul's DNA.

Which was why Jake had no idea how to even begin to process the fact that she would leave…again. The talk they'd had about the baby, about losing the baby, had made him feel closer to her than he ever had—a feat he would have thought was impossible. Sleeping with Tessa—or more accurately, making love to Tessa—would send things spiraling into an entirely different stratosphere.

Deciding that sitting here and dwelling on it was not helping the situation or anyone involved in it, Jake decided to get the hell out of his office, which he'd been holed up in for hours. Things were quiet at the station house. It was two a.m., and the guys on his crew were upstairs sleeping. He knew he should really try and get some sleep as well, but every time his head hit the pillow, sleep was the furthest thing from his mind. All he could think about was the blonde-haired, blue-eyed girl who had stolen his heart all those years ago and still owned it.

Pushing through the swinging kitchen door, Jake stopped short when he saw Chris sitting at the large communal kitchen table. He was staring down at the phone he was holding in his hand. He hadn't seemed to notice Jake walking in.

For a split second, Jake felt as though he might be intruding on a private moment, but before he could turn and walk out, Chris looked up and saw him.

"Hey." Chris's voice was weak and his skin pale,

apparent even though the only light source came from the moonlight shining in through the kitchen window.

"You all right, man?" Jake asked. The flu had been going around, and if Chris was coming down with it, he needed to get the hell out of the station before he got everyone sick.

"I just"—Chris swallowed hard—"got some news."

Even though Jake wasn't a betting man, he would wager that he already knew the answer to this. He asked anyway. "Is everything okay?"

Chris stared back down at his phone. In a monotone, zombie-like groan, he said, "She's pregnant."

"Who's pregnant?" Jake had no idea that Chris was seeing anyone. Seriously, that is.

Chris let out a huff as he ran his fingers through his hair. "Sydney."

Jake still had no idea who Chris was talking about.

Chris must have read the confusion on Jake's face because he explained, "That brunette that I've been hooking up with for the last few months."

"Oh, right." Jake remembered seeing Chris leave JT's with the same brunette several times.

"I just… I always wanted to be a dad, but I didn't want it to happen like this." Chris sounded tortured. "I mean, I like Sydney well enough. But, I barely know her. Most of the time we've spent together has been in bed, and I don't even think I've been around her when I haven't had a decent buzz on. Now we're going to be parents?!"

"Look." Jake pulled out a chair and took a seat across from Chris. "This may not be what you planned, but it's happening. So my advice, not that you asked for it, is to be as supportive as you can to Sydney. She's having your baby. Spend some time with her, preferably when you're not intoxicated. I mean, you've got nine months before the kid's here. Getting to know the mom would be a good use of that time. What's done is done. All you can change is the present and future."

Chris looked at Jake like he'd just grown another head. "Who are you and what have you done with Jake?"

"Shut the fuck up." Jake pushed off his chair. He didn't need Chris giving him a hard time when he was just trying to help.

"I'm serious, Chief. That was deep. And also really good advice. I was expecting you to give me shit about this. I figured you would say it was my own fault or hadn't anyone told me about the birds and the bees. But you didn't." Chris stood with renewed energy. "Thanks. I'm going to go call her back." And with that, he left the kitchen area.

"I'm not always an asshole," Jake said under his breath as he opened the fridge to look for leftovers.

Pulling out some guacamole dip, he grabbed a bag of tortilla chips and leaned against the tiled counter top. Chris was going to have a baby. His sister was going to have a baby. Was something in the water?

Growing up, Jake had figured that, by this age, he'd be a dad. Have been a dad for years by now. He remembered that in second grade, his class had been asked to write a paper on what they wanted to be when they grew up. It would have made sense that he would have written that he'd wanted to be a firefighter. Or if not that, then an astronaut, a doctor, a cowboy, a baseball player, or something that little boys dream about being. But no. Jake's paper was titled: When I Grow Up I Want To Be A Dad.

That's what he'd always wanted to be. It hit him now that he'd lost sight of that once Tessa had left. He'd not only lost her and their unborn baby, but he'd also lost his lifelong dream of being a father over the course of three days when he was seventeen.

Since that fateful Monday when Tessa had screamed for him to get out of her room, he hadn't given fatherhood even a passing thought. Sure, he'd participated in the act that could lead to pregnancy more times than he could count, but he was always careful because the last thing he wanted was to be a dad…unless it was with Tessa.

20

"You can lose the shirt now," Tessa said as she pulled the oil from her bag. Turning, she posed the question to the now shirtless brown-haired, blue-eyed man standing in front of her. "Would you like to do the honors or shall I?"

He held out his hands and, with a flirty smile, answered, "I would never turn down the chance to be oiled up by a beautiful woman."

Tessa laughed as she squeezed the plastic bottle and squirted some on her palms. Rubbing them together, she warned, "I have *really* cold hands."

"I think I can handle it, sweetheart." The too-smug-for-his-own-good cop winked at her.

His cocky expression vanished the moment her hands made contact with his chest. The big, tough policeman hissed and jumped back.

"Told you," Tessa shrugged as she quickly made work of greasing up his muscled upper body.

In the last two days, she'd touched more men than she had in the previous thirty years of her life—combined.

When she'd approached Mary for any extra work she might be able to throw her way, she hadn't expected to be handed the annual policeman and fireman calendar shoots. But Mary had said that she'd scheduled it the month before and now she was ill. The proofs were due at the printers this Friday, and Mary had only shot March and June for the policemen's calendar so far. That left twenty-two sessions between the two calendars that needed to be fit into a four-day window.

So of course Tessa had jumped right in. She really needed the money. Lauren had gotten back to her with estimates on the roofing and plumbing. Even if she maxed out her credit cards, she was still about four thousand short for the bare minimum of contract work the house needed before they could put it on the market.

So for the last few days, she'd gotten up early—like four a.m. early!—worked on Gran's house, and then come to Say Cheese at nine a.m. She would fit in as many sessions as she could before she headed to JT's for her night shift. After her shift ended, she would rush home and edit until she couldn't see straight.

She was exhausted and running on almost no sleep, but on the bright side, between this gig and bartending, she was quickly reaching her financial goal. Also she'd had hardly any time to think about Jake. Well, actually that was not true. She always thought about Jake, but she'd had very little time to dwell and overanalyze, which was working out well for her sanity and general wellbeing.

"All right, you are adequately oiled up." Tessa crossed to the sink to wash her hands before taking her place behind her camera. She was old school and still looked through the viewfinder, although her camera did have the option of looking on the screen.

Stepping back, she adjusted her lamp reflector and

looked at the readings. "Okay, so I just need you to give me your most badass-cop face."

After getting a few shots, she saw that her subject was not as comfortable in front of the camera as he had been hitting on her when he first arrived. Part of being a good photographer was pulling out of your models what they needed to give you.

"So, Julian, do you have a girlfriend?" Tessa asked as she unscrewed her camera from the tripod.

"No," he answered, the spark in his eye renewed.

"Really? That surprises me." Tessa lifted the camera up, looking through the viewfinder, and she began snapping pictures.

Julian shrugged as a cocky half smile appeared on his face. And there it was—exactly what she needed. "Well, you know how it is. I work a lot."

"Oh, I bet you do." She kept snapping. "I can't even imagine how dangerous what you do is."

Sticking out his chest like a proud peacock, he hooked his thumbs on his Sam Browne duty belt and his fingers fell loose down his waist. It was a great pose for the calendar because he looked in charge and totally comfortable.

"It can be," he answered proudly.

Two more shots and she had it. She looked down to check her screen. She flipped through the session, just to confirm that she'd gotten everything she needed. The one thing she absolutely adored about digital photography was that she didn't have to wait to see what she had until the film developed. Just hoping against hope that she had, in fact, gotten amazing shots.

Everything was at her fingertips. And not only that, but through the magic of technology, she could basically tweak and twist her image any which way until she was happy with it. She loved it.

"Awesome job, Julian. We got what we needed." Tessa moved to the Mac computer that was sitting on the back table in the studio to download the photos and get ready for the next session.

"So how does dinner sound? Friday night?" Julian moved beside her. *Close* beside her. Clearly he wasn't a fan of personal space.

"Oh thanks, but I'm actually working this Friday." Tessa tried to keep her voice as friendly and upbeat as possible. She hated awkward social situations, and she found that if she just stayed happy and clueless they would work themselves out.

"How about Saturday?" His voice dropped an octave.

Or not.

Okay, time to pull out the tried-and-true, old-faithful, get-out-of-jail-free-and-pass-go rejection. "Actually," she said as she turned, "I'm kind of seeing someone."

"Really." Julian looked at her like her pants were about to burst into flames from lying.

Was it really so *hard* to believe that she might be seeing someone? Her brows lifted and she tilted her head at his challenging tone. "Yes, really."

Julian backed away and held up his hands in mock surrender, perhaps sensing her irritation. He pulled his shirt back on and winked at her before leaving. "Well, if you ever want to give a *real* man a try, call me."

Tessa turned back to her computer. She heard footsteps and then the door shutting.

"Right," she mumbled under her breath as she pushed her camera's flash drive into the side of the computer, "like that would ever happen. Seriously, why do guys think that's even remotely attractive? News flash, Romeo. Girls do not like assholes."

"Are you sure about that?" a deep voice sounded from behind her.

Tessa screamed as she jumped at least a foot off the ground and spun around to find Jake dressed in full firefighter gear, leaning casually against the closed doorframe.

"What are you doing?!" Tessa asked as she clutched at her chest.

"Listening to you talking to yourself." Jake pushed off the doorframe and began walking towards her.

"When did you get here?" Tessa hadn't heard him come in.

"Right before you shot Officer Douchebag down." Jake stopped about a foot in front of her.

"Oh." Tessa nodded, looking up into the dark pools of his brown eyes. Her heartbeat began picking up for an entirely different reason than fear. "I didn't hear you come in."

"Clearly." A smile tugged at Jake's lips and Tessa felt it spread through her like cream in her coffee. "Where do you want me?"

"What?" Tessa wanted him naked and on top of her, but she didn't think she should just blurt that out.

His brow lifted and a knowing look flitted across his eyes. She couldn't prove that he could read her mind, but she had always suspected as much. As she tried to clear it of anything X-rated, he put his hand out towards the white backdrop beside him. "The photo shoot."

"Oh right! That." Jake was here for his photo session. Duh. Her only excuse for totally blanking was that she'd barely slept and, as Gran liked to say, "had been busier than a one-legged man in an ass kicking contest."

Shaking her head slightly, she said, "So we're gonna start with your full Bunker gear on. Then just your pants and boots. We're doing side-by-sides of uniform and shirtless. Go ahead and stand there."

Tessa's hands were shaking as she pulled the now cleared flash drive from the computer. She wasn't sure if they were shaking from nerves or arousal, but either way, she needed to lock it down and do her job. These calendars helped raise a lot of money for the city of Hope Falls.

Her heart was pounding and her mouth grew dry as she took her place in front of the backdrop. She began to lift the camera to her eye but realized that the shaking was getting worse. Tripod. Jake's shoot could obviously not be done freehand.

"Are you okay?" Jake asked with amusement lacing his voice.

"Yep," Tessa answered perhaps a tad too enthusiastically. She looked up to decide which pose to put Jake in and her breath caught in her chest. He stood totally naturally, his weight on his right foot, his left hand holding his helmet against his side. Not only was his body's pose picture perfect, the look in his eye was…sizzling.

If it were possible to spontaneously combust from a look, Tessa would have burst into flames by now. Clearing her throat, she focused her attention on screwing the base of her camera onto the tripod. It was difficult when she could feel the heat of his stare all over her skin like she was lying on a beach and the sun was shining down on her.

Pressing her eye to the viewfinder, she began clicking. Jake didn't need direction or emotion to be pulled out of him like the other models she'd been shooting. He naturally moved, just slightly every few moments, keeping the shots alive and full of life. Tessa adjusted her shutter speed and focusing ring and kept shooting.

"That's great," Tessa said. "I think we've got everything we need with that setup."

Tessa was relieved when Jake began taking off his jacket. She wasn't sure she could ask Jake to "lose the shirt" or "take it off" without her voice cracking, and as much as possible, she did want to, at least, have the appearance of professionalism.

Leaning down, she grabbed the oil out of her bag. When she stood, her eyes felt like they were popping out of her head, like in the cartoons when the wolf sees the pretty lady. Jake was pulling off his white undershirt, revealing his rippling abs and the hard planes of his muscled chest.

She walked slowly towards him, her heartbeat pounding in her own ears. Tessa knew that it was impossible for him to hear it, but it was so loud she felt like it was equally as impossible for him not to hear it.

Every other model had been given the option of whether or not they wanted to apply the glistening oil to their own bodies. Jake was not going to get any such option. Professionalism was one thing, but passing up a chance to touch Jake was just stupid. Or maybe touching him would be the stupid thing to do. She couldn't really decide, but she knew one thing for certain—it was going to happen.

Taking in a calming breath, Tessa squirted some the oily liquid in her palm and rubbed her hands together.

"I like where this is going," Jake said lightheartedly. Her eyes glanced up to his. The look in his eye betrayed his teasing tone. It was deadly serious.

Tessa smiled and let out a little nervous laugh as she rubbed her hands together, the slippery liquid causing them to slide easily. Her hands reached out and touched his body. The skin-to-skin contact sent a bolt of zings all the way to the top of her head and down to the tips of her toes.

Moving across his defined chest, her hands began to

tremble. Maybe this wasn't such a great idea after all. "Okay, okay, okay, okay," she whispered under her breath, trying to get some kind of a reign on her raging hormones. It wasn't really helping.

---~---

Jake knew that Tessa was just as affected by what was going on as he was. Her hands were shaking and he'd just heard her whispering barely audible "okays." More than anything, he wanted to cover her mouth with his and swallow her nervous rumblings in a kiss that was sure to cure all of her anxiety.

He was doing the best he possibly could to remain perfectly still while Tessa's soft hands roamed his chest and torso. There was one part of his anatomy that was not cooperating. His shaft was growing harder by the second and there was absolutely nothing that he could do about it.

The sensuous feeling of Tessa's touch gliding across his skin was too much for Jake to handle. Add to that the visual of her face concentrating as she worked, her pale hands against his olive skin, and the hint of cleavage he could see from her V-neck sweater and he was toast. There was no way his body was going to listen to his mental "down boy" command.

Closing his eyes didn't help matters. Just like before, all of his other senses became hyper aware. Her scent, her touch, even the nervous way she whispered "okay" were all sensual torment causing unrelenting desire to consume him.

"Done." She stepped away quickly, and he saw her

body tremble as a visible chill ran the length of her body. Turning, she quickly made her way to the small sink to rinse her hands. Jake's attention was solely focused on her perfect heart-shaped ass as it swayed back and forth while she crossed the room.

A small smile tugged at his lips as he heard her whispering to herself while she wiped her wet hands on her jeans. He watched, mesmerized, as she moved behind the camera. Her slim fingers reached up, turning a few knobs, and then she pivoted and adjusted an umbrella-looking thing behind her.

Tessa was sexy no matter what she was doing. She could be doing absolutely nothing at all and easily be the sexiest woman Jake had ever laid eyes on. But watching her work, in her element, turned him on something fierce. The way her brows furrowed in concentration. The way her eyes narrowed until she found just the right angle to get the exact shot she wanted.

Jake remembered when he used to take her up to Mountain Ridge when she was just learning about photography. He could spend hours upon hours just watching her with a camera. He'd thought, at the time, that he would be doing that for the rest of his life. Things obviously didn't turn out as planned.

Tessa cleared her throat bringing him back to the present. He looked up at her and she immediately began snapping pictures. Even though the camera was blocking Jake's view of Tessa's entire face, he could still see the smooth skin of her cheeks, her full pink lips, and the fine baby hairs that fell on her forehead. She wore her shoulder-length hair back in a ponytail, and wisps of fine tendrils framed her angelic face.

"Okay, chin down. Shoulders back," she instructed as she continued snapping.

A need unlike any he had ever experienced before was raging through him like an inferno. He was burning up inside with heated desire. He knew that Tessa had a job to do, but if she came back to oil him up again, he couldn't make any promises. He was holding on by a very thin thread.

"All right, we've got that." Tessa moved from behind the camera and grabbed a chair that had a wooden frame and an open back. She set it down directly in front of him with the seat facing him. "Straddle it," she said as she scurried quickly back to her camera.

"I like it when you talk dirty," Jake teased as he watched her move with lightning speed. She obviously didn't trust herself to be close to him any more than he trusted himself to be close to her.

She let out a puff of breath that sounded like a forced laugh and dismissively waved her hand at his comment. When she turned, he saw that a light pink blush had crept up on her cheeks.

While she adjusted the lighting and her camera, he pulled the chair slightly towards him and did as she asked. Placing his legs on either side, he straddled it and sat down, leaning his forearms on the frame.

"Good," she said, her voice sounding strained. "That's perfect."

She snapped several more shots and moved the tripod to the left. Jake assumed it was to get another angle of the pose. He could hear more mumbling under her breath and she sounded a little frustrated.

"Is everything okay?" he asked.

Jake was pretty sure that *he* wasn't doing anything that would cause her aggravation. He'd been doing these calendar shoots since he'd moved back home from college and they were pretty straightforward. Take your shirt off and look into the camera like you want to have sex with it. Normally, with Mary standing behind the lens, he had to do a bit of acting. But not today. No acting required today.

"Yep. Everything is fine," Tessa said a little too brightly through clenched teeth.

His brow rose in question. "You sure about that?"

Pursing her lips, she nodded her head determinedly. She dipped her head, looking at the base of the camera, and Jake noticed her unscrewing something, then pulling the camera off the tripod with purpose. Jake saw a fire in Tessa's eyes that made his body stand even higher at attention and salute. Luckily, in his new seated position he didn't think it would be quite as obvious. Not that he really gave a damn.

Jake watched as Tessa alternated holding the camera in her right hand then her left, simultaneously shaking the hand that was empty. Then, taking a deep breath, she knelt to the ground. His eyes followed the lens. He saw the shutter closing and opening rapidly as she tilted her head and spread her legs farther apart, moving lower towards the ground. Her action caused Jake's dick to twitch in his pants, begging for attention.

After another torturous half hour or so Tessa pulled the camera from in front of her face and smiled as she looked down at it. Her thin finger swiped the flat screen on the back as she announced proudly, "Got it."

As she continued looking, her eyes widened. "Wow, Jake. I've been tempted to tell every other guy I've shot over the past few days not to quit their day jobs. But holy smokes! If you ever wanted to change your profession, you could *definitely* be a model."

She crossed the room, heading towards the computer he'd seen her standing at when he'd come in. As she passed by him, the sweet scent of fresh flowers drifted through the air. Tessa always smelled good. Sometimes she smelled like vanilla or watermelon. Other times, it was flowers or just pure clean and fresh. And somehow, no matter what the scent, she smelled uniquely like…Tessa. Jake had no idea how she managed to do that.

Standing, he followed her like she was the Pied Piper and her ass was the flute. He mindlessly crossed the room, Tessa only a few steps in front of him. She stopped and pulled out a small card before feeding it into the side of the computer. He continued, only stopping when he was directly behind her. He wasn't touching her but he was so close to her that he'd be surprised if a piece of paper could fit between their bodies.

Jake noticed her hand shaking as her fingers moved over the mouse and she clicked the right side. She stood a good foot shorter than him at five foot two, but he could still smell the flowery scent of her shampoo. His fingers itched to reach out and stroke her silky hair, the same way he had when they'd spent the night on his couch. He'd stayed up the entire night just watching her as she slept.

It was still so unbelievable to him that she was actually back in Hope Falls. Even if it was just for a short time. He didn't want to waste a moment he had with her by sleeping. Like his dad always said, "You can sleep when you're dead." Jake had always considered that a morbid saying, but that night, with Tessa lying in his lap, he understood it perfectly.

"See?" She looked up at him and sucked in a breath of awareness when she saw how close he was standing. Her eyes widened and her lips parted. She swallowed audibly and then looked back to the large screen.

Tearing his gaze from the sweet spot in her neck, Jake forced himself to look at the pictures.

He couldn't believe what he saw. "What the—"

"Don't worry," she quickly explained. "I can Photoshop it out."

"I hope so," Jake said. He wasn't sure if he should be embarrassed or proud. Since it was Jake, he went with proud. His pictures looked more like they'd be featured in Playgirl than a community calendar. He was standing at full attention, tenting his turnout pants something fierce. "My mom buys this calendar."

Tessa giggled a little as she scrolled through the shots. "I know. I'll take care of it. I promise."

Jake placed his hands on Tessa's jean-clad hips and pulled her against him. Leaning down, he whispered suggestively in her ear, "You promise, huh?"

Jake knew that this wasn't the time or the place, but at this moment, neither of those things really mattered to him. He gripped her hips tighter as her backside pressed against his throbbing manhood.

"Jake." His name came out as a plea, her voice threaded with need.

His body immediately recognized hers. His responses had always been, and still were, so much more intense with Tessa than any other woman he'd touched. This was the real thing. Everything else had just been a cheap, not even remotely satisfying, imitation.

"God, you feel so good." They were fully clothed and Jake felt more connected to her than he had with hundreds of women when he'd been naked and inside of them.

Tessa whimpered and she melted back against him. Her fingers reached up and wrapped around his biceps as if to anchor herself to him. Feeling her holding on to him as her nails dug into his skin caused Jake to feel a primal surge of arousal spread through him. So much stronger than merely being turned on.

He needed to touch her. Skin to skin. His palms slid to her stomach as his fingers dipped beneath her jeans.

"Jake…my…next appointment—" Tessa feebly protested through choppy breaths.

"I locked the door when I came in," he growled.

Her head fell to the side against his shoulder, and he took the opportunity to press his lips to the soft spot on the base of her neck. She moaned as his lips grazed her sensitive skin. Needing to taste her, he gently licked and kissed a trail up the side of her neck.

She gripped him harder as she moaned, "Are you sure…we should… Is this…a good ide—"

"Do you want me to touch you?" Jake interrupted, getting right to the point. That was all that mattered in this moment.

During these past few days that he'd been at the station house, he'd had a lot of time to think. There was nothing Jake or Tessa could do to erase the past. And he knew that he had no control over the future. All he had—all they had—was right here, right now.

"Yes," Tessa whispered as her body melted against his.

"Tell me," Jake demanded. He wanted to hear her say it.

"I want you to touch me," she said breathlessly

Urgency swept through Jake as he made quick work of her button and zipper. The second it was down, his fingers slid beneath her satin panties. He felt a sprinkling of hair at the top of her femininity, sending a jolt of need to shoot through him.

"Spread your legs," he commanded roughly as his fingers continued their erotic path to her core. Tessa whimpered as she did as he'd asked. His fingers dipped lower and he groaned as they glided against her soft, moist lips. "You're so wet."

"You're so hard," she moaned in a soft, anxious sigh. As the candid words left her mouth, she tilted her hips back, pressing her ass into his erection and almost causing him to come in his pants.

The motion also caused her distended nub to brush against the pad of his finger. She cried out at the contact. He moved his finger in a circular motion, spreading her wetness as he slid over her nub again and again until he felt her legs begin to shake.

"Oh God…Jake…I'm gonna—"

"I know." Jake's finger moved at a steady rhythm as he felt her growing wetter and wetter. His other hand slid beneath her sweater. His palm grazed over her ribs and continued up until he felt the bottom of her bra. His hand cupped her breast beneath her bra and he felt her hardened nipple rubbing against his palm.

Squeezing her plump flesh in his hand just once, Jake removed his hand from beneath her sweater and bra knowing, exactly what he needed to do to send Tessa up and over the edge.

A small smile of amusement spread across his face at her sigh of disappointment as he pulled his hand back. Didn't she know him better than that?

Her body pressed against his hand moving faster and faster, seeking release. His fingers were covered in her growing arousal.

Moving his large hand to her collarbone, he trailed his fingers down over her chest, slipping beneath her sweater and pulling it down, taking her bra with it. When he looked over her shoulder at her now exposed breasts, his breath caught in his chest. She was just so damn beautiful. Her rounded mounds, the pale pink areola that surrounded her hardened nipples. His heart beat erratically in his chest as desire spiraled through his body like a hurricane.

Lifting his fingers to her mouth, he traced her lips before slipping his index and middle finger inside. "Suck," he harshly instructed.

She moaned as her lips covered his fingers and her soft, wet tongue licked along the length of his digits. He moved his fingers in and out of her hot, wet mouth several times and could feel her body shaking at the erotic act. Then, pulling them out slowly, he spread the moisture from her mouth over each tight peak of her breasts.

Jake's balls tightened at the sight of her glistening nipples. His mouth covered her neck as he alternated rolling first her right nipple, then her left, between his fingers.

Tessa's entire body was shaking now as she came apart in his arms. Her fingers clutched him even tighter as she muttered words of encouragement. Saying how good she felt. How good it felt for him to touch her.

His fingers continued their erotic caresses until he felt her body go limp against him. He might still be strung tight with need, but he hadn't felt this sexually satisfied since…the last time he'd made love to Tessa.

---~---

Tessa could only hear the loud pants of her breath and a faraway ringing sound in her ears as she came back down from her earth-shattering release. Jake's arms and body were the only things that kept her from falling to the floor. Her legs felt like wet noodles. She felt like all of her strength and stress had just drained out of her.

Never before in her life had she experienced such a powerful orgasm. It didn't surprise her, at all, that it would be at Jake's hands. As a teen, she'd enjoyed sex with Jake, and he'd always made sure that she came at least once, but it had never felt like the orgasm she'd just had. Even though Jake had always made her feel safe and loved, she was young and she had insecurities like any other teenage girl and that made her inhibited.

But she wasn't inhibited anymore.

A second wind of desire swept over her as she drifted back into the present. Tessa could feel Jake's rock-hard member pressing firmly against her butt. Not suffering from any of the shyness that she had when she was younger, Tessa turned in Jake's arms, excitement and anticipation flooding her system. Looking up into his gorgeous, heavy-lidded brown eyes lined with dark, thick lashes, Tessa sweetly smiled. "Hi," she said.

"Hi," he repeated as he grinned down at her, his thumbs sensually rubbing up and down her lower back.

Standing in front of him, breasts hanging out, pants unzipped after just coming at his touch, Tessa would have thought that a small bit of embarrassment might have tried to creep in. But the opposite actually occurred.

She felt sexy. Powerful even. Leaning forward, she pressed her lips to the strong plane of his chest. He took in a deep breath through his nose, and his palms moved down, cupping her rear and kneading it in his hands.

Peppering kisses across Jake's muscular chest, she stopped to pay extra attention to each one of his nipples, her tongue passing over them before lightly nipping each bud with her teeth. Then she moved lower, sucking and licking her way down his ripped abdomen. Tessa felt her sexy, powerful energy increasing by the second.

She'd never done what she was about to do with him before. As an adult, she'd gone down on the few boyfriends she'd had. And she'd enjoyed it. But she'd always regretted that she hadn't experienced this with Jake.

Time to put that regret to bed, so to speak, Tessa thought as she bent down on her knees and her fingers grazed the top of his turnout pants.

"Tessa," Jake gritted out in what she assumed was meant to be a warning, but his deep, gravelly voice came out sounding hotter than a firecracker lit on both ends.

As she ignored his wannabe warning, a thrill raced through Tessa as she unzipped Jake's pants and saw the outline of his impressive length in his black boxer briefs. Her hand moved over it like metal drawn to a magnet.

Jake moaned and his head dropped back as her fingers molded around his erection, stroking up and down his length. Tessa was almost giddy at the thought that she would finally be able to do *this* with *Jake*.

Somewhere in the back of her consciousness, she was aware that they really didn't have much time, so as much as she would like to draw this out, to explore every inch of him, she knew that if she wanted to do this, she needed to move things along.

So without further ado, she slipped her fingers beneath the elastic waistband of his BVDs and pulled out his shaft. Firmly wrapping her fingers around it, she felt him throbbing in her palm and the sensation sent a burst of bliss exploding in the crux of her thighs. Her mouth watered as she watched her hand move up and down his heavy, rock-hard member. The smooth silkiness of the skin felt like it was covering a steel rod. She loved the feeling of her hand gliding up and down him.

A small white bead of liquid appeared on his engorged tip and Tessa leaned forward and licked it off. A deep groan ripped from his chest, and she felt his fingers thread through her hair. God, she loved it when he ran his hands through her hair.

Just as she was about to open her mouth and take him inside, he fisted his hand and tugged so she was looking up at him. The sensation caused her to cry out as pleasure washed over her, emanating from the sting where his fingers were knotted.

Tessa thought there was a very real possibility that she might come again. Kneeling before Jake while holding his manhood in her hands, her breasts exposed as she looked up at him, his strong chest heaving, his abs tense and showcasing his rippling muscles, the primal look in his eye as he gazed down—all of this was hands-down the most erotic experience she'd ever had.

"You don't have to do this," he said with an almost tortured look in his eye.

She knew that he was just trying to protect her because when she was younger she'd never been interested in doing this. But she was all grown up now, and he might not know it but she *absolutely* had to do this.

She felt a wicked smile spread across her lips as she held eye contact with him and opened her mouth over the large head of his hardened groin. A guttural sound filled the air as she pulled him into her mouth with a wet suction. She slid her tongue up and down his length as her lips tightened around him.

With one hand, she held on to his hip for balance as the other stroked the base of his erection, her fingers clasped around it. His fingers spread out as he guided her head up and down. She felt his fingers tense, and his member began growing larger and larger in her mouth.

Picking up the pace, Tessa tightened her lips and fingers around him as she bobbed her head up and down.

"Fuck, that feels good," he groaned as she continued her sensual assault. She tasted the salty goodness of his arousal just before he warned, "Tessa, I'm gonna come."

He might have thought that would cause her to pull away. But it had quite the opposite effect. She wanted Jake. All of Jake. Instead of backing off, she doubled her efforts, squeezing him tighter and swirling her tongue in a suctioning pull.

She felt his entire body tense with release as he came. He jerked his head and it fell back as his fingers clenched tightly in her hair. Tessa rode out his orgasm until she had sucked the very last drop of his arousal from him.

Just as he leaned forward and held the desk for support, Tessa heard a knock at the door. Standing, she smiled up at a still-recovering Jake.

"Perfect timing." She patted his chest and began adjusting her sweater as she moved under his arm to make her way to the bathroom. Calling over her shoulder, she said, "Can you get that? I need to freshen up."

She didn't know how he did it, but the next thing she knew, she was turned around, being held in Jake's arms, and pressed flat against his half-naked body. The corners of his mouth turned up and he had a look in his eye that reminded her of a predatory wolf. "This isn't over," he stated.

As much as she wished they could continue this afternoon delight, she had a job to do. "Jake, my next session is here," she explained as she tried to pull out of his hold.

"When are you done here?" he asked, not letting her go.

"Around six, but then I have to be at JT's 'til at least midnight."

"Fine. I'll see you at JT's, and I am coming home with you tonight." His voice sounded like he was trying to lay down the law or convince her of the inevitable.

What she wanted to tell him was, *Yeah, no shit, Sherlock.* But she decided her behavior today had been shocking enough, so instead she just said, "Good."

His eyes filled with even more fire at her easy acquiescence. Releasing her from his grasp, he swatted her rear playfully as she hurried to the bathroom.

"Hey, Tessa."

She stopped and looked over her shoulder.

"I'm gonna kill this," as he minimized the screen with his images, "I don't think anyone should see these until you Photoshop Mr. Happy."

Tessa burst out laughing at the nickname he's chosen to give his junk. She nodded as she went into the bathroom and closed the door. Just like the first night she'd been in town, she almost didn't recognize the image staring back at her.

Her face was flushed, her lips were swollen, her clothes were rumpled in undress, and her hair was a mess. Her heart beat rapidly in her chest as the realization of what had just occurred sank into her.

She'd just had a sexual encounter…with Jake…at Say Cheese…in the middle of the day. Tessa waited to see if she would feel regret. Embarrassment. Shame. Nope. Nope. And nope.

All she felt was excitement and happiness. She had about eight more hours until she and Jake could finish what they'd started in the studio and Tessa couldn't wait.

21

JAKE WALKED INTO JT'S AND HIS EYES IMMEDIATELY LANDED on Tessa. She was laughing at something Levi had just said as she poured several drinks at once. A small twinge of jealousy crept up in Jake's chest. He didn't like it.

Jealousy was a useless emotion in his book. And he'd never had to deal with it with any other girl he'd been with. Only Tessa.

Jake waved to a couple of guys from the station as he made his way between the tables and chairs. He crossed the room and took a seat at the only empty stool at the bar.

Before he even sat down, Levi had a longneck sitting in front of him. "Hey, Jake. Haven't seen you around."

"I've been working," Jake said as he brought the bottle to his mouth and took a swig.

He had been working for the last few days but normally Jake would have been at JT's at least two nights a week. Instead, he'd been with Tessa or home brooding about her return. Which had just been a week ago.

It was only last Wednesday that his world had stopped spinning and he thought he'd seen a ghost. Jake looked over to the exact spot in the room that he'd laid eyes on her. It felt like a lifetime had passed in that time.

"Hey, Jakey," he heard a whiny voice say from behind him, "do you want to play some pool?"

He turned and saw Courtney, who had somehow managed to wear an even more revealing outfit tonight than the last time he'd seen her. Tonight, she was wearing a netted, form-fitting dress, and although she had the appropriate undergarments on, the peek-a-boo effect of the fabric left little to the imagination.

"Not tonight, sweetheart." Jake winked at her and swiveled back around on his stool.

He felt hands running over his shoulders and down his chest as he heard Courtney purring in his ear, "Please? Play with me, Jake."

Jake had to stop himself from turning around and pushing her off of him. Hard. It was just that the feeling of another woman's hands on him, now that Tessa had touched him again, made him almost sick to his stomach.

Still, he didn't want to be a *dick*. So instead of jerking away from her, he stood, causing her hands to fall at their sides, and said, "I'm with someone, actually."

Was it technically true? No. But there was a truth in the statement. He'd always been with Tessa. Even when she'd left. His heart had gone with her, because she owned it.

An irritated look crossed Courtney's heavily made-up face. "Who are you with?"

"Doesn't matter," Jake said, not wanting this conversation to continue. It was not headed in a good direction. He nodded as he moved past her. "Have a good night."

Luckily, he spotted his sister, Nikki. She was seated by herself on a two-top and had her laptop open. He pulled out the stool on the opposite side of the table and sat down. Looking up, she smiled and took out earphones that he hadn't noticed she'd been wearing.

"Whatcha doing?" he asked as he scooted his chair closer to the table and set his beer down.

"Studying," she said with a sigh.

"In a bar?" He hadn't been in school in a while—granted, he hadn't been the best student when he was in school—but he honestly didn't think that this environment would really be the most conducive to retaining and processing knowledge. "Is the library closed?"

"Ha ha ha, very funny." His sister shut her laptop and ran her fingers through her hair. "I had to get out of my house and be around people. I was going stir-crazy."

Jake had wondered about the transition from flight attendant to full-time student. Nikki was social with a capital S. She needed interactions. Things happening. She got bored faster than five-year-olds.

Jake motioned towards the computer. "How's it going?"

"Good. Really good," she beamed, and Jake honestly couldn't be happier for her.

"And how are things with Maxim's Most Eligible Bachelor?" Jake asked even though it didn't take a psychic to figure out the answer.

"Good." Nikki's smile grew even brighter as she added, "And he won't be an eligible bachelor for much longer."

"True. Poor guy," Jake said, teasing his sister.

"Shut up," Nikki said as she swatted his arm, reverting to their go-to comeback as kids. "A *lucky* guy is what he is."

"Who's the lucky guy?"

Jake turned and saw Tessa standing beside the table, and like always, his heart picked up speed. His eyes dropped to her jeans, the ones his hand had been inside just a few hours earlier.

"Mike," Nikki smiled up at Tessa.

"Oh, yes he is," Tessa nodded in agreement. "I was just checking if you needed anything. I didn't want to bother you before. You looked busy."

"I would *love* a Coke." Nikki let her head fall back dramatically. "I need a caffeine fix."

"Got it." Tessa smiled as she looked over at Jake. "What about you?"

"What about me?" he asked as her brilliant blue eyes landed on him and awareness sizzled between them.

"Do you need anything?" A blush crept up her cheeks, and Jake noticed her giving him the don't-you-dare-start stare.

"Yes. I need something." His eyes wandered down Tessa's body.

"To drink," Tessa clarified in her I'm-serious-knock-it-off tone. Jake loved that tone. In fact, he lived to hear that tone. It was sexy as hell to him for some reason.

"Oh, to drink," Jake said as if he'd had no idea that was what she had been asking him about. "No, I'm good. Thanks," he added with a wink, and she shook her head, trying not to smile as she walked back behind the bar.

His eyes followed her until he could no longer see one of his very favorite things in the world to look at—her jean-covered ass. Well, her ass in any state, really. Naked was preferable, and later tonight, he was planning on seeing it in that exact state.

When he glanced back at his sister, she was squinting her eyes at him. "What the hell is wrong with you?"

"Looking at you two is like looking into the sun. You're so hot that I couldn't look away, but now it's burned into my retinas," Nikki said as if she were in pain.

Now it was his turn to sound like a middle-schooler. Jake smiled as he told her, "Shut up, smartass."

---~---

Tessa could not believe how Jake was acting. No, scratch that—she could. He always liked to push the envelope with her. He had always loved to walk that fine line between embarrassing her just a little bit and making her mad. Sometimes he stepped over the invisible line that separated the two, but as always with Jake, one smile and a kiss and all would be forgiven.

If Tessa looked up "irresistible" in the dictionary, she was sure that she would find a picture of Jake smiling with his trademark wink. She shook her head back and forth as she grabbed some glasses and filled the orders she'd taken out on the floor.

Two cranberry and vodkas, three Jack and Cokes, a Tequila Sunrise, five Snake Bite shots, and finally, Nikki's Coke. She placed the drinks along with the bottles of beers she needed to deliver on a tray, grabbed it, and held it high, turning sideways as she slid between the small opening between the end of the bar and the wall.

First, she stopped by her V.I.P. table and dropped off Nikki's Coke. Sure, she'd been the last person to give her an order, so reasonably that would mean that she should be the last one served, but screw reasonable. Nikki got her drink first.

Then she made her rounds without incident, dropping off the Jack and Cokes, cran and vodkas, and the Tequila Sunrise. Finally, she ended at the table with the twenty-something pricks who'd ordered the shots and beers. She dropped them off without making eye contact and quickly began to move away from the table.

Tessa didn't mind dealing with drunk guys, even if they

were hitting on her. But these assholes were taking inappropriate commenting to a whole new level. Just as she pivoted away from said assholes, one of them reached out and grabbed her wrist.

"Hey now, not so fast, blondie," the red shirted asshole said as he rubbed his thumb across her wrist, making her skin crawl.

Tessa tried to keep her patience as she turned back around and pulled her arm away from him. "I have to get back to work, boys." She monitored her tone, making sure to keep it light, but her patience was wearing extremely thin.

"Nah." The dark-haired asshole in the flannel shirt shook his head. "You can hang out for a minute."

"No, I can't," Tessa stated firmly as she once again turned to leave.

Then, Red Shirt grabbed her again, saying, "Now, now. The customer's always right, sweetheart. Didn't they teach you that in Cocktailing 101? Or did you take Cockteasing 101? 'Cause you certainly seem good at that. Consider my cock officially teased."

Tessa tried to pull her wrist away, but Red Shirt tightened his grip. Through clenched teeth, Tessa said with a deadly serious tone, "Let. Me. Go."

"Nah, I think it's time you take a seat." Red Shirt scooted away from his chair and patted his thigh. When she pulled away again, he gripped her harder and lifted up his shirt. That's when Tessa saw his limp dick lying outside of his jeans.

His friends burst out in laughter and cheers, and just as Tessa was about to hit Mr. Limp Dick over the head with her tray, she saw a fist fly beside her head and land straight on Red Shirt's jaw. Tessa could feel the impact of the punch through the hand that was still wrapped around her wrist right before the fingers released their grip.

The next thing she knew, she was behind Jake's back, one of his arms holding her securely in place. She tried to look around his large bicep but it wasn't happening. He had her plastered up against him.

She heard yelling, probably from the guys at the table, and felt Jake's body shake from what she assumed was him landing another punch. Within seconds, several other guys Tessa recognized from the fire station were there, as well as Levi.

Everyone in the small table area was on their feet and suddenly Nikki was at her side. "Are you okay?" Jake's sister asked, concern etched in her face.

Tessa nodded against the hard planes of Jake's back. Adrenaline was racing through her and her heart was pounding.

Jake turned around. Wrapping both arms around her, he pulled her in and held her snugly against him. And just like that, the entire bar disappeared. It was just her and Jake. The two of them.

He drew back and cupped her face in his hands. "Are you okay?"

"Yeah, I'm fine. Really," she assured him, bringing her hands up to rest over his.

He searched her eyes for a moment more before they both heard Eric's deep voice asking, "What's going on?"

She turned and saw that, just like the week before, Eric was dressed head to toe in uniform.

"Damn." Jake released her face but slipped one arm around her waist, pulling her to his side. "Did you teleport here?"

"I was in the parking lot," Eric explained.

Tessa stood beside Jake as he, Levi, and Nikki all

explained what happened. The peanut gallery of assholes kept trying to interject, but Eric was having none of it.

After hearing the entire story, Eric told Julian, who had shown up a few moments after Eric, to watch the guys at the table. Then he turned to Tessa, "I need to talk to you."

Tessa nodded and began following Eric. Jake was right by her side. They hadn't even made it two steps when Eric turned back and said to his brother, "Alone."

Jake did not like the sound of that. "Hell no. I'm going—"

"It's fine." Tessa patted him on the chest. "I'll be fine."

She looked right in his eyes and smiled. Of course she would be fine. She'd be with the Chief of Police, who also happened to be Jake's big brother.

Jake nodded, but he didn't look happy about it.

Eric stopped at the end of the hall that held the bathrooms and turned around. "Do you want to press charges?" he asked, wasting no time with pleasantries.

"No." Tessa shook her head.

Hopefully, Jake had taught those guys a lesson they wouldn't forget anytime soon. Besides, she didn't really feel like they'd ever been a real threat to her.

Eric stood silently in front of her. It got a little awkward, so she asked, "Is that all?"

He still didn't answer for several moments. Then he nodded once.

Oookay.

Tessa turned to leave and was stopped by Eric's voice. "Be careful."

She immediately turned back around at his cryptic warning. She looked up at him and had no idea what he was talking about. "Of what?" she asked.

"With Jake." Eric's brows furrowed. "I know you care

about him, but you have no idea what you leaving did to him."

With that, he left the hall. Leaving her alone.

His words hung in her head. This wasn't the first time she'd heard that. But she'd seen him in the back of his truck with that girl. Only *two weeks* later. He had been fine. Right?

Tessa knew that the only way she would know for sure was if she just asked him. They needed to talk.

Just then, Jake rounded the corner and pulled her into his arms. "Come on. I'm taking you home."

Tessa couldn't make sense of everything right now, but the one thing she knew for sure, was that home with Jake was the only place she wanted to be.

22

Tessa walked in the front door of Jake's condo, all of the trepidation she had felt about him since she had been back in Hope Falls melting away like snow under the rays of the bright, springtime sun. Far from feeling timid and unsure in his presence, she now felt bold. Sexy. Daring.

Their encounter at Say Cheese had started her down that path, but the scene in the bar had clinched it. Wow. She knew it was a little cliché that she'd gotten so turned on by Jake's hyper-masculine, testosterone-fueled display—but she couldn't help it. When he had stormed up to save the day with his "Me Tarzan, You Jane" routine, she just hadn't been able to help herself. Her body—and even her brain—had jumped right on board and responded with, *Um, yes, Me Jane. Now bring me home, Tarzan, so I can take a ride on your big swinging vine!*

As soon as they stepped past the threshold, the clatter of claws on hardwood filled the space, and seconds later, Lucky dashed pell-mell into the room. He leapt into Tessa's arms as if she were his long-lost best friend and he were about one-tenth his actual size.

She felt Jake's arms behind her, holding her up under the assault of the dog's heavy body, and then he quickly moved around in front of her and lifted Lucky down. He scolded Lucky, telling him never to do that again, but Tessa could hear the undercurrent of affection and amusement in his voice. From the way Lucky was wagging his tail, Tessa guessed that the dog was picking up on it as well.

She giggled. “He seems very intimidated.”

Jake shook his head. “Well, apparently I'm not nearly as adept at putting my own dog in his place as I am drunk assholes.”

Tessa grinned widely. “Well, those guys deserved to be put in their place. Lucky, on the other hand…he's a good boy!"

Obviously, Lucky did not grasp the meaning of her entire speech, but he did clearly pick up on the words "Lucky" and "good boy," which caused his tail to sweep back and forth with even greater speed and intensity as he rose up on his haunches, placing his front paws on Tessa's chest and beginning to lick her face.

Tessa laughed, ruffling the dog’s fur affectionately. She murmured to him as she petted his silky coat, assuring him that he was, indeed, a good boy.

Jake called Lucky to him and the dog happily followed his owner.

“You’re going in the laundry room, boy.” Jake patted the yellow lab’s head as he looked over his shoulder at Tessa. “I have *plans* for you and they don’t include my dog getting more affection than I do. I don't care if his name is 'Lucky.' But don't worry. I'm going to put plenty of his favorite treats in with him. He'll be more than happy.”

“Okay.” Tessa liked the sound of *plans*. “I'm just going to go freshen up. I would like to be dog-spit free for your plans.”

"Use the upstairs. The downstairs is connected to the laundry room and I want to get him settled."

Tessa practically skipped up the stairs, through the bedroom and into the bathroom. She turned on the water and washed her face, the cold temperature bringing her back down to reality a little bit, piercing the lust-and-adrenaline fog that had been firmly holding her brain in its grip since Jake had touched her in the photography studio this afternoon. However, far from giving her second thoughts, this moment of bright-eyed clarity only served to make her even more excited about what was about to happen.

This had been too long coming. It was time. She wasn't sure if this was the smartest move they'd ever made, but she knew she needed Jake and he needed her. And this was going to happen. Tonight.

Tessa assessed her freshly scrubbed face in the mirror and saw a woman who was surer of herself than Tessa could remember being in years. That was partly attributable to Jake's influence, sure. But the strong, clear-eyed determination she saw in her own eyes came from deep within, and she was proud that she had that reserve of strength inside, just waiting to be tapped.

She smirked. *Speaking of waiting to be tapped.* She smiled as she dried off her face, immensely amused by her own pun. Then, as she reached for the doorknob, all of the self-assuredness and confidence she'd been so happy to be feeling vanished. Poof! In a span of three seconds, it was gone.

What if being with Jake tonight somehow further damaged their relationship instead of bringing them closer? They were just getting back to being friends. Yes, they'd gotten frisky in the studio, but this was different. And on the flipside of that coin, what if it did bring them closer? What then? It didn't change anything. Right?

"Okay, okay, okay, okay," she whispered to herself, shaking her hands to try and release some of her anxiety. She knew that she couldn't stand in the bathroom all night intellectualizing and overanalyzing her and Jake being together. So, taking a deep breath, she reached her now trembling hand out and turned the doorknob.

As she stepped out of the bathroom door, she saw that Jake was already waiting for her in the bedroom, sitting casually on the edge of the bed. He looked up as she walked towards him and the expression in his gorgeous big brown eyes stopped Tessa in her tracks. They were so full of emotion, but they appeared to be conflicted. She couldn't quite get a read on what he was feeling, and it made her anxiety skyrocket.

"God, you're so beautiful," he rasped.

And just like that, Tessa wasn't thinking about her nerves or anxiety. Jake's compliment rushed through her like white water rapids. It had always been like that. Whether it was four little words, a touch, a smile, or a look, Jake affected her on a primal level.

Staring at him as his hungry gaze raked over her, she attempted to reply, but her voice came out as a whisper. "So are you."

"Come here," Jake responded, his voice growing thick with lust.

The sound of his voice like that, the sudden fullness of it, the catch in his voice, the rapidness of his breath—it washed over Tessa in a tidal wave. Suddenly, she was on fire from head to toe. She needed Jake. To be close to him. To feel his skin against her skin, his mouth on hers, or she felt like she would explode.

Spontaneous human combustion. Yep. She'd heard of

it, and she didn't think it could be caused by mere lust—but wow. After tonight, if she heard that such a thing were possible, she certainly wouldn't question it.

She moved across the room in two steps on unsteady legs, her heart feeling like it would beat right through her ribs. She stopped only when she was standing in front of him, and his mouth turned up into a sexy half smile.

"Straddle it," he directed, repeating the instruction she'd given to him earlier at the studio.

Tessa let out a little laugh, and the last tiny bit of anxiety and nervousness dissipated completely. This was Jake. Her Jake.

She placed her hands on his shoulder as she lifted one knee up on the side of his thigh. Before she could move the other one, Jake's hands were on her, pulling her up on his lap, his mouth crushing hers in a passionate kiss. She could feel his hands roaming up and down her back, dipping down and cupping the firm globes of her backside.

Her hands moved over his strong shoulders and down his back. There was a thought in the back of her mind that there were too many layers of clothing between them, but Tessa couldn't bring herself to break their kiss to remedy it. Even through the cotton of his shirt, she felt his muscles rippling beneath her touch, but she wanted to touch skin.

So she moved her hands up and cupped his face. The bristly hairs of his panty-melting five-o'clock shadow beneath her palm sent a shock of tingles straight to her femininity. She gently dug her fingers into his skin at the powerful sensation.

Breaking their kiss, Jake's mouth moved to the base of her wrist. He moved one of his hands and cradled hers as he lavished sensual attention on the sensitive area just beneath her palm. Tessa began feeling dizzy with arousal.

The room was spinning so she closed her eyes. Then, suddenly, everything stopped.

Jake's hand was no longer roaming up and down her back. His magical mouth was no longer kissing her flesh. He was perfectly still. The only movement she could feel was his chest rising and falling against her.

Opening her eyes, she found his jaw locked and fury in the eyes that had just been filled with lust and desire. His gaze was laser-focused on her hand that rested in his.

"Jake?" she spoke through choppy breaths.

"I'm so sorry," he rasped.

"For what?" Tessa had no idea what he was talking about. Was he sorry they were about to have sex? Was he so sorry that he was putting a stop to it? Panic began to rise up inside of her.

"I should have got there sooner." Jake closed his pained eyes and softly kissed her wrist again.

Okay, time out!

Tessa needed to know what the hell Jake was talking about. She pulled her arm away from his soft lips and that's when she saw it. There was a discolored, raised outline of fingers from where Red Shirt had held her wrist.

Looking back at Jake, she tried to assure him. "I'm fine. Honestly. You know I bruise easily."

He was breathing only through his nose, and if he were a dragon, he'd definitely be shooting fire out of his nostrils. "I should have killed him."

"No, you shouldn't have!" she exclaimed.

He stared at her with all the pent-up anger of a bull ready to charge.

"Oh, stop it." She smiled as her eyes widened. "And you say Nikki's a drama queen. You trying to take her crown, killer?"

Normally, Jake was the first one to let something go or

joke around about things, but he looked *far* from amused at her teasing comment.

Scrunching her nose, she tilted her head and asked, "Too soon?"

Luckily, that comment was rewarded with Jake's mouth twitching at the corners and his eyes softening as he said, "You're a brat."

"I know," Tessa said as a sense of pride welled up in her. She loved that she, too, could affect Jake. Maybe not as much as he did her, but she would take it. Leaning forward, she softly kissed the corners of his mouth that had just turned up.

He let out a small sound of resignation. "Are you trying to distract me?"

She continued pressing kisses along his jawline. "Yes, I am."

Her lips trailed down to his neck and she felt his vein beneath her kiss. True, it could be protruding because he'd just been angry. Its appearance didn't necessarily mean that he was still turned on, but she figured, either way, she would enjoy it.

Slowly, she licked from the base of his neck where the vein began, all the way up to the sensitive spot just beneath his ear. A moan vibrated through his chest, and she felt his hands move back down to her butt, his fingers kneading her.

Leaning back, she asked as innocently as possible, "Is it working?"

A fire of arousal once again sparked in Jake's eyes as he picked her up and flipped their positions. She was lying flat on her back on the bed now and he hovered over her.

Then he moved to her side, Jake's hand roaming up and down her body as he leaned over and whispered, his lips brushing against her ear, "Yes. It is."

Tessa took in a deep, shuddering breath and reveled in the sentiment, loving the feel of Jake's hands on her body and the sound of his voice in her ear. On so many nights over the past thirteen years, this was a scene that had played out in her dreams. It had seemed too much to hope or imagine that it might one day come true. But now, that was exactly what was happening. Her dream, her wildest fantasy, was coming true at last. She was making love to Jake Maguire again.

Tessa felt Jake's hand slip under her shirt, caressing the smooth, flat skin of her belly. Tingles exploded throughout her torso, zipping out to her extremities with the power of electric charges, until her body felt like one giant fiery mass of charges.

"Good. I'm glad." Tessa's strained voice was threaded with need.

She felt his tongue on the skin of her neck as he trailed his mouth lower and sensed his intensity increase with each kiss. Tessa felt totally consumed. She was torn between the impulse to slow things down to stretch the encounter out as long as possible and the equally strong drive to rush headlong through the building intensity and the explosion that would inevitably occur. The tension between these two mutually exclusive desires had stretched her taut, like a rubber band about to snap, but it was the sweetest torture she could imagine being subjected to.

In reality, she did not surrender herself to either one of the conflicting impulses, deciding, rather, to simply surrender herself to Jake. As difficult as it was, she forced herself to lay back, relax, and just enjoy the sensations that the touch of this deliciously sexy man was sending through her body.

She felt alive for the first time in a long time, and Jake

was the reason. When it came to taking good care of her, Jake was a master. It had always been that way.

Tessa threaded her fingers through Jake's hair as he moved his head lower and lower, kissing down her neck as he went. She felt his hands slide behind her back and unhook her bra. Then he slipped her shirt up and brought them off together in one fluid movement. She moaned as his rough palms traversed her smooth skin, and she pushed her body even harder against him, needing to get closer—as close as she possibly could.

Jake rose up on his elbow and surveyed her now-bare torso. His gaze caressed her, moving slowly from her smooth, flat belly up to the plump, round mounds of her breasts. She felt her nipples harden under his scrutiny, which she felt like a physical touch. Jake must've seen this, as well, because she heard his breath draw in sharply as he eyes landed on her hard, pointed nipples. Then he dove for them hungrily, enveloping first one and then the other in his hot, wet, mouth.

Tessa could feel the intensity of his need for her the instant his tongue made contact with the tight, hard peak of her nipple. The sheer power of it was so strong that it caused her to arch her back and let out a cry. It was more than the pure physical pleasure of having his tongue caressing the sensitive nubs that caused her to cry out, although the pleasure was fierce. It was the connection, the electricity that was flowing back and forth between them, not just within their bodies, but also within their souls. That was what really got to her and made her lose control.

She could have handled the pleasure. Pleasure was wonderful and she enjoyed it, but she had been given pleasure by other guys. She had also given herself pleasure on more than one occasion. Simple pleasure was a cheap imitation of the soul-consuming sensation that was currently streaking through her entire being, and that sensation could only be imparted to her by one person—Jake. That was the way it had always been, and it was abundantly clear to Tessa that that was the way it still was.

She tangled her fingers in his hair, pressing herself even harder into his mouth, unable to get close enough to him to satisfy the white-hot fire that was burning within her belly.

"Jake..." she whimpered as she reached for his shirt. She wanted to feel him. Skin to skin. "I want this off…"

Jake lifted his head and looked hungrily into her eyes, the naked lust she saw there stoked her inner fire to even greater heights. He reached one hand behind him and yanked his shirt up and off of his body.

Then, moving over her, he covered her mouth with his, plunging his tongue inside. Tessa thought that she might explode from the burst of white-hot electricity that surged inside of her at that moment. She wrapped her legs around his waist, feeling her core tighten at the touch of his hardness through the layers of fabric that still separated them. The bare skin of his chest rubbed erotically against her sensitized peaks, only increasing the pleasure bursting between her legs.

She had forgotten how powerful this was with Jake. She had forgotten what it felt like when she wasn't just having sex, but when she was making love.

She never wanted to forget again.

--- ~ ---

Jake kissed Tessa with all of the pent-up sexual energy that had been building for the thirteen years since she had left. Sure, he had had sex since then. But those girls hadn't been Tessa. None of them had mattered. He hadn't *felt* anything except the most fundamental biological response to the act of two people having sex. It had felt empty and lonely.

Not like this. Not like he felt with Tessa. She was a part of him. When they were together he didn't know where he stopped and she began.

A part of Jake couldn't really make himself believe that this was actually happening, that he was actually here—in bed with Tessa—after all of these years. He couldn't stop touching her, running his hands over her smooth, soft skin. He simply loved the feel of her, couldn't get enough of touching her. Admittedly part of this was an effort to convince himself that he wasn't dreaming, that she was actually here, that this was real.

Jake began peppering small kisses down her neck again, then her chest, moving past her breasts this time, and continuing down her belly. He trailed his tongue down the flat expanse and reveled in the feeling of her muscles jumping underneath her skin at his touch. He loved that he affected her that way. He just loved the fact that he could bring her that much pleasure with a simple touch.

When he reached the waistband of her jeans, he unbuttoned them and slipped them down her legs, bringing her lacy panties with them. He needed to see her naked before him. He needed to have nothing covering her, nothing hiding her from him, nothing between him and her gorgeous body.

When he had completely undressed her, his eyes traveled slowly up her naked flesh and he could see her trembling, whether from arousal or vulnerability—or a combination of both—he was not sure.

Without a word, he knelt at the side of the bed. Looking down he saw that her toenails were painted red. She was happy. He ran his finger over her toes.

"What's wrong?" she asked as she lifted up on her elbows.

"They're red." He looked up and answered. "So that means you're happy."

Her brow knitted in confusion. "What?"

"The night you got here, they were purple, so I knew you were sad. Now they're red, so I know you're happy."

Her lips parted as she shook her head a little in disbelief. "You remembered that?"

"I remember everything about you," Jake said as he ran his fingertips up the outsides of her perfectly shaped legs and over her hips, feeling her skin shudder deliciously at his touch.

When his hands had reached her waist, he grasped her firmly and pulled her closer to the edge of the bed. Her arms gave out and she was once again flat on her back. Then, slowly...ever so slowly...he pushed her knees apart and positioned himself in between them. He sharply drew in a breath at the glistening wetness he saw there.

Unable to wait even a moment longer, he buried his head between her legs, covering her entirely with his mouth, tasting her sweet arousal, devouring her, and running his hands up and down her body as his mouth moved furiously on her core.

Tessa began to wriggle and shudder underneath his hands, and he could feel the passion building inside of her minute by minute. He worked his tongue, stiffening it and moving it up and down and in circles around the center of her pleasure, building her up to a stunning climax.

He felt Tessa's fingers grasping his hair in her fists, felt her raising her hips to meet his mouth, pressing herself into him and encouraging him onward. He continued his steady pace, nearly as desperate to bring her to release as she obviously was to get there. He'd always known it—he lived to give this woman pleasure.

He could go for the rest of his life and never get tired of making love to her. Night after night, day after day—every time he looked at her, every time he touched her, he was amazed by some new aspect of her body and soul that he had never before fully appreciated. He knew with ever fiber in his being that it would always, always be that way.

He loved Tessa. Not just a little bit. Completely and totally, down to the core of his soul. He was entirely and irrevocably in love with Tessa Hayes and he always would be, for every moment until the day he died.

He didn't know what the future held for them in the long run, so he didn't know if that was a good thing or a bad thing, but he did know that it was true. In fact, it was probably the truest and most definite thing about him.

He felt her coming up to the edge of climax, and he continued his efforts to push her blissfully over, but she yanked on his hair to pull his head up and gasped, "No, Jake. Inside me. I want to come while you're inside me."

He grinned at her. Far be it from him to argue with a beautiful, naked woman.

Jake stood, shedding his pants and boxers as quickly as possible and then reached into his nightstand and grabbed a condom. He unwrapped it and smoothly slipped it on, turning back to Tessa to see that she had scooted back and repositioned herself in the middle of the bed. She held out her arms to him and he happily climbed into her embrace.

Jake leaned on his elbow, framing her face, his manhood positioned at her tight, wet opening. Her beautiful blue eyes looked up at him as she panted for breath and her hands roamed up and down his back.

Jake was overwhelmed with love as he stared into the sky blue pools of her eyes. He knew that he couldn't say those words to her, so instead he said, "I've missed you."

She nodded as tears filled her eyes. Her lip quivered as she said, "I've missed you, too."

Holding her gaze, he pushed himself slowly inside of her, groaning as her tight wetness fully enveloped him. His body shook from the power of the love, pleasure and satisfaction that filled him so fully and completely. Tessa's eyes closed as her hips rocked into his and she let out a needy moan. He felt a slight sting in his back as her nails dug into his skin, her thighs trembling against his hips.

Resting his forehead against hers, Jake rocked his hips, moving inside of her, slowly building up his pace. He didn't want to rush this no matter how incredible it felt. He wanted to stay like this forever. Connected to Tessa. Body and soul.

With the pleasure intensifying unbearably as Jake felt the inner fire of his passion begin to build to a peak, he recognized the telltale signs in Tessa's body that the same thing was happening to her. Her hips matched his rhythm, thrust for thrust. Her hands raked up his back as she arched her breasts against the hard planes of his chest. Her gasps and moans became ever more desperate as his pace increased.

All too soon, he was at the very edge of climax. It was simply a matter of holding himself back until she was also ready so that they could experience that physical and emotional explosion together, entangled in one another's arms, the way that it should be. He hoped he would be able to. The intensity of sensation he was experiencing was so extreme that he was afraid it was going to overtake him and he would be carried away in an uncontrollable rush of pleasure.

Thankfully—because he honestly did not know how much longer he could've held out—after just a few moments, he heard her cry with encouragements as her body convulsed around him. He felt her arms and legs encircle him and grasp with steel-like strength, and her inner walls pulsed tightly around his shaft.

Jake moaned and surrendered to his own climax, grateful that he had been able to wait. Happy that he had been able to do that for her. He'd needed to share that with her. It felt significant to him. It felt like it meant something.

When their bodies had exhausted themselves and he looked up and into her eyes, he could see that he was not the only one who felt the significance of what had just happened between them. Tessa did not say anything, but her eyes said it all. He'd always been able to read her like an open book, and this had meant something to her. It *was* significant.

A little voice in the back of his head popped up. *But...does it mean that she will stay?*

He pushed the thought from his mind. He didn't want to ruin the present moment with worries about the future. He had wasted too much time doing that. Instead, he simply kissed her softly, held her, and enjoyed the knowledge that—for tonight at least—he was falling asleep while holding the woman he loved in his arms.

23

Tessa could feel Jake's eyes on her as she sat in the passenger seat of his SUV, headed to Gran's memorial service. She still couldn't believe that Jake had put this together in just the short time she'd been back. She'd been totally shocked when he'd told her about it yesterday. He said that the town needed to say goodbye, too. Tessa couldn't get over how amazing Jake was being. Especially after how long she'd been gone.

She stared out the window, pretending to be even more lost in thought than she actually was because she simply didn't have the emotional strength to deal with saying goodbye to her grandmother, *again*, and to deal with anything Jake-related on the same day.

Of course, she had "said goodbye" to her grandmother months ago—hell, if not years ago. So, in that respect, it didn't really make sense that she was so emotional today. But who said emotions have to make sense? When she had dealt with her grandmother's passing before, it had been a highly personal thing. It had been a solitary grieving. The only people who'd even known she had been going through it or sympathized with her were her roommate and the staff who had been taking care of her Gran. Although they, of course, had felt bad for what she'd been going through, they had not *known* her Gran. Not really. Not when Gran had actually *been* Gran.

Today was different. Today was when a lot of people who loved Grandma Adie– really, truly knew her and loved her—were going to stand up and grieve for her right along with Tessa. Tessa knew that she should be grateful that her Gran had been so well-loved, and she was—seriously, she was. Still, there was a little part of her that selfishly wished that she didn't have to go through this today. It was going to hurt like hell.

Tessa shook her head a little to herself as she looked out the window at the beautiful pine trees they were passing. She knew that the pain wasn't the worst part. What Tessa was really afraid of was that today's service was going to make Adeline's death seem *real*.

Tessa sucked in a breath as that epiphany hit her. Damn. That was it. That was the core of it. She'd recognized it as soon as the thought had occurred to her.

There was a tiny corner of her mind that clung to the thought of Gran alive, in a different place or something. As if Tessa were just off on a photo assignment and would pop in to visit her after she got home. Of course, that idea wasn't rational, but it wasn't a rational part of her mind that harbored it.

And that was the real issue. That was why today was so hard—Tessa was afraid that going to the memorial service was going to shatter that one, tiny, last remaining illusion she had that she would ever see her Gran again.

She felt tears dropping into her lap and was surprised. She hadn't even realized that she had been welling up. Jake, who kept giving her long and concerned glances—

longer, in fact, than what was probably safe while driving! —reached over and squeezed her hand.

"You're sure you're okay?" he asked, his warm brown eyes melting her heart.

"I'm fine," she assured him, realizing even as she said it that her shaky tone of voice belied the certainty that her words implied.

Jake just smiled at her sympathetically. She sighed. It was a great smile. It was a smile that made her want to tell him to stop the car, pull over, forget the memorial service, and just curl up in his arms and stay there—forever.

She turned her head and stared resolutely out the passenger's side window as they pulled into the church parking lot. She was not sure how she was going to get through this. There had been so much going on since she had been back. Physically and emotionally exhausted, she was running on empty.

Jake pulled into the closest parking space available and turned off the ignition. He immediately opened his door and got out, walking around to Tessa's side and opening her door for her. She took a deep breath. She would have preferred to sit in the car for a few moments and take the time to gather her thoughts, but this was probably better in the long run.

Reaching out to grasp the hand Jake was offering her, she gingerly stepped to the ground. Immediately, she was struck by the power and strength she felt emanating from his hand. It poured into her, strength she could lean on, strength she could depend on. She instantly felt calmer. She could do this. She could do this for Gran because today was not about her at all—today was for Gran.

As they walked towards the front door of Hope Falls Community Church, Jake held Tessa's hand in his, and she loved how familiar and safe it felt. The years between them melted away, as did every painful thing that had ever transpired between the two of them, and suddenly they were just Jake and Tessa, holding hands. Normal. Natural. Meant to be.

She sighed at the deep sense of loss that thought engendered in her, and Jake put a protective arm around her shoulder. Tessa instinctively leaned against him. It seemed her body wasn't waiting to see what her mind or heart thought about leaning on Jake—literally and figuratively.

As the two of them stepped through the doors of the church, they were met by a sea of people gathered to honor her Gran. Seeing her there, they began coming up and expressing their condolences. Tessa was extremely grateful to have Jake with her, holding her up, offering silent support. If Jake had not been there, she would've certainly felt overwhelmed. She was, after all, a largely solitary person. She had been, by necessity, for nearly her entire life—the one year she had lived in Hope Falls being the notable exception.

Although she was certainly getting back into the "groove" of the small-town Hope Falls lifestyle during the time she had been back, there were still times that it was a shock to her system. Now, was one of those times. The outpouring of love was so wonderful but would definitely have been too much to process if Jake had not been right by her side, being her rock as he always was.

Well...when she let him be, anyway.

"Is this too much? Do you want to go sit down now?" she heard him whisper in her ear, and she nodded gratefully. God, it was amazing how that man always seemed to instinctively know exactly what she needed at any given moment!

At her response, Jake took control of the situation, as

he was so good at doing. He made polite excuses to everyone who came up to them, excuses she barely heard, and ushered her to her reserved seat and sat beside her.

When Pastor Harrison stepped up to the podium and began to speak, Tessa tried to focus on what he was saying, even if it was painful. Gran deserved that. Tessa needed to honor her by being fully present, she knew, even if it hurt.

"When I was a kid," the Pastor was saying, "I used to walk my dog, Bullet, by Adeline's house every day. Many of those days, she was outside working in her yard. She would always say 'hi' to me and Bullet. Always with a smile on her face that seemed like she was truly glad to see us. One day, she called me over to ask if I would like to earn a little money by taking care of her yard. I was happy to do it and showed up the next day, ready to start my job. When I had finished working, she met me on the porch with cookies and milk and we had the best talk. That day was the beginning of a lifelong friendship. Adeline always seemed genuinely interested in the things that were going on in my life, and that meant a lot to me.

"In fact, the sense of caring that she showed toward me was a big inspiration for me when I was deciding what to do with my life. It was a big part of what steered me to a life of service. I wish that I had told her that while I had the chance."

Tears flowed freely down Tessa's face as she listened to the pastor's story and all of the stories that came after from people who had been touched by Adeline's kindness and her willingness to listen and to care.

Tessa had been nervous, at first, that no one would get up to speak when offered the opportunity. After all, although Gran was wonderful, she had been gone from the community for many years.

However, in the end, the opposite happened. Far more

people wanted to speak than there was even time for, and that fact truthfully touched Tessa's heart nearly as much as the actual words they spoke.

Finally, Pastor Harrison returned to the podium. "Now," he said in his melodic and authoritative voice, perfect for ministry, "Adeline's granddaughter, Tessa, is here. Tessa, would you like to say a few words about your grandmother?"

Tessa's eyes widened and her back stiffened. Oh, God! Why hadn't she thought about this when Jake had told her about the service yesterday? Why hadn't it even crossed her mind? Of *course* she was going to be asked to speak! That was a no-brainer! But she had been so wrapped up in the emotions of the event—and of Jake, if she were being perfectly honest—that it hadn't even entered her mind.

Jake, sensing her mounting panic, put a hand to the small of her back in a tiny, comforting gesture. He leaned over to her. "Just speak from the heart," he whispered in her ear. "You're in a safe place. Everyone in this room loves you."

Tessa's throat went dry at the words.

Everyone? she felt like asking. *Everyone...including...you?*

She stood up from the pew and made her way up the platform steps on trembling legs. She did not think she had ever felt so many competing emotions at once. But the one that was quickly taking center stage was simply a burning desire to get through all of this without passing out.

She took her place behind the podium and adjusted the small microphone. She looked up at all of the faces staring back at her. They were, down to the last one, tear-stained. She saw real and sincere pain and regret on the visages of every single person in every single pew.

Suddenly, an overwhelming sense of calm washed over her.

Jake was right. This was a safe space. These people loved her—that was true. And they loved Gran, and this was about her.

Suddenly, Tessa smiled. She felt joy bubbling up inside of her unexpectedly, incongruously. She let out a short laugh and knew exactly what to say.

"I can't tell you how much Grandma Adie would have hated this," she chuckled, and several more people joined in with her laughter. "All of us standing around, talking about her excellent qualities, putting her at center stage. Oh, she would not have liked that one bit."

Now the entire chapel was laughing, warmly, and Tessa felt her grandmother's presence in the room, more strongly than she had felt it in years. Tears slipped down her face, but she didn't mind them. There was also a smile on her lips, and that was the important thing.

"I can't begin to express how much it means to me to be able to talk about her with people who knew her," Tessa said as her tears freely fell. "She was the warmest, most caring, most giving person I have ever known. She was the first person to ever love me completely and without judgment or expectation. She was actually the person to teach me what that felt like, and she was the person who taught me that I deserve that. It didn't matter how big or small an accomplishment was—she was proud and let you know it. I miss her every single day, and... Well, I just can't tell you how much it means to me to know that there are so many other people who feel the same way."

As Tessa sat back in the pew next to Jake, she was grateful for the comforting touch of his arm around her shoulders and had to resist the urge to simply bury her face in his neck and collapse against him, seeking the comforting solace only he could provide.

Yes, it was true what she had said—Gran had been the

first person to love her completely and without condition. But she hadn't been the only person to love her that way. Jake had, too.

Gran had been torn from Tessa by a terrible disease beyond either one of their control. But Jake? Well, he was right here. Tessa had thought she had done the right thing by giving him up, that she had done what was best for him. Tessa had been so sure that she had done the only thing she *could* do if she'd loved him. She had been so convinced there hadn't been any another option.

Now, she wasn't so sure.

If losing Gran had taught her anything, wasn't it that love—true, unconditional, complete love—was a rare thing in this world and she should hold on to it? Or had she been right the first time, that loving Jake had meant stepping aside so he could have what he really wanted—a family?

Tessa had no idea, and after feeling like she'd been through the emotional wringer, she knew that this was not going to be the day to figure it out.

As the service wrapped up, Jake's mom rushed to Tessa's side and threw her arms around her. Tessa loved Rosalie and appreciated her and Sean being there today.

Pulling away, Jake's mom smoothed down Tessa's hair. "Oh, my *Tesero*, I'm here if you need me. You know that, right?"

Tessa nodded.

As more people began surrounding them, offering condolences, Jake's mom excused herself to go get the food set up in the dining hall, but not before making Tessa promise that she'd be at Sunday dinner.

Tessa really wasn't sure that she could handle it, but of course she had agreed. She didn't have the heart to disappoint Jake's mom, even if it meant breaking her heart even more.

24

"GOOD ON YA, BOYO." JAKE'S DAD PATTED HIS SHOULDER with enthusiasm after Jake finished telling them about the incident in the bar a few days ago after his mom had asked him if he'd really pulled a gun on someone. The Hope Falls rumor mill was no joke.

"And what about you?" Jake's mom wagged her finger at her oldest son. "Why weren't those boys arrested for harassing our girl?"

Tessa tried to jump in. "Oh no, Mrs. Maguire, Eric was gre—"

Eric lifted his hand, halting Tessa's defense. "Well, since *boyo* over there decided to take matters into his own hands, I was mainly concerned about making sure those assh—"

"Language!" Rosalie snapped at her son.

"That those *jerks* didn't press charges against Jake."

Jake's mom's hand flew up in the air, "What do you mean?! That's crazy! That man exposed himself and left a bruise on my *Tesero's* wrist. Jake was just defending her!"

"Jake dislocated that guys jaw and knocked out another guy's teeth, Mom," Eric said in a flat tone.

Rosalie shook her head. "Ah, self-defense."

Tessa could see that Eric's tension was building, and it was feeling a little odd that Jake was so quiet. In fact, he'd been quiet since they'd arrived at his mom and dad's house for Sunday dinner.

"So, Amy, how are the wedding plans going? Just one more week!" Lily said excitedly, smoothly changing the subject.

"Good," Amy smiled. "I think everything is set. Asking Lauren to get involved really helped. I remembered how amazing she was when Amanda's wedding fell apart just two days before she was supposed to walk down the aisle. And hers was a much bigger affair. We just want simple."

Matt, leaned over and kissed Amy. Tessa felt her heart fill and a smile tug at her lips. They were so cute together. Matt seemed to adore Amy and vice versa.

"Actually"—Amy snapped her fingers as if something had just occurred to her, her gaze falling on Tessa—"the one thing I was supposed to take care of, I keep forgetting. I have been meaning to ask you… Would you mind taking some pictures at the wedding?"

"Yes, of course I will," Tessa agreed. "I would love to."

"Just a few. I don't want you to feel like you're working. I want you to enjoy yourself," Amy quickly added.

"Are you kidding me? I *love* being behind the camera," Tessa said emphatically, hoping to put Amy's mind at ease.

"Okay, just let me know how much you char—"

"No," Tessa interrupted her, shaking her head. "No charge."

"No, of course I'm going to pay. Just let me kno—"

"I can't charge you. You're family." The second the words left Tessa's mouth, she wished that life had a remote control button and she could rewind. The room fell silent and she could feel everyone's eyes on her and Jake. Attempting to lessen the awkward level of this situation at least a degree or two, Tessa offered, "Consider it a gift from me to you."

"Thank you," Amy said, smiling sweetly.

Nikki, who was now Tessa's favorite person in the whole world, moved the conversation along. She asked Amy about how her pregnancy was going and Lily and Eric about how the wedding plans were coming along.

While everyone was discussing all of the exciting news in the family, Tessa took the time to regroup mentally. The past couple of weeks had felt like both a whirlwind and an eternity. She had no idea how that was even possible. Everything had gotten so confusing and complicated.

Especially the past few days since she and Jake had started sleeping together. She'd meant to talk to him. She really had. Her several attempts at a serious conversation had been thwarted by their insatiable hormones. The second they were alone with each other, it was like erotic dynamite exploded. They couldn't seem to keep their hands—and other body parts!—off of one another. Which was great except that Tessa wasn't sure what it meant. To Jake or to her.

The fact remained that they needed to talk. She'd just been so scared to ruin what they had going on right now. Which, on the surface, seemed simple enough. They were attracted to each other and acting on it. But Tessa wasn't foolish enough to believe that. What was going on between her and Jake was anything but simple.

Which was the main reason she hadn't wanted to rock the boat. Bringing up the past or the future would definitely change the present. But maybe that wouldn't be such a bad thing. Every second, every minute, every hour, every day, Tessa was doing something she would have thought was impossible. She was falling more in love with Jake Maguire.

The first time she'd left, it had come very close to destroying her. Thirteen years later, sure, she was older and wiser, but neither of those things meant that walking away from Jake would be any easier. As far as she knew, nothing had changed the fact that she had to leave. She had to leave for him.

Jake placed his arm around Tessa and ran his thumbs in circles on her shoulder. Instantly her body relaxed. He leaned over and whispered softly, "You okay?"

"Yeah," she lied.

His eyes narrowed and she knew that he saw right through her. Luckily, his mom asked him about his house and told him she'd made curtains. Tessa tried to pull herself out of the drama that was going on in her own head while his family discussed all of the decorating options he had for the amazing space. She didn't know how many more of these Sunday dinners she would be attending so she wanted to enjoy every second she could with these incredible people who she *did* consider her family. She needed to be present.

"…would make a great nursery. And I picked neutral colors, so it doesn't matter if it's a boy or a girl," Jake's mom announced proudly.

Tension radiated from Jake as he spoke. "Shouldn't you be busy planning Amy's nursery or even Lily's or Nikki's?"

"Hey!" Nikki threw a crumpled up napkin hitting Jake in the temple. "Bite your tongue."

Jake held up his hands in surrender. "I'm just saying, why not focus on babies for your children who are in serious relationships?"

Rosalie looked confused. Her eyes darted back and

forth between Jake and Tessa. She threw her hands up in exaggerated display. "What are you talking about? You are."

Nikki once again flew to the rescue—Tessa was seriously considering ordering her a cape that read: Super Subject Changer—and moved the conversation to drama going on with Mike's family. Apparently, after all of the scandal at the hands of Mike's Mother and ex-campaign manager, Mike had distanced himself from his family. But they had been reaching out, and he and Nikki were going to be going to dinner with them this week.

Tessa listened as everyone put in their two cents about whether or not that was a good idea but refrained from giving her opinion. She wasn't doing such a hot job at running her own life, so she really didn't think she should be giving anyone advice on how to live theirs.

Thinking about what she and Jake were doing made her cheeks flush with both embarrassment and good old-fashioned anxiety. After hearing that there were already curtains made for Jake's—as of yet—nonexistent nursery, Tessa knew more than ever that she had to leave when the house was sold. But she knew that Jake's family would never understand when she did.

They would hate her. And she would hate that. But she could handle it. For Jake.

---~---

Lucky jumped off of the couch, startling Jake out of a sound sleep. Barking and pounding followed. Even without opening the door Jake knew exactly who was on the other side.

As he stood slowly, his body ached in protest. He'd just gotten home from being at the station for the last few days, where he'd gotten about two hours of sleep a night. There'd been a lot of calls due to the weather. They'd gotten a lot of rain over the past week. Drivers in Hope Falls were much more conditioned to deal with snow than rain. There'd been several accidents per night and they'd been the first on scene, every time.

Normally, he could make up for his lack of sleep with one nap. He'd catch a few and be up and raring to go. That had not happened today, however. As Jake walked—or more like shuffled at a snail's pace—to the front door, he thought of why he wasn't bouncing back.

Maybe he was coming down with the flu that was going around? Nope. He never got sick. Even as a kid, he had never missed even one day of school due to illness. His immune system was Superman status.

It could be because he's getting old. His thirty years might actually be catching up with him. Or, it could be because not only had he gotten next to no sleep for the past few days at the station, he had gone into his shift after getting even less sleep than that. Since he'd taken Tessa home from JT's the night of the "incident," they'd spent a lot of time in bed but *none* of it had been for sleeping.

Could lots of sex and no sleep cause Jake's body to feel like it had been hit by a Mack truck? Nah. Jake dismissed the idea. But even if it was the reason, he wouldn't have changed a thing. And if Tessa were standing in front of him right now, he'd have her naked and up against the wall before she could blink.

Jake wasn't sure what all this crazy-hot, mind-blowing s-e-x they were having meant, but he sure as hell knew he didn't want it to stop. Sore body or not, he wanted as much of Tessa as he could have.

The pounding was growing increasingly louder as Jake turned the knob and opened the door. "Seriously? Do they teach you that knock in the academy? Here's a thought," Jake said sarcastically. "You don't *have* to knock like you're about to break down a door when you're not on duty."

A small, smug smile tilted Eric's lips as he stepped past Jake. "Where would the fun be in that?"

Jake watched his brother's retreating back as he made his way into the kitchen. "Come on in," Jake announced sardonically.

Eric ignored him as Jake followed him into the kitchen. He came around the corner to find Eric pouring himself a cup of coffee from a pot Jake had made when he'd gotten home a few hours earlier. Jake thought about offering to make him a fresh pot, but he figured his brother was a big boy who obviously had no problems whatsoever making himself at home in Jake's house. If he wanted a fresh pot, he could brew one his damn self.

Jake leaned against the counter, waiting to see what wise words of wisdom his brother had come by to drop on him. He knew this probably had to do with one blonde-haired, blue-eyed girl who was none of his brother's business.

The kitchen chair squeaked as his brother casually sat down and began sipping his freshly poured cup o' joe. He looked in no hurry to get this convo started.

Jake grabbed his navy blue HFFD sweatshirt that was hanging off the chair and pulled it on. Then he rubbed his hands over his face.

"So, what's up?" Jake asked, leaning back on the counter again, putting his hands in the front pocket of his sweatshirt.

"You ready for this weekend?" Eric asked.

"Yep." Jake wasn't sure if he was referring to the Policeman/Fireman Ball on Saturday or Amy's wedding on Sunday, but either way he was good.

"You taking Tessa to the Ball?"

"Nope. I have to take the winning ticket holder." Jake had been raffled off as a date to raise money for the station.

"That's right," Eric nodded. "What about to Amy's wedding?"

"Tessa's the photographer and I'm in the wedding, so we'll both be there if that's what you're asking."

Eric set his cup down. "That's not what I'm asking."

"What exactly are you asking?" Jake asked crankily. He hadn't slept and his body felt like an eighty-year-old man's. Plus his brother had interrupted his nap, and Jake *loved* his sleep.

"Have you talked to her?"

He knew his brother just wanted to help, but Jake was not in the mood. Part of his crankiness probably had to do with the fact that the answer to Eric's question was no. Jake hadn't talked to Tessa. They'd been busy…gettin' busy.

Jake pushed off the counter. "I'm tired, Eric. I've got to get some sleep."

His brother just stared at him. Jake was about to tell him that he didn't have to go home but he needed to get the hell out of here, when he stood. Finally.

"You need to talk to her," Eric stated in his most intimidating I'm-a-cop-you-have-to-do-what-I-say voice.

"Yes, sir, Officer," Jake said in his most sarcastic I-totally-don't-give-a-shit-what-you-say tone.

Eric just shook his head at his little brother as he left. Jake knew Eric was right. He did need to talk to Tessa. But he *didn't* need to talk to Eric about needing to talk to Tessa.

Just before the front door shut, Eric said, "I hope you know what you're doing."

After it was closed, Jake looked down at Lucky's big, brown puppy-dog eyes. "So do I." He petted the top of his dog's head. "So do I."

25

TESSA RANG THE DOORBELL AT AMANDA'S HOUSE, A BOTTLE of wine in hand, grateful that she heard happy, loud chattering already coming from inside the house. Thank God for Amy and her well-timed wedding—and baby—announcement! They meant that Tessa was not going to be the center of conversation at tonight's book club meeting, and that was exactly the way she liked things—with the attention firmly focused on someone else.

Amanda opened the door and gave her a hug, ushering her inside. When she walked into the living room, the faces of the women lit up at the sight of her. "Tessa!" exclaimed about half of them, focusing on her face, while the other half yelled, "Wine!" as their eyes traveled down to the bottle she held in her hand. Tessa laughed. She would have been hard-pressed to say which group was more excited.

Tessa held up the bottle with a flourish, eager to focus the attention of all of the women on the thing that was not her. They might be distracted by the alcohol and the wedding and baby plans right now, but if she knew these ladies—and she most certainly did—the slightest little thing would be enough to redirect their attention to her and, more specifically, to her relationship with Jake.

No thanks. Tessa would take a pass on that extremely complicated topic. Better to keep them distracted with shiny objects like babies, weddings, and wine.

"So," Tessa said to Amy as she sat down, adopting her best let's-dish-some-gossip voice, "how are the wedding plans going?"

Amy's face lit up. Clearly, she was delighted about the opportunity to talk about her favorite subject. "Well," she revealed, face glowing, "it's going okay. I may have underestimated how much work it was though. But I want to get married before I'm showing, because, well, not that I'm a vain person or anything, but—"

"She wants to look smokin' hot in her dress," finished Nikki.

"Yes, that," agreed Amy readily, an even wider smile crossing her face. "And I just want to be Mrs. Kellan."

"So is everything okay? Do you need me to help?" Tessa asked.

"You're doing enough. Thank you so much for agreeing to take the pictures." Amy then explained, "Nikki, my mom, and Lauren are doing most of the heavy lifting. Even though I feel fine and I keep trying to explain to everyone that I'm not sick, I'm just pregnant, they still want me off my feet and out of the winter cold as much as possible. And I do appreciate that. I haven't been dealing with much in the way of morning sickness, but it definitely has been a drain on my energy reserves."

The thought popped into Tessa's mind, unbidden, of the daydreams she used to have about planning her and Jake's wedding. Then for some reason, the thought that if she *had* married Jake, the little baby that was, right now, nothing more than a drain on Amy's energy and a warm spot of love in her heart, would be an adorable little moppet who would call her Auntie Tessa.

Tessa's eyes closed involuntarily with the strain of pushing those thoughts away. She absolutely could not indulge in that kind of thinking. It was far too dangerous. It led her down paths that were too difficult to come back from. Tessa knew that being here in Hope Falls was only temporary. The day was going to come—and it would probably come sooner rather than later—when she was going to have to pack up her PT cruiser and drive right back out of town.

It was going to be hard enough as it was. She had to protect herself. Leaving Hope Falls—and leaving Jake—had nearly destroyed her once. She had been so empty inside that fleeing to one war zone after another had actually been a welcome relief. That capturing the unimaginable pain on the faces of people whose lives and worlds had been ripped to shreds had seemed like a natural extension of the wasteland that had lain inside her.

She couldn't go back there. She had barely survived it. She didn't know if she could survive it again. Especially now that Gran was gone.

She shook herself mentally and returned her focus to the topic at hand—Amy's wedding.

“So you’re all set then?” Tessa asked.

“Actually, Karina”—Amy turned to their dark-haired friend—“I have a favor to ask you, with regards to the ceremony, as a matter of fact.”

Karina lifted her wine glass in a mock toast. “Ask away, girl! You know I'd do anything for you!”

Amy smiled. “Excellent! Then would you mind singing “Hold Me Tighter” at the ceremony? Matt and I both love that song.”

“You got it, babe!” Karina readily agreed.

"Oh!" Tessa exclaimed. "That's always been one of my favorites! I just love the chorus. It's so romantic. It makes me melt!"

Karina's face took on a knowing expression, and she sent Tessa a conspiratorial wink. "Well, I should hope so," she laughed. "I think you might be able to relate."

Tessa was confused. She looked around at the rest of the ladies in the room, wondering if she was the only one who didn't get the reference, but no one jumped in to explain and everyone looked equally as confused as she felt. Finally, she asked, "Why? Why would I be able to relate?"

Karina grinned, clearly eager to fill her in as she held out her hands in a grand ta-da fashion. "Because I wrote that song about you and Jake."

Tessa froze. She could see from the shocked expressions that no one else had been aware of this either.

"What do you mean?" she asked quietly.

"Well, I remember the exact day in high school. I saw you by your locker, and you were looking kind of sad. Then Jake walked up behind you and wrapped his arms around you. You sank back against him, and you just looked so peaceful and radiant... And he looked so protective and"—Karina shivered—"male. Then the chorus just played in my head. At that moment, it all just flowed. 'Hold me tighter than I've ever been, save me from this world within. The way you wrap me in your arms, tells me all that's in your heart. I feel your love when I feel your touch, so just hold me tight tonight.' I mean, seriously, I couldn't grab a notebook fast enough to get it all down!"

Tessa was shocked, and she didn't know how to react. She felt as if her skin were made of spun sugar, as if even the slightest tiny movement would cause her to shatter into a million pieces. She didn't know if she was going to laugh, or cry, or hyperventilate, or...

Luckily, she was saved the embarrassment of doing either of the latter by Amy, whose facial expression had just turned distinctly queasy.

"Wait a minute." Amy's face grew serious. "Do you mean to tell me that I've been…um, making out…with my fiancé to a song that is actually about my *brother*?"

"'Fraid so, darlin'." Karina winked. "And I doubt you'd be that shade of red if *all* you and Matty boy were doing was 'making out' to that song."

The room exploded in laughter and Karina's face lit up excitedly as she clutched her chest.

"I feel like Al Green! Did you make the baby to my song?"

Amy just shook her head. She was smiling but obviously embarrassed by the unwanted attention. She touched the top of her nose as if she were pushing up nonexistent glasses as she answered, "No."

"Do you want to pick another song for the wedding?" Karina asked, letting Amy off the hook.

"No, I still love that song," Amy answered.

So did Tessa. So. Did. Tessa.

26

Jake looked down at his date and pasted a plastic smile on his face. Inwardly, he was doing anything but smiling. The last thing he wanted was to be here with this card-carrying member of the Bleached-Blonde Bimbo (B.B.B.) club, but fair was fair. Her ticket had been pulled in the "Win a Date with the Fire Chief" raffle his guys had put on without his knowledge. It wasn't her fault that his thoughts—along with his heart and his soul—belonged only to Tessa. Nope, she had paid her money and won her prize, and he was going to do his best to be a decent companion this evening.

Still, he found himself glancing around every two seconds to see if Tessa had arrived. He just couldn't stop himself. He knew that she was going to be here this evening. She was working, taking photos on assignment from Say Cheese. Just the thought that he was going to get a glimpse of her beautiful face was enough to lift his spirits and make his heart expand—not to mention other parts of his anatomy. He just wished that she were here with him. Damn.

"Who do you keep looking around for?" his date pouted. "You're supposed to be paying attention to me!"

Jake winced inwardly. She was right. The truth was that she had won this. He was her date and he should be paying attention to her. It was just that grating, wheedling tone she used was annoying the shit out of him.

He turned to her and smiled, doing his best to look sincere. *Stop grinding your teeth, Maguire,* he warned himself. *Just be nice.*

"Sorry. You're absolutely right," he conceded and saw the ghost of a slyly triumphant smirk grace her lips. That annoyed him, but he fought to maintain his pleasant demeanor. "I promise, for the rest of the night, I will be completely and totally focused on—"

He trailed off mid-sentence, not even grasping the irony, because at that moment, he caught his first glimpse of Tessa. His breath caught in his throat and his eyes widened.

She looked like an angel.

The smooth black satin of her dress skimmed her trim curves like a glove. She moved effortlessly through the crowd, her smile lighting up the room as she snapped photos and chatted with everyone she came across. Her hair was pulled up, showcasing the gorgeous, sexy slope of her neck. The sight of her exposed skin made Jake's mouth water, and he was having a hard time drawing in a full breath.

Breathtaking. That was the only word for it. Tessa was breathtaking.

"Only focused on what?"

Jake barely registered the words, and he definitely was not aware that they had been aimed at him until he felt a sharp poke in his ribs.

He looked down, unable to hide his annoyance now

that physical pain was part of this torture ritual, AKA "date."

"What?" he snapped.

B.B.B. stuck her bottom lip out, playing up a fake tremble for full effect.

"You're only going to be focused on what?" she whined.

Great. Now the pouting was back. *Is this chick for real?* He sighed to himself as he clenched his teeth.

It didn't matter. Jake knew he had to pull his head out of his ass and fast. It wasn't Rib Poker's fault that he was here with her instead of Tessa. Jake just needed to man up and follow through with his commitment.

"Only focused on you," he admitted, doing his best not to show how tightly gritted his teeth were as he said the words.

She smiled and winked in a way she must have thought was seductive. "Good boy," she purred. "And if you're *really* good, maybe you'll get a treat later."

What the hell? Did she have him confused with Lucky? Is this the sort of thing guys went for?

Well, yeah. He guessed it was. Sadly, this inane-banter-as-foreplay routine was exactly the sort of thing he used to go for in his man-whore days.

Eric appeared next to him at that very moment, as if making it a point now to be in Jake's business at all times.

"How's it going, bro?" Eric asked with a sly smirk.

"Great," Jake replied flatly.

"It absolutely is. It's going so great," the blonde said, possessively slipping her arm through Jake's.

Eric looked at her for a moment then put his hand out. "I'm Eric," he said, "Jake's brother."

When the blonde raised her heavily mascaraed eyes to meet Jake's, waiting for him to make the introductions, he realized he didn't have a clue what her name was. Shit! He knew she was part of the B.B.Bs. But out of the group, he only knew Courtney's name, and this wasn't Courtney. It was also something with an 'eeeee' sound at the end. Trixie? Cookie? Zoey? Crap! Something like that. Everything sounded close, but nothing sounded right.

Jake saw the exact instant that Eric realized what was going on, but he never had any illusions that Eric was going to rescue him. He couldn't really blame his big brother. Jake would not have rescued Eric if the situation were reversed.

"Jake, why don't you introduce me to your date?" Eric asked, an undercurrent of amusement coloring his tone.

"Yeah, Jakey," the blonde pouted. "Why don't you introduce me to your brother?"

"Really, Jakey," Eric continued, faux sincerity filling his voice. "It's just poor form. So rude."

"Yeah, it's so rude!" the blonde continued to pout.

Damn it all to hell. Jake was honestly trying to do his best to get through this night and be a half-decent date. He was going to kill Eric the next time they were alone, and he did his best to convey that sentiment with his facial expression.

Far from looking intimidated, however, Eric appeared highly amused.

Just then, Lily walked up, wearing a red gown that left nothing to the imagination. Jake could see Eric's reaction to her written all over his face. In fact, right then, Eric's face probably looked quite a bit like how Jake's had just moments earlier when he'd laid eyes on Tessa.

Well, good, Jake reasoned. *Maybe he'll be distracted enough by Lily that he'll stop being a dick.*

No such luck.

Eric looked back to the blonde, his face open and full

of warmth. Jake knew it was false, but the blonde would certainly fall for it.

"This is my fiancée, Lily," he introduced. "And, Lily, this is Jake's date..."

Eric looked pointedly at Jake, who opened his mouth to form some sort of reply, but Lily ruined Eric's gag, turning to Jake with genuine surprise and blurting out, "Oh, I thought you were here with Tessa?" before covering her mouth with her hand.

"Who's Tessa?" the blonde spat, her eyes wild with fury.

It's none of your damn business.

"A friend," he replied firmly. He looked back at Lily, who was mouthing, "Sorry," a worried expression on her face. Jake nodded. He knew that his soon-to-be sister-in-law hadn't meant to cause any trouble and he didn't want her thinking she had.

He felt his arm being tugged on and he turned to see that the pouty lip was back in full affect—it must have been her go-to move. "Tonight, I'm supposed to be your friend," she whined.

Jake's head was pounding from all of the conflicting emotions. He felt like telling her straight up, "Seriously, I don't even know your damn name! Stop whining!" But of course, that was not an option. He simply bit back his frustration and smiled.

He needed to take control of this evening before it spiraled any further out of control. Thinking that he might have figured out a way to stop the flow of endless conversation coming at him from all sides, he summoned every last drop of charm he could. "You are. Do you want to dance?"

--- ~ ---

Tessa was having a hard time maintaining the sunny and friendly façade she had been determined to keep up throughout the course of the evening. When she left the house, she had been pumped up and feeling strong, having listened to her Girl Power playlist the entire time she was getting ready. From “Don't Need You To Tell Me I'm Pretty” by Samantha Mumba to “Independent Women” by Destiny's Child, she had rocked out to female empowerment anthems for an entire hour while doing her hair and makeup. And, yes, she did recognize the irony. Still, she needed the boost.

Her playlist had ended on “Extraordinary” by Liz Phair, and by the time she’d walked out the door, she had been feeling confident and ready to go to this event, and Jake's presence was not going to throw her in the least. He would be there with a date who had won the honor through a raffle, and Tessa could handle it. She was going to be working and Jake was raising money for a good cause.

Much to Tessa's disappointment, however, that strong glass-half-full momentum she’d built up lasted for about .5 seconds after she laid eyes on Jake in his tux. She was disappointed with herself, obviously, for falling prey to her hormones. But she was equally disappointed in her playlist for giving her false hope that she might be able to withstand them when she so *clearly* could not.

Still, Tessa had a job to do. And she couldn’t let it suffer because of how much seeing Jake affected her. So, she put on a bright smile and began to mingle and take pictures. If there was one thing that she had learned during the endless parade of weddings, birthdays, graduations, bar mitzvahs, and quinceañeras she had photographed over the years, it was that people came out looking much more natural and organic in photographs if you chatted with them first. It was always best to get them relaxed and smiling and happy and then shoot away.

She was here to take photos tonight—that was her job. But moreover, she was here to take *great* photos tonight. That was her work ethic. She didn't care if she was photographing a prom for a high school or a war zone for *Time*—she did her best work every time she got behind the lens. No exceptions.

So, yes, it was tearing her apart inside that Jake was across the room with a gorgeous—a little flashy but she had to admit, gorgeous—blonde on his arm instead of her. Oh well. That didn't matter. What did matter was that she was going to put on a happy front and do her job.

"Hey, girlie girl." Tessa heard Amanda's familiar perky voice beside her. "How are you doing?"

Tessa turned and looked into Amanda's eyes, reveling in the warmth and concern she saw there. It was good to see a friendly face and be able to drop the plastic, professional façade for just a moment.

Tessa shook her head. "Well, I have to admit, it's a bit exhausting pretending to be happy and bubbly," she laughed.

Amanda enfolded her in a quick hug and then said, "Well, why don't you take a little break from capturing the festivities and sit and have a glass of watered down wine from the open bar with me?"

Tessa nodded gratefully. "Honestly, the promise of weak booze has never been so welcomed."

It took a while to make it through the crowded room. Especially with people stopping her every two feet either to tell her how great it was to see her again—which was nice to hear—or to comment on the fact that they thought she would be Jake's date tonight—which was not so nice to hear.

When they did finally sit down together at one of the tables that had been placed around the perimeter of the dance floor, Tessa held up her glass of wine and said wryly, "I think I'm going to be needing more than one of these tonight."

Amanda reached over and rubbed her shoulder in support, and Tessa appreciated it. However, that relief was short-lived, because at that instant she looked up and saw something that, even though she had been expecting to see something like it all evening, sent her into an emotional tailspin.

Jake and his beautiful blonde date were out on the dance floor and she was clinging to him for all she was worth.

Tessa's insides clenched. She knew it wasn't real. She knew that Jake was only there because this was a professional function and the girl had won a raffle. It wasn't *real.* And yet...

Tessa couldn't help it. The emotional reaction she had to seeing Jake with his arms around another woman—to seeing Jake with another woman pressed tightly against his body—was horrible. It made Tessa feel as if she wanted to die—or more accurately, like she wanted the other woman to die.

When she looked at the picture they made out on the dance floor, it made her wonder, *Is that the kind of girl Jake is going to end up with?* Was that really what Tessa wanted for him? Would that girl, who was rubbing up against him like a cat in heat, be a good wife, a good mother? Would *she* love Jake like Tessa did? Would *she* be willing to sacrifice her own personal happiness for him?

"Hey, Levi!" Amanda's voice pulled her out of her inner turmoil. "How are you tonight?"

"Great," Levi answered with a smile. "Just wondering if I can interest either one of you lovely ladies in a dance?"

"Love to, boss," Tessa immediately replied, surprising even herself as she shot to her feet. Both Amanda and Levi looked shocked at the speed and enthusiasm with which she had answered, but Tessa didn't care. All she knew was that, right now, she needed to get her mind off of the incredibly sexy man and well-endowed blonde she couldn't seem to tear her eyes away from. Dancing seemed like a better solution than wallowing in a glass of wine.

Levi led her out to the dance floor and placed his hand loosely on her waist, standing about a foot and a half back from her and taking her hand in his free one. Clearly he knew that this was a purely platonic dance. Unlike big-boobed blondie.

She and Levi moved across the dance floor with an easy grace, and he even dipped her. Although Tessa had originally only agreed to dance with Levi as a distraction, it was actually turning out to be pretty fun. In fact, she would go as far as to say it was the highlight of her evening. Levi was a great dancer.

Just as she as really beginning to let go and enjoy herself, Levi spun her around and Jake came into view again. What she saw made her cringe just a little.

Jake was staring at her with laser-focused intensity, and he did not look happy. Nope. Not one little bit. In fact, if anything, that man looked jealous.

Tessa didn't want Jake to be upset. She'd only been dancing with someone else to get her mind off of *him*. Shoot. She couldn't just walk away from Levi mid-dance. It would be incredibly rude for one thing, not to mention ridiculous.

As the song played on and she and Levi glided around the dance floor, she could sense Jake's eyes on her every single moment. She had always been attuned to his presence and his attention, ever since they had met as teenagers. If he entered a room, even if her back was turned, she could sense him. The small hairs on her arms and the nape of her back would stand up as if shocked by static electricity. Now, thirteen years later, that bond had not been severed. It had not even been weakened. She felt Jake's eyes on her like a physical touch.

When the music slowly faded out and the couples on the dance floor, including herself and Levi, began to wander away back to their tables, Tessa smiled up at him and said sincerely, "Thank you for the dance. I really needed it."

“No problem,” he said as they arrived at the table that now held not only Amanda, but Nikki, Amy, and Karina as well. “Ladies.” He nodded before walking away.

“Dang, Levi can really move,” Karina observed as she sipped a glass of white wine.

“I know, right?!” Amanda agreed.

Amy sat down, joining them and holding the firefighter calendar Tessa had shot last week. “Wow, these pictures are… Wow.”

Nikki looked over her shoulder as Amy flipped the page and immediately recoiled from what she saw. “Oh my God! I’m scarred for life. A sister should never see that expression on her brother’s face.”

“I agree,” Amy said, looking a tad horrified herself.

Tessa hadn’t seen the final product but she knew the proofs she’d sent to the printers and Jake’s photo had been, well…hot. For his shirtless pose, she’d chosen one where he'd been straddling the chair, looking down into the camera.

She felt a blush rising on her cheeks as she remembered how *hot* the entire session was—and more to the point—how hot the after session was, too.

Amanda and Karina scooted around so they could see what all the fuss was about. As soon as their eyes landed on the photo, Amanda's jaw dropped as her cheeks turned bright red while Karina's mouth turned up in a mischievous smile and she fanned herself, saying, "Holy hot tamale."

Tessa didn't think it could be *that* bad. He wasn't any more naked than any of the other guys in the calendar. "Can I see it?" Tessa asked, and Amy nodded, handing it over to her.

Oh my.

She must have gotten desensitized by seeing frame after frame of Jake in all of his sexy glory because looking at him now, not in the context of editing, her entire body was engulfed in tingles. It wasn't just his muscular body, which was amazing. It was the look in his eye. That was how he looked at her when he was buried deep inside of her.

"Okay, you know it's a hot pic when it even makes the photographer blush," Karina teased.

Tessa shook her head, smiling. As her friends took back the calendar and flipped through the other pages, Tessa's eyes automatically roamed the dance floor. Jake was still out there with the blonde draped all over him.

He'd texted her earlier and told her he was coming over after he dropped off B.B.B. She'd been a little confused about the B.B.B. part, but the one thing she knew for sure was that he might be *here* with someone else, but he'd be with her later tonight. In bed. She could hardly wait.

27

JAKE WALKED UP THE FRONT WALKWAY TO HIS HOUSE. TESSA opened the front door before he reached the welcome mat.

"Hi," she said softly.

"Hi," he repeated as he stepped into the house, a bundle of pent-up nerves. He felt stretched tight and on the verge of snapping.

He and Tessa had not said one word to each other during the entire event, so he had no idea what she was feeling—but he knew that he was about to explode with a complicated mix of emotions that he could not even begin to unravel. He'd dropped off his date and drove straight here.

Watching her dancing with Levi was absolute torture, plain and simple. It had made an instinct well up in him to protect her, although he knew that was silly. Levi was one of his good friends and he knew, intellectually, that he posed no threat to Tessa. Still, his base instincts were not clued into his intellectual thought process, apparently. It also gave him a powerful urge to claim her as his possession, his territory.

He realized the idiocy of the jealousy he had felt because he had been watching her dance with Levi while he, himself, had been on the dance floor with another woman in his arms.

Ridiculous.

That didn't change the facts, though. His emotions were running high and he felt as if they were about to boil over. He could feel the tension in the pit of his stomach. He usually only felt this kind of adrenaline buildup when he was about to go battle a fire. Hell, maybe that was actually a good analogy. His jealousy was like a metaphorical fire. The trick was that he needed to actually put it out or—just like the real thing—it would consume him.

Jealousy aside, he still did have his wits about him enough to realize that he didn't want to say something to her that he would regret. Words can hurt, and sometimes words were something a person—or a relationship—could not come back from. He didn't want to say anything to Tessa in the heat of anger that would be impossible to take back—especially when he realized his anger was unjustified. She had done absolutely nothing wrong.

He recognized that he needed to take a moment to cool off before engaging with her. He began to walk up the stairs towards his bedroom as he loosened his tie, not looking back at her. He knew that if he looked at her, it would all be over. He would not be able to keep himself from engaging, and he wasn't in a frame of mind to do that, rationally, at the moment.

"Where are you going?" He heard Tessa's tight voice behind him.

"Shower," was his clipped reply.

His stride didn't stop until he reached his bathroom. He

turned on the water in the shower, setting the temperature to as high as he could stand it. He then peeled off the layers of his formal clothing, dropping them onto the floor—not caring about the disarray or the condition of the clothes. He just needed to get his body underneath that steaming stream of water and let the physical sensation bring his head back down to earth. He instinctively knew that it was exactly what he needed to come back to himself. Even the simple act of breathing the steam the water had already generated was beginning to calm him just a bit.

Jake climbed underneath the red-hot spray, letting the sting of the water penetrate his skin, breathing the steamy air deep into his lungs, and attempting to let it clear his mind.

Jake ducked his head under the stream coming from the showerhead, letting it drench his head and body. He did his best to lose himself in the pounding rhythm of the water hitting the ceramic floor and the pulsing needles where it landed on his skin.

He became so lost in the sound and sensation of the shower, in fact, that it was a complete surprise to him when he heard Tessa's voice, less than an inch from his ear as she hissed, "Wow, you really like it *hot*, don't you?"

Then, without giving him time to turn around, she pressed herself against his back. He felt the soft pillows of her breasts against the hard, rippling muscles of his back and felt the beads of her hard nipples as they slipped along his wet skin. She snaked her arms around his waist, sliding her hand down to grasp his engorged erection in her slick palm.

Every ounce of anger and jealousy dissolved and was replaced with desire and arousal. Tessa was magic like that. With her, he had absolutely no control. He saw her body, heard her voice, or felt her touch and sprang to life. Every single time, without fail.

He pressed his palms up against the tile walls of the shower as her hand moved faster and faster up and down his shaft. Her other hand ran up his chest. She spread her fingers out and held him tightly as she pumped him hard. He could feel himself growing larger and larger in her firm grip.

Then suddenly, she was in front of him, lowering to her knees in one fluid motion. He moaned in anticipation of her sweet lips on his shaft.

He dropped his gaze to her mouth as she encircled the tip of his sex with her lips and he felt her tongue swirling around it. Moaning again, this time from pleasure, he placed one hand on the back of her head to guide her and the other he pressed firmly back against the tile. He was definitely going to need some help maintaining his balance. This was one of the best feelings he had ever experienced. He was almost dizzy with desire.

His eyes closed as his head fell back from the sheer power of ecstasy that was coursing through his veins, but immediately he realized that he didn't want to miss even one moment of watching her head move up and down along his manhood. He looked back down on her and was mesmerized by the combination of erotic sights. He couldn't decide what was sexier—her plump, red lips wrapped around his massive erection as it glided in and out of her mouth, her slick wet body that was kneeling on the shower floor in front of him, or her big blue eyes as she stared directly into his as she sucked him.

All of them equally, he decided. Or all of them together. She was such a total package of sexiness that he simply couldn't separate the elements of it out into parts.

Jake grabbed her hair even more desperately, a guttural

moan ripping from him as a spasm of pleasure rocked through him. He was on the edge of coming, and he didn't want to do that right now. He wanted to be inside her. The instinct that had taken hold of him earlier, the one that drove him to claim her, to possess her, hadn't faded. It was still going strong. In fact, it was pumping through his veins like hot lava, spurring him on to take action.

He reached down and placed his hands under her arms, pulling her up to stand in front of him. "I don't want to come yet," he rasped, "I want to make love to you. All night."

She drew back and looked into his eyes, a sexy little half smile playing on her lips. He grinned back. He recognized that wicked little gleam in her eye. He had seen it on several occasions before. Tessa was a good girl 99.9% of the time. That gleam showed up the .1% of the time that she was bad.

He grinned even wider. When Tessa decided to be a bad girl, the results were always amazing.

"That sounds nice," she said sweetly, her voice low and seductive, "but first I want you to do something for me."

He stepped closer to her, leaning his face down so that he was looking directly into her eyes. Their breathing intermingled, indistinguishable from each other and from the steam that billowed around them.

"Okay," he asked her slowly, "what do you want me to do?"

She continued to look unabashedly into his eyes, the naughty gleam intensifying as she stated clearly, "I want you to fuck me."

Jake shuddered at the erotic thrill her provocative request sent through him, but he did not hesitate to act on it. He grabbed her firmly by the waist and lifted her up and off of her feet, carrying her two short steps until her back was pressed against the tile wall of the shower. She gasped and her eyes widened. Her breathing quickened, and she bit her bottom lip.

Jake drove into her with a power he hadn't even known he possessed. There was so much driving him as he pushed himself into her again and again—his love for her, the fierceness with which he had missed her, his uncertainty about their future, and yes, even his jealousy at seeing Levi's arms around her.

He needed her. With every cell in his body, down to every corner of his soul, he needed her. He needed to possess her, if only to even the scales, because she so completely possessed him.

Yes. It was true, and he knew it. Body, mind, and soul—he was hers. He belonged to her. She owned him, down to the core of his being, and she always would.

--- ~ ---

Tessa loved the pure carnal pleasure of Jake driving himself into her over and over again. She loved his losing his tight grasp of control and taking her. She let herself be taken over by this erotic fantasy come to life.

Her body was filled with a tingling ache. Hot lust whipped through her. The decadent pleasure sent her soaring to a higher level of sensation than she'd even known was possible.

But there was a lot more than just the physical reactions to being with Jake that was consuming her senses. She felt the intensity of his feelings toward her and her feelings toward him. She felt the traces of poignant melancholy from all of the years they had been apart and the sweetness of the joy that coming back together had brought. She felt the urgency generated by the fact that what the future held for them was uncertain. And yet, she felt the security of certainty as well, because she was so sure of her total and unwavering devotion to him, no matter what the future would bring.

All of these feelings rocketed around inside of her, crashing into one another like bumper cars, mixing and melting and forming one giant miasma of intensity.

Suddenly, it was simply not enough to be a passive participant in their coupling, held up against the wall with very little room to maneuver. She felt the need to move, to grasp, to raise her hips in order to meet his thrusts. She needed space. Her body needed the freedom to follow her instincts, to move with him and touch him in whatever way felt right in the moment.

"Take me to bed, Jake," she moaned, "I want to be in bed with you."

Without even taking time to respond or shut off the water in the shower, Jake pushed aside the glass shower door and carried her with him as he stepped across the bathroom tile and then walked the remaining steps to his bed.

He put her down in the middle of the bed, not on her back as she would have predicted, but rather on her hands and knees. She felt the indentation of the bed as he climbed up behind her, placing his hands on her hips and leaning down over her. She felt the strong, hard muscles of his chest press against her back.

"I want you like this," he explained simply, as if no other explanation were necessary—and it wasn't. The erotic thrill that ran the length of Tessa's body at his forceful words was unprecedented. In fact, she was surprised that she even managed to stay conscious under the weight of it.

She heard the sound of plastic tearing and realized that Jake must be slipping on a condom. She appreciated that he was levelheaded and responsible enough to remember to do that, because she was so dizzy with lust that she wasn't sure she could even remember her middle name.

Her mental musing was short-lived when, a few seconds later, she felt him thrust into her, penetrating her with a passion that took her breath away. She looked down at the sheet she was kneeling on, seeing water drip and shake free from her hair as Jake pounded into her again and again. She watched the dark puddle of water spread farther and farther out on the light grey sheets and was inordinately turned on by the sight.

She loved this. She loved every part of it. She closed her eyes to just feel. Feel his rock-hard erection as it plunged again and again into her hot center. Feel his incredibly strong hands gripping her hips and waist, making her feel tiny and safe as he pulled her back against him over and over. Feel his fingers digging into her skin.

Her arms began to shake from the sheer pleasure Jake was giving her body, and she didn't think she would be able to support herself on them much longer. When she did collapse onto her elbows, she turned her face to the side, pressing her cheek against the dark cotton of Jake sheets, wet from the water that had dripped off of her from the shower. Just one more sensation to add to her list of things that were conspiring to send her spiraling over the erotic edge.

Just then, Jake decided to up the ante, and Tessa did not know how she was going to maintain her sanity, let alone her consciousness. He leaned down over her, pressing his chest against her back as he continued to move inside of her, and slid one of his hands up to her breasts. He began moving it from one breast to the other, tweaking her nipples and rolling them in turn between his thumb and forefinger as he continued the punishing rhythm of his thrusts.

Tessa heard a moan escape from her mouth. The sound was so desperate, so carnal, and yet so intimate. In fact, it perfectly captured the way she was feeling inside, right now, in the way that no words ever could.

Without breaking his rhythm, Jake moved his hand down between her legs and began to manipulate her sensitive flesh as he continued steady, hard strokes in and out of her. She began to shake everywhere. She marveled at the way that, despite the fact that they had been apart for so long, he knew every single thing about her—how she would respond, what she needed from him, how to elicit any reaction that he wanted, and how to give her the most mind-blowing pleasure she had ever known.

It was pleasure she would never have been able to imagine was possible had she not experienced it herself, pleasure she never would have believed was real if it had been described to her. She would've thought it was an exaggeration, a fantasy. She would never have thought that it was within the realm of possibility for her body to produce the sensations that were now tearing through her with abandon.

She knew that the only reason she was able to experience this, now, was Jake. With anyone else, this kind of feeling would be an unattainable ideal. She knew instinctively, beyond any shadow of a doubt, that what she was feeling right now was nothing that could ever be replicated in the future. Anything she would ever try to do with anyone else, she would ever try to attempt it with, would be nothing else but a pale imitation of the connection and intensity Jake was giving her right at this moment.

Tessa closed her eyes as her inner muscles spasmed as the waves of climax begin to crash over her. She surrendered herself to the sensation completely, letting the feelings wash through her as if she were nothing but an empty vessel that was meant for this—which, in essence, she was at that moment.

She felt Jake's hands roaming all over her body as wave after wave of orgasm shook through her, little earthquakes of pleasure that he kept going even longer by the expert touches he administered to her flesh as she came.

Just as the waves began to calm and she was a bit more aware of her surroundings, she felt Jake's hands tighten on her and his muscles tense against her body. He let out a guttural moan that let her know that he was beginning to ride the same crest of pleasure she was, and that knowledge sent another erotic wave shooting through her.

When every last bit of energy had been expended from her muscles, she collapsed forward on the bed, breathing hard and still trembling. Jake rolled to the side and pulled her with him, snuggling her into her absolute favorite place in the world to be—within the safe circle of his strong arms.

He stroked her still-wet hair and lovingly kissed the top of her head. She would do anything to have this moment stretch on until eternity. She wanted to stay here, just like this, forever.

She sighed. She had often heard the phrase that all good things must come to an end. Tessa just wished it weren't true in this case.

28

Tessa felt like she was floating on a cloud. She could hear Jake's voice but it was coming from far away. Her body felt light and airy, like she was drifting down a lazy river.

"Wake up, beautiful." Jake's voice seemed closer now.

She tried to open her eyes but the suckers were heavy.

A chuckle sounded, and she was pretty sure it was coming from Jake. She felt a featherlight touch brush against her cheek as Jake's deep voice sounded again. "That's it. Open your eyes."

As her eyes fluttered open, she was met with a smiling Jake beaming down at her. "Good morning."

Tessa *loved* Jake and she *loved* waking up to Jake's smiling face. The problem here was she wasn't ready to wake up. Her eyes began closing again.

"Uh uh. I've got something to show you, baby." At those words, she felt herself being lifted off the bed in Jake's strong arms.

Tessa tucked her head in the crook of Jake's shoulder

and took in a deep breath through her nose. She loved how he smelled. Fresh, like soap and man.

Curling her body closer to him, Tessa closed her eyes as she snuggled against the solid planes of Jake's muscular chest. She was still sleepy and she felt her body totally relax and revel in the feeling of being carried by the man she loved. She felt so treasured. So special.

When they reached the bottom of the stairs, Jake gently set her down. Then, kneeling before her, he picked up one of her feet and began putting it in a boot. She reached out and held on to his shoulder to steady herself when suddenly the entire scene felt like déjà vu.

Tessa gasped and covered her mouth. "It snowed!"

Jake smiled brightly as he looked up at her, winking. "You're not quite as quick on the uptake as you used to be."

"Shut up!" Tessa swatted his shoulder. "I was sleepy."

He stood and pulled her into his arms, kissing her like he needed her as much as he needed his next breath. His hands roamed up and down her back. His tongue explored her mouth expertly, his lips the perfect balance between firm and soft.

Damn, the man could kiss.

When Jake pulled away from Tessa, he heard a protesting moan escape from her mouth. A satisfied grin spread across Jake's face as he put on her the same jacket he'd put on her the first night she'd arrived. After he zipped her up, he pulled a beanie out of his pocket, stuck it on her head, kissed her on her nose, and said, "Come on, sleepy."

He opened the door, but before she could see anything, he covered her eyes. She reached up and tried to pull his hands away. "Hey!"

His large hands didn't budge. "Nope. No peeking."

As he was navigating her outside and down the stairs, telling her to take three steps here, four steps there, she mumbled, "I liked it better when you just carried me."

"If I did that, you would peek," Jake answered.

"True," Tessa sighed as she felt her boots sink into snow as she walked across Jake's front yard. She wanted to *see* it.

"Okay, two steps up." Jake's voice sounded excited and it caused Tessa to get even more anxious—in a good way!—for whatever he had planned.

"Stop," he said and she did.

She felt his warm breath fan down her neck, sending a delicious chill down her spine. His lips brushed against her outer ear, causing a deep pull in her core as he whispered, "Are you ready?"

She was ready for *something*, but she didn't really think it would be appropriate for outdoors.

"Yes," she said as she nodded her head.

He removed his hands from her eyes and her breath caught in her throat as tears immediately filled her eyes. They were standing on her Gran's porch. A brand-new swing was hanging from the rafters, and there were two insulated cups sitting beside the swing and a box of donuts.

"Oh my gosh!" Tessa flung her arms around Jake's neck as tears poured down her face. "When did you do this?"

His arms came around her and he rubbed up and down her back. "I've had the new swing in the garage since the day we all worked on the house. I was just waiting for the first snow. I got up a few hours ago and hung it. I wanted it to be a surprise."

Tessa took in a shaky breath as she wiped her eyes. "You didn't have to do that."

He pulled back and looked down at her, his eyes and tone growing serious. "Yes. I did."

As she stared up into Jake's big brown eyes, she felt warmed from the inside out. It might have been thirty degrees outside, but when Jake looked at her like that, she was more than warm—she was hot.

"Come here." He tugged her with him and they sat on the brand-new swing. He handed her a cup, and before the liquid even hit her mouth, she could smell that it was hot chocolate. And it might have been a figment of her imagination, but it smelled and tasted exactly the same as it had all those years ago.

Tessa looked out over the unclouded view of the face of the mountain and was momentarily paralyzed by its beauty. As snow fell on the majestic Sierra Nevadas, sprinkling it with white powder, it gave it an almost fairytale-like appearance.

She felt the swing move beneath her as Jake reached behind it. Tessa turned her head just in time to see him pulling out the very same patchwork comforter they'd snuggled underneath the first time they'd done this. It looked like it was in perfect condition. She'd asked her Gran for it when she'd first moved to Arizona and she'd told her that she didn't have it anymore.

"Where did you…? How did you…?" Tessa couldn't believe her eyes.

Jake didn't answer as he draped it over her shoulders and wrapped her up in it like a burrito, only her hands wrapped around her mug sticking out. Turning towards her, he circled his arms around her and pulled her snugly to him, her back resting against his chest.

Tessa closed her eyes, so overwhelmed by…everything.

She couldn't speak. She just sat against Jake's solidness,

sipping her hot chocolate as he rocked them slowly in the swing.

Everything in Tessa's world, right at this moment, was…perfect.

"I've had this"—Jake's hand grazed the comforter that was covering Tessa—"since the night that I came looking for you after I went back to the hospital and you weren't there. I took it with me after I searched the whole house."

Okay, maybe not perfect.

Tessa swallowed hard as her stomach dipped—and not from the motion of the swing. Sitting up, she placed the cup down on the small table that sat next to the hanging swing and turned back to face Jake. If they were going to talk about this, she needed to be looking at him.

"Why did you leave?" Jake asked. She saw moisture filling his eyes and her heart broke all over again.

She'd known this moment was coming. It was inevitable. Jake needed to hear the truth. The whole truth.

Taking a deep breath and reaching inside herself, she tried to stay calm as she spoke. "When we were in the truck, I only told you half of what the doctors told me—"

"What?!" Jake interrupted, "What do you mean?"

Tessa felt like she was going to throw up. This shouldn't be that hard. They were both adults now. They'd moved on with their lives. They weren't lovesick teens with idealistic views of what their futures held. But apparently her heart and body had not gotten that memo because they were both behaving as if that was exactly what they were.

Tessa shook her head a little, trying to pull it together, as tears, again, fell unbidden down her cheeks. She sniffed. "They told me that I had been born with a congenital abnormality in my fallopian tubes. That alone would have made it difficult to conceive. But when I had the miscarriage, my fallopian tube burst and they said that in all likelihood I would never be able to conceive children." Tears were pouring down her cheeks now, and she felt like her heart was being ripped out of her body as she said, "I can never have a baby."

Jake's arms were around her, holding her tightly against him just like the night in the truck when he had held her while she'd sobbed. The soothing tone of Jake's voice as he whispered against her hair, the safety of being held in his arms, and the lulling feeling of being rocked back and forth all worked together to heal a part of Tessa that she'd thought would be broken…forever.

She stayed in the safety of his embrace until she felt a small bit of strength renewing in her. It grew with every gentle caress, every encouraging word, every rock of the swing. When it felt like the emotional storm inside of her had finally passed, Tessa sat up and wiped her eyes a final time. Although it had been painful to revisit the memory and finally say the words out loud to Jake, it had also been almost therapeutic.

Now Jake knew. He knew the truth and he understood why she'd done what she had done. The invisible weight she'd subconsciously been carrying around for the last thirteen years had been lifted off of her shoulders and she felt lighter than a feather.

"I'm so sorry, Tessa," Jake said as he smoothed some stray hairs off of her damp cheek.

Leaning into his palm, for the first time in a long time, Tessa felt a spark of hope that even if they still couldn't be together, they could still be friends. That Jake understood, now, and could forgive her for what she'd done.

Looking earnestly into her eyes, he said, "But I still don't understand why you left."

Or not.

She spoke slowly, making sure he understood the finality of her words. "I can't get pregnant. I can *never* have children."

He was still staring at her like she was speaking another language. She really hadn't thought that she was going to have to connect the dots, but obviously she did.

---~---

Jake saw that questioning Tessa was making her upset, and honestly, that was the last thing he wanted to do. But he needed to know. Once and for all. No matter how painful. She might be the one crying, but he felt like his heart was being ripped out of his chest.

"Wanting to be a dad is all you talked about." Tessa's hands flew out of the blanket. "And not just being a dad. But about your Irish-Italian heritage. And how much you loved having siblings and wanted that for *your* kids. The ones you had already named!"

"That's why you left?" Jake honestly could not believe what he was hearing. He tried to remain calm. "You left because you couldn't have kids."

"Yes!" Tessa threw up her hands in frustration, as if that point should have been clear.

The swing rocked a little, and Jake stared at Tessa. He'd played this talk—the "why Tessa left" talk—over in his mind countless times, but not in a million years had he thought *those* would be the words coming out of her mouth.

Jake tried to clarify. "You still loved me. And you left."

"Yes," she said, tears pooling in her eyes again. "I never stopped loving you. I still love you."

Jake took in a deep breath as he leaned forward and rested his elbows on his knees, dropping his head in his hands. It had been hard enough for him to deal with the fact that she'd stopped loving him and left. To find out that she *hadn't* stopped loving him, that they *could* have been together, infuriated him.

Raking his fingers through his hair, he counted to ten in his head. He remembered, as a kid, his mom counting to ten when she thought she was going to lose it. It had never really worked that well for her, but he figured he'd give it a try.

After he got to ten, he looked up, straight ahead at the mountain, and asked, "And you're leaving again. Just because of *that*."

"Why are you acting like it's a little thing, Jake?" Tessa raised her voice, which she rarely did. "I wanted you to have a full life, with kids and a family. You can't have that with me!"

"And you just made that decision all on your own?! I don't get a vote in my own life?!" Jake yelled.

Tessa flinched at his words—or at the volume of his voice—and then quietly said through tears streaming down her face, "I know…er...um…knew what you would have said if I'd told you."

"Really? So you're a mind reader now, too?" Jake could hear himself being a total asshole and he just couldn't stop it. "So tell me, mind reader! What would I have said?!"

Tessa's lip trembled as she took a deep breath. "You would have said that you loved me and it didn't matter. That we would figure it out."

"Damn right that's what I would have said!" Jake stood and the swing creaked and swung back. He saw Tessa grab the side as he glared down at her. "Because that's the truth. It was then and it is now!"

"Jake." Tessa's voice pleaded as her big blue eyes looked up at him and she shook her head. It felt like a knife was twisting in his gut. He saw it then. There was not going to be any changing her mind. She'd decided both of their fates. This one time, the time that he needed it most, there would be no reasoning with her.

But he still had to try. "I wanted to have a family with *you*, Tessa. Not anyone else." His arms flew out. "I'm thirty years old and *you* are the last girlfriend I've had."

She continued shaking her head. "You would have ended up resenting me or hating me."

"And you think I *don't* now?" Jake wished he could take the words back as soon as they'd left his mouth. He didn't resent her and he definitely didn't *hate* her.

A sad smile lifted on the corners of Tessa's mouth as she stood and shrugged her shoulders. "No, I know you do. And you may never believe this"—she took in a shaky breath and wrapped her arms around herself protectively—"but I only wanted to do what was best for you. I still only want what's best for you."

Jake sat back down. His legs felt unsteady and he didn't trust them to hold him up. How could she not know that she was what was best for him? He just couldn't reconcile the things she was saying to him. "Are you honestly going to stand there and tell me that *you* leaving was really the best thing for *me*?" He could hear his anger, confusion, and pain bleeding into his voice.

Tessa spoke through the huge tears flowing down her face. "I know that I hurt you, Jake. I see that, now, more than ever. But can *you* see that doing what I did, that decision I made, cost me *everything*? You were my whole world. I walked away from you, from love, from a life that I knew was better than any dream-come-true I could have imagined, because I loved you *that* much.

"When I left, I willingly chose a broken heart"—she sniffed, her breath catching in her throat—"and a broken *life* because I truly believed it was the only way that *you* could have a whole life, a life you deserved…deserve to have. I sacrificed everything I ever wanted so you could have everything you ever wanted. And as painful as it was for me, so painful sometimes I didn't think I could survive it, I would do it again. For you. I would do anything for you."

Jake reached out and wrapped his arms around Tessa, pulling her close to him. His face was pressed up against her belly. "Then be with me. Stay in Hope Falls. Marry me. We'll figure everything else out."

"I wish it were that simple," she said softly through broken breaths as her fingers ran through his hair.

Looking up at her, he knew that somehow he had to make her see. "It is that simple. Nothing else matters. You are everything to me. *You* are my family. If you leave, I'm not going to just meet someone and start a family."

Tessa shook her head. "You don't know that."

"Yes, I do! Tessa, I haven't wanted anyone since you left."

Pain slashed through her eyes as her jaw tightened and she pulled away from him. "Don't, Jake." The tears were falling faster than they had just moments before. She held up her hand to stop him when he reached out again and tried to hold her. "After everything we've been through. Just don't."

Again Jake was lost. "Don't what?"

"You haven't *wanted* anyone?" she repeated his words.

"No." Jake shook his head emphatically.

Tessa tilted her head and crossed her arms in a

defensive stance. "Really? Because I came back to Hope Falls *two weeks* after I left the hospital, before I went to New York, and I saw you."

"Wait." Jake stood back up. "You came back?! And you *saw* me?!"

Tessa's voice shook as she said, "Yes. You were having sex with some blonde girl. In your truck. I saw you."

"And?" Jake really didn't know what her point was.

"And it was *two* weeks after I left." Tessa's voice rose with every word she spoke.

He couldn't believe that she was actually throwing the fact that he'd been with someone else in his face. He was *not* the asshole here. "So? What's your point?!"

Tessa's face flinched like his words had slapped her in the face. Her eyes widened and she shook her head like she couldn't believe the words that had left Jake's mouth.

"What's *my* point?!" Tessa asked with fury in her voice.

"Tessa, stop." Jake took a step towards her but she moved away.

"No. My *point* is you moved on! How long did you wait?! A whole day? Two days?" Her voice kept rising. Lunging at him, she pushed his chest. Hard. "'You haven't *wanted* anyone!" Letting out a forced laugh, she said, "Are you kidding me?! Your sisters had to buy you new furniture that was 'slut-free.'" Tessa put up her hands in air quotes. "Just how many girls have you *not wanted* since the girl in the truck?!" Then she pushed him again.

Jake grabbed her hands and pulled her towards him. "Is that what this is really about?! You stayed away because you saw me with some girl in my truck?"

"What? No!" Her brow furrowed in anger as she took a step back.

Jake followed, closing the distance between them. "Because yeah, I did sleep with girls. A lot of them. And to answer your question, it was three days. Three days before I fucked Jessica in the back of my truck. And then I think Gretchen was next a couple days late—"

"Stop it!" Tessa pulled out of his hold, shaking her head. "I don't want to hear this."

"No! You asked, so here it is! Yes! I had sex with a lot of girls. Hundreds, actually. But do you actually think I *wanted* any of them?! I didn't even know most of their *names*! I never *saw* any of them. I only ever saw you! It was always about *you*!" Jake grabbed her hand and put it flat against his chest. "Every time I was with one of them, I was only trying to fill the empty black hole where my heart was before you left and ripped it out of my chest."

"Don't say that." Tessa's lips were trembling, and her hands was shaking under his.

"Why not? It's the truth. I didn't give a *shit* about any of those girls. I know that makes me an asshole. But I don't give a shit. I have loved one girl and only one girl. It's only ever been you, Tessa!"

Jake could see her battling with what he was telling her.

He didn't know what else he could possibly say to make her see, to make her understand. "Do you want to know why I don't live in my own house? The one I've wanted since I was a kid? Because I can't without you! That was supposed to be our house. Yeah, maybe I wanted it before I even met you, but after you left, even that dream was nothing if I didn't have you."

Lifting his hands, he cupped her face and wiped her tears from her cheeks. She reached up and placed her hands on top of his. Leaning down, he kissed her forehead, her nose, her cheeks, and then each eyelid before brushing his lips against hers. The only sound that filled the air was their labored breathing as they stood on the small porch.

Resting his forehead against hers, he closed his eyes as

he cradled her face, desperately begging in a whispered voice, "Just stay. Please. Stay."

Her chin started shaking and he felt tears puddling beneath his palms. Lifting his head, he looked down into her tortured blue eyes. He saw his answer. She was leaving.

Cursing under his breath, he walked off the porch as Tessa called his name. He really hadn't believed, until this moment, that she would actually leave him. Again.

29

Jake stood to the side of the small altar in Hope Falls Community Church, trying to put on a good show, but he felt miserable. The bridesmaids had just walked down the aisle and Amy was next. He still couldn't believe that his baby sister was really getting married today. He still thought of her as, basically, a little kid, even though he knew that was ridiculous.

He looked around, trying to distract himself from all the rioting emotions he was feeling. Everyone was dressed in their Sunday best. He smiled at Nikki, who was Amy's maid of honor. Next to her stood Sara and Shelby, Matt's sisters. He, himself, stood next to Eric and Matt's brother-in-law, Sara's husband. His mother sat on the front pew, already weepy even though the ceremony hadn't yet begun.

Jake was also having a hard time keeping from misting up, but not for the same reasons as his mom. Sure, he loved his kid sister, and yeah, he was happy for her. And yes, of course, there was the fact that both sides of his heritage—Irish and Italian—had imbued him with more than a healthy sense of passion and emotion and very little inhibition about showing it. But that wasn't it either.

No, the reason why Jake was having a hard time keeping his emotions in check was currently scurrying around the back of the church, camera around her neck, snapping pictures like a woman possessed.

Tessa. Damn. He hadn't talked to her since he'd left her this morning on the porch. He'd been on wedding duty the entire day.

All day had been consumed with running last-minute errands for his mom and sisters. It had been wedding, wedding, wedding every minute. And each task he'd completed had brought Tessa to his mind. What their wedding would be like.

Tessa in a wedding gown. Tessa walking toward him down the aisle. Tessa, her face radiant as he lifted her veil. Tessa with tears running down her face as they spoke their vows to one another from the bottoms of their hearts. Tessa as he leaned down to give her their first kiss as husband and wife. And finally, he and Tessa walking hand in hand back up the aisle after Pastor Harrison announced them as Mr. and Mrs. Maguire.

Damn.

He seriously needed to get a grip!

Jake was snapped from his reverie as he heard the opening strains of Pachelbel's Canon fill the church. *Time to focus.* He needed to be there for Amy. He couldn't spend the day thinking about him and Tessa. It would show on his face, and that would take away from the special quality that the day should have. This was Amy's day, and Matt's, and Jake was determined not to do anything to detract from it.

As the dramatic strains of the bridal march burst forth

from the organ, Jake was momentarily taken aback by the beautiful sight of his sister in her wedding gown being led down the aisle by their father, who was continually pausing to wipe tears from his eyes.

Jake smiled. Yep. He had definitely inherited his tendency to feel his emotions deeply. The apple did not fall far from the weeping tree.

When they reached the altar, the music died down and Pastor Harrison said, "Who gives this woman to be married to this man?"

His father wiggled his brow, a twinkle in his eye. *Uh oh,* Jake thought, *that's his 'I have something clever to say' look.*

Amy had, apparently, made the same observation, because she elbowed their dad in the ribs and gave him a significant look.

"Well, now, let me see," his dad began, and Amy closed her eyes resignedly. Jake smiled. Their father's brogue was even more exaggerated than usual, which meant he was playing it up for effect.

Then, *thankfully*, Jake's dad said simply, "Her mother and I do."

Pastor Harrison nodded, a small smile playing on his lips as their dad placed Amy's hand into Matt's. From that instant on, her face was glowing, completely focused on Matt, as if no one else in the world existed.

Again, Jake felt a twinge in his chest. He recognized that expression. He had seen it on Tessa's face in the past, and he knew that he had worn it, himself, when the two of them were together. He sighed and resigned himself to the fact that he was probably not going to be able to push out all thoughts of Tessa and their relationship from his mind. It was probably naïve of him to have thought he could pull that off in the first place.

He decided, instead, that his new goal was simply going to be that, no matter how much his "Tessa turmoil" invaded his mind and soul, he was not going to let it show on his face or in his body language. He'd been hiding how he felt from the world for thirteen years. One more day wouldn't kill him.

Just as he was settling on this new resolution and committing fresh to the idea of controlling his feelings, Karina and Ryan stepped up to a microphone that had been set up to one side of the platform, Ryan with a guitar slung over his shoulder. Ryan began to pick and strum the strings, and then Karina opened her mouth to sing a lovely melody with her beautiful, bell-like voice.

As Jake listened to the lyrics about holding tight to the person you loved and knowing that all would be right with the world as long as they were in your arms, Jake started to feel a new tightening and aching his chest. Shit, the song made him think about Tessa even more than the rest of the ceremony had. He knew it was completely ridiculous to think that the song had any sort of special significance for his relationship with Tessa. Jake was pretty sure that everyone who'd been in love could probably relate to the universal theme, thinking every song written about love was somehow particular and special to their situation.

Still, Jake couldn't chase away the nagging sensation that this song perfectly captured the intense feeling that passed between himself and Tessa every single time he held her, and it became even more difficult to keep a happy or even neutral expression on his face.

It also became very difficult to stand where he was and stay still, because with every fiber of his being, all he wanted to do was run to the back of the church, scoop Tessa up in his arms, and hold her like the song described, begging her from the bottom of his heart and soul for her to stay. To just…stay.

--- ~ ---

Tessa made the rounds at Amy and Matt's wedding reception, a—hopefully convincing!—smile plastered firmly on her face and a heart that felt ready to shatter, beating within her chest. Getting through the ceremony had been difficult, especially listening to Karina and Ryan's beautiful duet rendition of "Hold Me Tighter" with the bittersweet knowledge that Karina had written it about her and Jake.

It was odd, actually, to know that piece of trivia. Tessa had listened to the song so many times in the past, feeling connected to the sentiment but also feeling oddly jealous of the fictional couple in the song.

It's so simple for them, she had thought to herself. *They were so sure of themselves and their love. The couple in this song would never end their relationship. No. They would see a clear path through the pain.* They *would come out triumphant and stronger than ever.*

Yeah, not so much.

Still, as difficult as the ceremony had been, the reception was proving to be even harder. At the ceremony, she had been able to focus on just doing her job. The world didn't exist for her in any form except through the lens of her camera. Every moment, there was a new shot to frame, a new angle to perfect, a new vantage point to hurry over to and claim. As tough as it was, emotionally, to block out the more sentimental parts of her surroundings, at least she had the work to focus on.

Here at the reception, it was different. She was still working, but it was a completely different process. This was a more casual environment, and as such, her process needed to be more casual in order to fit in well and make people comfortable. She had to talk to them, to chat, to give them instructions about where to look and how to smile.

At any other event, in San Diego, where she knew no one, that would've been a snap. Here, in Hope Falls, where she knew everyone, it was proving to be somewhat more problematic. It seemed that at every single table she stopped at, everyone wanted to talk about her and Jake. In fact, from her perspective, it seemed to be a much more common topic on people's minds even than Amy and Matt's ceremony.

Deciding to take a break from human subjects, Tessa moved her photographic attention to the cake table. After that, she would move on to the lighting and centerpieces because ambience shots didn't require interaction.

As she was snapping away, she pressed her eye to the viewfinder and Jake's face came into focus across the room. He was sitting with his parents, laughing at something his dad had said, and Tessa felt her heart slam into her chest.

All day she'd had to actively stop herself from running and throwing herself into his arms. Kissing him senseless and then making him finish their conversation. The only thing stopping her was that she couldn't be sure if he was still really mad about this morning. Since before today, he'd never even raised his voice to her. Tessa had no idea how he'd react if she approached him now. And she absolutely did not want to make a scene at Amy's wedding.

Now wasn't the time or place, but Tessa was not done

with their discussion. Not by a long shot. She hadn't been when he'd abruptly stomped off the porch, gotten into his SUV, and driven away. She'd stood staring down the street for what felt like an hour, thinking he would come back. That he just needed to cool down and any second his Yukon would appear at the end of the street. But…it hadn't.

Maybe that was for the best, she thought as she redirected her attention to lighting and centerpieces. She'd had all day to think about the things he'd said to her. To try and process all the things he'd told her.

Tessa had always known how much *she* loved Jake, but she hadn't realized until this morning how much he'd loved her. In her mind, Jake was Jake and he would be the same passionate, loving, caring, strong man with whomever he was with. There was no doubt in her mind that he was irreplaceable in her life, but it had never dawned on her that she might be irreplaceable in his.

She'd honestly thought the only option she'd had was to let him go and move on with his life.

After she'd gotten all the inanimate object shots, Tessa dug in her bag and grabbed her panoramic lens so she could get some crowd pics. Her mind was swimming with thoughts of Jake, of her and Jake—the past, the present, the future. Luckily, she'd been shooting receptions for so long that getting everything she needed was second nature and required zero brain power.

Which was good because her mind kept drifting back to that day in the hospital when she'd told Gran what she was going to do. Gran had told her not to make a hasty decision. To give it some time. To talk it over with Jake.

At the time, Tessa had thought that Gran just hadn't understood how important having children was to Jake. She'd tried to explain that there was no decision to make, there was no choice—if she'd really loved him, she'd had to let him go.

When she'd left the hospital and stayed with her aunt, Gran had insisted that Tessa was making a mistake. Gran kept telling her she couldn't leave him like that and not tell him the whole truth. Tessa could hear her voice now. "*That boy's been nothing but good to you and he doesn't deserve that.*" Gran had also said that she couldn't tell her what the right decision was for her or for Jake and their life but that she was sure what Tessa was doing was wrong and that he, at least, deserved the truth.

So she'd listened to Gran and decided to go talk to Jake before she got on the flight and took the internship with a photographer in New York. On the way to his house, she'd even started thinking that maybe they could work things out, that the shock and finality of losing the baby might have caused her to make a rash decision, and when he found out the whole truth, Jake would be Jake and magically make everything better.

She never ended up making it to his house that day. Driving along the highway, she'd spotted his truck down by the river parked in "their spot." She'd gotten off the highway and pulled in behind him. That's when she saw it. Jake…having sex…with another girl. Devastation didn't even scratch the surface of what she'd felt. Anger, disbelief and betrayal ripped through her soul.

She'd put her car in reverse and driven straight to the airport. She'd cried the entire drive because she'd known, then, that she'd been absolutely right in her decision. Jake would move on and find happiness with someone else. And that knowledge had shattered the remaining pieces of her heart into a million pieces.

Tessa placed her camera back into the bag once she'd gotten several usable crowd shots. Now she just had to wait for the cake cutting. Her feet were killing her because she'd made the idiotic decision to dress for style instead of comfort today and now her toes were paying the price.

She spotted an open seat at a table with her friends and she made her way to it. This particular table held four couples—Ryan and Karina, Amanda and Justin, Ben and Lauren, and Sam and Luke. She dropped into the one empty seat next to Shelby, Matt's sister, looking adorable but uncomfortable in her bridesmaid's dress.

Tessa smiled at her sympathetically. "Not a formalwear kind of gal, huh?" she guessed.

"Oh, God, no!" Shelby cried, horrified. "I'm a jeans-and-T-shirt girl all the way. I mean, don't get me wrong. I can get hoochie-fied up for the club as good as the next girl, but skinny jeans and stiletto boots are a long way from taffeta. Only for my brother. Seriously. There is literally no one else in the world I love enough to wear this getup for."

Tessa laughed. She liked Shelby. She liked anyone who would say whatever was on their mind in a given moment. It kind of reminded her of Nikki.

Tessa looked back at her to continue the conversation and found that Shelby's attention was focused elsewhere. She was seemingly transfixed by something across the room.

Tessa followed her gaze but didn't see anything. She looked back. "What's so interesting?"

Shelby's eyes widened. "Who's the hottie behind the bar with the tattoos?" she breathed.

Tessa looked back, and then her eyes brightened. Happy for the distraction, she answered, "Oh, that's Levi. Do you want to meet him?"

"Hell. Yes." Shelby said decisively.

Tessa smiled as she waved and got Levi's attention,

motioning him over. She liked that Shelby didn't put up any façade of protest. She was a straight-up kind of a girl.

When Levi reached their table, Tessa made the introductions, saying, “Levi, I'd like to introduce you to Matt's sister, Shelby. And, Shelby, this is Levi. He owns JT's Roadhouse, the bar just outside of town.”

“I'm not surprised that you own a bar,” Shelby flirted shamelessly.

“Why's that?” Levi asked, amused and clearly enjoying the interaction.

Shelby shrugged provocatively—well, as provocatively as the fluffy gown would allow, at any rate. Her eyes narrowed as she said with a bit of a challenge in her tone, “It suits you. Let me guess. You ride, too.”

“I do,” Levi laughed, clearly charmed and wanting to get to know Shelby better. “Do you want to dance?” he asked, holding out his hand.

A slow smile crossed Shelby's face as she stood and took it in her own. “Don't mind if I do.”

With that, they were off to the dance floor and Tessa felt like she’d just seen an instant love connection. Or lust connection, at the very least. Clearly, those two were infatuated with each other. As she looked around the table, all she saw were her friends paired up. Deliriously happy in relationships. Damn. Maybe there *was* something in the water in Hope Falls.

“Okay”—Karina leaned forward in her seat—“I think we all just witnessed the opening scene to a porno happen in real life.”

Tessa laughed. “There were definitely sparks flying between those two.”

All the couples began reminiscing about the first time they’d laid eyes on each other and Tessa silently remembered the first time she’d seen Jake. She’d only been in Hope Falls for a few hours and Gran had needed to run errands. So they'd headed into town and Tessa was given a list of groceries to get while Gran went to the dry cleaners.

Tessa remembered how good the cold air conditioning had felt when she'd walked into the Pack 'N' Pay on the hot, summer day. She'd grabbed a cart and had pushed it to the produce section. That's when she'd seen Jake. He had been stocking the lettuce, and Tessa remembered feeling like the rest of the world had disappeared. She'd stood there, paralyzed, until he'd looked up at her and smiled. She'd turned her cart away and began picking tomatoes, embarrassed to have been caught checking him out. Before she'd even gotten two in the bag, he'd walked over, introduced himself, and made her forget all about being embarrassed.

He'd asked if he could see her when he got off of his shift. She'd told him she was staying with her grandma and she'd have to ask. When he'd found out who her Gran was, he'd just winked at her and told her to tell Adeline he'd see them for dinner. She'd been so tongue tied, she'd just nodded.

He'd shown up at six o'clock sharp that night. And the rest was history.

"May I have this dance?" Tessa sat up straight at the sound of the familiar voice in her ear. She turned to see Jake smiling down at her. Suddenly, the realization of the song that was now playing swept over her. Peter Cetera's "Glory of Love."

And just like it had all those years ago in the Pack 'N' Pay, the rest of the world disappeared and there was just Jake. "Yes," she answered, smiling from ear to ear.

Jake led her out to the dance floor and enfolded her in his arms. "I'm sorry for this morning," Jake said, deep regret tingeing his voice.

Tessa looked up at him in surprise. It took her a moment to catch up with the conversation, and then she let out a little laugh.

"What's so funny?" Jake asked, a small frown of puzzlement furling his brow.

Tessa shook her head. "Nothing," she explained with a smile. "It's just that, for a minute, I had actually forgotten about our fight this morning. I was remembering when we met."

"That was the best day of my life," Jake said a small smile tilting his lips.

At his words, Tessa's pulse picked up speed. Relief and hope filled her. Jake didn't seem mad at all anymore, and he'd even apologized. Maybe they could talk here after all. "Thank you, Jake. And I'm sorry, too. I've been wanting to talk to you all day—"

A sharp buzzing sound came from Jake's pocket, interrupting their dance. Jake pulled his phone out, a disappointed look crossing his face. He exchanged a few words with the person on the other end before replacing the phone in his pocket and explaining with regret, "I have to go in and cover a shift. Now. There's nobody else. This damn flu that's going around."

Tessa tried not to let the disappointment show in her eyes.

Jake took her hands in his. "Just promise me one thing. Promise me that you won't leave town without saying goodbye to me first," he said earnestly, looking into her eyes.

Tessa was taken aback. Why would he ask her to promise that? But before she had a chance to ask, his phone buzzed again and he cursed under his breath.

"I have to go," Jake said as he was already moving away from her. "Just promise me."

"I promise," Tessa agreed, still not understanding why he would ask that.

As she watched him walk out the door of the reception hall, she knew that it would be a few days before he'd be off. She hated knowing that she couldn't clear the air with him before that, but trying to look at the bright side of things, she told herself it had been thirteen years. What would a few more days hurt?

30

TESSA LEANED HER ELBOWS ON THE KITCHEN ISLAND, trying to concentrate on editing Amy's wedding pictures. She wanted to do the best job she possibly could for her. She'd weeded out the duds and only had a few more that she needed to crop and color correct for the slideshow.

She hadn't slept, at all, last night after the wedding. Part of the reason was that she wanted to get the slideshow uploaded before Amy and Matt left for their honeymoon tomorrow morning. But the main reason was because she kept replaying everything that had happened the last few weeks in her head. Over and over again.

A few things more than others. Of course every time Jake had touched her, kissed her and made love to her was getting a lot of review time.

But also the almost cryptic words Jake had spoken to her before he left the wedding last night, kept haunting her as well. Why would he ask her to promise him to say goodbye before she left town?

Did he think that she was just going to leave, forget about Gran's house, just because of the fight they'd had?

Did he think that she was the same scared seventeen-year-old who had left the hospital without telling him?

There were so many questions flooding Tessa's mind that she knew what she had to do. She needed to talk to Jake. Now.

Wait. Maybe the mature thing to do would be to wait until he was off on Wednesday, make him a nice dinner, and discuss all of the questions that were on her mind.

Nah. Tessa grabbed her keys and purse off of the counter and headed out the door. Maturity was overrated.

Thirteen years was long enough to wait. She couldn't wait another second to find out if she and Jake had a real chance, a real shot at this.

Excitement and adrenaline flooded her system as she jumped into her PT Cruiser and headed to the station. Her heart was racing and her palms were sweaty with anticipation as she drove through the small town of Hope Falls. She had butterflies in her stomach, but they weren't gracefully flitting about. Oh no, it felt more like they were having a full-blown roller derby of destruction in there.

"Okay, okay, okay, okay," Tessa whispered to herself to try and settle down.

Just as she was starting her second round of 'okays', her phone buzzed in her purse.

Jake.

Grabbing her phone as she pulled up to the intersection the fire station sat at, she felt her heart sink when she saw the call was from Lauren. Not that she didn't want to talk to her friend. It was just that, for a split second, she thought that maybe she and Jake did, in fact, have some kind of psychic connection and he was calling to tell her that he couldn't stop thinking about her and they needed to talk. Then she would have pulled into the parking lot and Jake would have been standing there waiting. It would have been like a scene from a movie.

Snapping herself back to reality, Tessa hit the answer button on her phone. "Hey, Lauren."

"I have some good news," Lauren said with a small amount of hesitation before adding, "I think."

Lauren's contradictory words and tone ratcheted up Tessa's nervous energy tenfold. The light turned green, and Tessa crossed the intersection and drove to the back of the station, pulling into one of the three empty parking spaces.

When she was no longer operating heavy machinery, she asked, "What good news?"

"We got on an offer on the house, as is. It came in at asking price and you can sign today. The buyer is pre-approved and going to be using it as a rental."

Tessa went numb. This was good news. Right?

"Oh, okay." Tessa's head was spinning.

"Do you want me to come by? With the contract?" Lauren asked.

"Um, I'm actually in town. I have an errand to run, but I will stop by after." Tessa felt like she needed to see Jake more than ever now.

"Okay, see you then," Lauren said, and Tessa disconnected the call.

Tessa stepped out of the car and walked in through the back door of the station, operating solely on autopilot. She wasn't even fully aware of the short trip from the lot to standing in front of Jake's door. Her hand fisted and she watched as it knocked three times. She couldn't feel the wood as her knuckles hit it. It was as if she were floating outside herself completely.

Jake's voice sounded from inside. "Come in."

Tessa tried to pull herself together before walking into

the office. After their fight yesterday, she really wanted to say exactly the right thing. Unfortunately, she had no idea what that was.

"Come in," he repeated, this time louder and with a hint of irritation.

Taking a deep breath, she turned the doorknob and stepped inside. He looked up, his deep brown eyes locking with hers. Like always, she felt his stare all the way down to her soul.

He didn't look mad, but he certainly didn't look happy to see her. He looked…sad.

"Are you okay?" she asked, shutting the door behind her and moving to sit in the green leather chair in front of his desk.

"Yep," he answered briskly and leaned back in his high-back leather chair.

The vibe between them was so strange that she got thrown off. Well she'd already been a little off balance by Lauren's call, but now she had totally gone off the rails.

Whether it was because she hated awkward silences or just because she just didn't want any more secrets between them, she blurted out, "I got an offer on the house."

His expression did not change one iota. Nodding once, he said with resignation in his tone, "I know."

Tessa felt her jaw, literally, fall open. Sure, she knew that news traveled fast in Hope Falls, but this was ridiculous. "Who told you?" After the question left her mouth, she realized it was a stupid one. Lauren had to be the one who had told Jake.

"No one had to. I made the offer."

"You made the offer?" Tessa asked out loud, thinking that she must have heard him wrong.

"Yes." Jake's voice, body language, even his eyes were giving no clues as to what this was all about. It was as if he'd put up invisible walls since she'd danced with him just yesterday to *their* song at his sister's wedding.

"Why?" she asked, searching his eyes.

"It's what you wanted, right? To sell the house so you could open up your studio. I just moved the process along for you." His cold tone caused a sinking feeling in Tessa's stomach. "Did you stop by to say 'goodbye'?"

Tessa couldn't feel her legs, so she wasn't sure that they would hold her, but she figured that, worst-case scenario, even if she fell flat on her butt, it wouldn't be any worse than sitting in front of Jake while he did everything but pack her bags for her to get her out of town.

Did she come by to say "goodbye?" No, she came by to tell him that she wanted to try. That if he really couldn't be happy without her, then she would stay. That she loved him and had only ever wanted what was best for him. That she was sorry that she'd wasted years of their lives that they could have spent together, but that if he wanted her, she wouldn't waste another second by not being with him.

Obviously she wouldn't be saying those things now, so she just nodded as she swallowed a huge lump in her throat. Standing, she was happy that her legs did not give out on her. Tessa tried to hold the tears that were threatening to fall at bay and keep her voice strong as she said, "I am so glad we got to spend this time together. Thank you, Jake. For everything."

He didn't respond. He didn't get out from behind his desk. The only indication that he'd heard her at all was his jaw locking tightly and the vein on the side of his neck popping out.

Tessa had no idea what he was mad about, but she didn't want their last conversation to be a fight. So she plastered on her best fake smile and turned to leave.

"Bye, Jake."

But as her hand touched the doorknob, something stopped her. It was the realization that she still had questions in her mind and she didn't want to live out the rest of her life wondering about them, even if that meant the last conversation she and Jake had would be a yelling match. She'd made the mistake of not talking things out with Jake when she was seventeen. She was not going to do that again.

Turning back, she asked quickly, before she lost her nerve, "Is that why you told me to say 'goodbye' to you before I left yesterday? Because you knew you were going to buy Gran's house?"

---~---

Jake didn't know why Tessa was dragging this out. He'd given her an out. She was free. "I met with Lauren before the wedding. I'd already put an offer on the house."

"Because you want me to leave?" Tessa asked, her voice shaking like *she* was the injured party here.

Why am I always the asshole?

"Tessa"—Jake raked his hands through his hair—"I saw it in your eyes yesterday on your porch. You *are* leaving. Like I said, I just sped up the process."

"Because you want me to go?" Now tears were falling down her cheeks.

This was ridiculous. Hadn't he asked—no, *begged*—her to stay just yesterday?! Jake did not want to fight with her again, but he was really getting pissed off. As calmly as possible, he said, "It doesn't matter what I want. You've made that perfectly clear."

Tessa still stood on the other side of the room in front of the door. Jake could see her shaking from where he sat, and she was white as a ghost. More than anything, he wanted to go to her, hold her in his arms.

But he couldn't. He had to start protecting himself. Because when she left, there had to, at least, be pieces of himself that he could try to put back together to make a life with. A miserable life, but a life.

He saw her draw in a deep breath before she asked, "What if it did matter?"

His heart jumped in his chest. "What do you mean?"

"I mean…" Shaking her head a little, she crossed back to the visitor chair, whispering, "Okay, okay, okay, okay," to herself and sat down. Her blue eyes looked up at him, and what he saw made a small glimmer of hope twist in his chest. She continued, "What I mean is, what do *you* want to happen here?"

Jake was confused. He'd thought he could not have made himself any clearer yesterday on the porch. As much as he wanted to see where this was headed, a small part of him was scared that he would pour his heart out and she would walk away. Again.

So instead of answering, he asked, "What do *you* want to happen here?"

She looked like a deer caught in headlights. Obviously, she had not expected him to turn the tables on her. It wasn't so fun when you were the one in the hot seat. He waited. Inside he was dying, but he sat there silently. Waiting.

"Well," she said after what felt like hours, "I was thinking about what you said yesterday…and…"

Jake's heart started beating faster.

She licked her lips, nervously, and her gaze dropped to her hands, which she was wringing in her lap. He thought he heard her mumble, "Oh screw it," under her breath before she looked back up at him with a new fire in her eyes. "I love you. I have never stopped loving you. I only left and stayed away because I wanted the best for *you*. I wanted you to have everything you'd ever dreamed of.

"But I was thinking about what you said about me, about the other girls, about you not living in your house. So, I came over here to tell you that if you still wanted to be with me, I'm yours. I mean, I've *always* been yours, but I'll stay. If that's really what you want.

"But *then* I got Lauren's call and I came in here and *you* said you bought the hou—"

Jake was up and around the desk, and before she had a chance to finish what she was saying, he had her in his arms. His lips found hers and he claimed her with his kiss. Her arms flew around his neck and her legs wrapped around his waist. She parted her lips and his tongue swept inside of her mouth. She kissed him back with equal fervor, meeting him lick for lick.

It had only been a day since he'd kissed her last, but damn, Jake had missed her mouth. He knew her kisses were like a drug to him that he would never get enough of. Jake took his time, pouring all of the love he had inside himself into this kiss.

Tessa's curves melted against him, and Jake knew he needed to get them out of there before he cleared his desk, stripped her out of her clothes, and took her on top of it. But before anything went further, Jake needed to confirm what he thought Tessa was saying.

Pulling away, he met her half-lidded gaze. She looked almost drunk. He smiled, liking the knowledge that he'd made her feel that way from his kiss.

"So you're staying?" he asked, his voice strained with need.

"If you want me," she said, still sounding a little unsure.

"I want you. Only you. Forever." Jake didn't know how much clearer he could be.

A smile spread across Tessa's beautiful face. "Then, yes. I'm staying."

"Marry me." Jake knew he wasn't on one knee and he didn't have a ring, but he had to know that Tessa would be his wife.

"Okay," she answered immediately, her smile spreading even wider.

"Today."

"What?" she said as she drew her head back and looked at him like he needed to be in a strait jacket. "We can't get married *today*."

"Why not? Let's drive to Tahoe. We'll get our license and go to a chapel. You can be Mrs. Maguire by sundown."

"But what about your family?" Tessa asked, her eyes wide as saucers.

"I told you. You're my family. It's me and you. It's always been me and you."

He could see a battle going on behind her beautiful blue eyes. Her mouth turned into a nervous frown as she said, "Your mom and Nikki will kill us."

"I'll deal with them." Jake needed her to say *yes*. With everything in his being, he needed Tessa to finally be his wife. He knew that begging had never helped before, but that didn't stop the plea from leaving his mouth. "Please. Marry me. Today."

Her eyes scanned his face and her chest was rising and falling rapidly. Tears formed in her eyes, her lips turning up into a smile as she whispered, "Yes. I'll marry you. Today."

Jake pulled her tightly against him, crushing her with

his arms and burying his head in the crook of her neck as relief and joy washed over him like a giant wave. "I love you," he whispered against her ear.

She held him just as tightly. "I love you, too."

"Let's go get married." He grabbed his keys off the desk and started towards the door.

"I can walk," she giggled as she held her arms securely around his neck.

"Good," he said, not putting her down. Jake didn't want to let her go. And now, thank God, he never had to.

THE END

BLURB: IN HIS KISS

Hope Falls - Dorsey Men Series: Book 1

For him, everything had fallen into place...

Levi Dorsey didn't want much and never complained. The private, sexy bar owner was content in his life and excited to move forward with his new business project. There was just one problem--he'd never been able to forget about that kiss...or about her.

For her, everything had fallen apart...

Shelby Kellan was once confident in knowing who she was and what she wanted. But recent events caused the gorgeous, blue-eyed beauty to barely recognize the woman she saw when she looked in the mirror. She knew she needed a fresh start. Could she do it with his kiss still lingering on her lips?

Eighteen months ago, Levi and Shelby shared the perfect kiss. Now, he wanted more, but would she be able to give that to him after already losing so much?

In His Kiss

OTHER TITLES BY MELANIE SHAWN

The Whisper Lake Series

Return To You

Always Been You

Let Me Love You

Made For You

The Southern Comfort Series

Panty Dropper

Sex On The Beach

Between the Sheets

Afternoon Delight

The Crossroad Series

My First

My Last

My Only

My Everything

Tempting Love

Crazy Love

Actually Love

Fairytale Love

My Love

The Crossroads Body Guards

All He Wants

All He Needs

All He Feels

All He Desires

The Crossroads Bachelorettes

Just One Night

Just One Kiss

Just One Look

Just One Touch

The Wishing Well, Texas Series

Teasing Destiny

Convincing Cara

Discovering Harmony

Taming Travis

Claiming Colton

Trusting Bryson

Seducing Sawyer

Unwrapping Jade

Borrowing Bentley

Loving Jackson

Educating Holden

Kissing Beau

Hope Falls

Feels Like Home

Coming Home

Carry Me Home

Home to Me

One Sweet Day

Hope Falls: Maguire Family

Forever and Always

Forever to Go

Forever With You

Forever Your Girl

Hope Falls: Dorsey Men

In His Kiss

When We Kiss

Last First Kiss

Every Little Kiss

Christmas Wish

Hope Falls:Station 8

Hot Summer Nights

Too Hot to Handle

Love So Hot

Coming in Hot

Hope Falls:Brewed Awakenings

Falling Into Fate

Tempting Fate

Resisting Fate

Flirting With Fate

The Valentine Bay Series

Protecting My Heart

Rescuing His Heart

Rocking Her Heart

Playing By Heart

Unbreak My Heart

The Steamy Weekend Series

Charming Cupid

Seducing Cinderella

Resisting Romeo

The Someday Series

Someday Girl

One Day His

Forever Us

Chasing Perfect

Book Boyfriend

Embracing Reckless

Meet Cute

ABOUT THE AUTHOR

Melanie Shawn is the writing team of sister duo Melanie and Shawna. Originally from Northern California, they both migrated south and now call So Cal their home.

Growing up, Melanie constantly had her head in a book and was always working on short stories, manuscripts, plays and poetry. After graduating magna cum laude from Pepperdine University, she went on to teach grades 2nd through 8th for five years. She now spends her days writing and taking care of her furry baby, a Lhasa Apso named Hercules. In her free time, her favorite activity is to curl up on the couch with that stubborn, funny mutt and binge-watch cable TV shows on DVD (preferably of at least eight seasons in length - a girl's gotta have her standards!).

Shawna always loved romance in any form - movie, song or literary. If it was a love story with a happy ending, Shawna was all about it! She proudly acknowledges that she is a romanceaholic. Her days are jam-packed with writing, being a wife, mom aka referee of two teens, and indulging in her second passion (dance!) as a Zumba instructor. In the little free time she has, she joins Melanie in marathon-watching DVDs of their favorite TV programs.

They have joined forces to create a world where True Love and Happily Ever After always has a Sexy Twist!

You can keep up with all the latest Melanie Shawn news, including new releases and contests, at:

http://melanieshawn.com
and
http://facebook.com/melanieshawnbooks

Made in United States
North Haven, CT
08 May 2023

36376312R00198